RUSTY BLADE

THE LOVE OF A FAN

SHAINA KEIBLER

NEWMAN SPRINGS PUBLISHING
320 Broad Street
Red Bank, NJ 07701

First originally published by Newman Springs Publishing 2021

ISBN 978-1-63881-023-0 (Paperback)
ISBN 978-1-63881-031-5 (Digital)

Printed in the United States of America

This book is dedicated to my favorite stuntman and actor, Ken Kirzinger, who has always been my inspiration to never let any fears or self-doubts stop me from pursuing my dreams. I am proud to be his fan. To Lauro Chartrand-DelValle, for never letting me fail myself. It's an honor having them both be a part of this book. Both are members of Stunts Canada located in British Columbia, Canada.

I also dedicate this book to my husband, Cory Keibler, for staying by my side and supporting my dreams with so much patience and love. To my mom, Helen Gore, for always being my biggest fan. To my stepfather, Wayne Hinkle, for loving and accepting me as his own. To Tonya Abrams, Colleen Marie Murphy, Jessica Freeman, and Dana Lambert-Hodge for being the best of gal friends a girl can ask for. To all my family and friends not mentioned here who stand by me, love me unconditionally, and believe in me.

I also want to send a special thank-you to everyone who was generous enough to help me publish this book. Thank you all for your support.

I love you all!

1

I t's a warm Wednesday August morning in Chicago, Illinois; and Shannon Keeler, a thirty-year-old over-the-road truck driver, is out making her first delivery since losing her husband of six years, Craig, unexpectedly. Even though everyone felt it was too soon, she knew that being back on the road would help keep her mind occupied more than just sitting at home grieving herself insane. With a long history of depression and a suicide attempt, she has to stay busy. It hasn't been easy adjusting to her now lonely empty life and unpredictable future without him and now the fear of facing the world alone. Her bronze-colored semi that was once filled with his endless laughter, heavy metal music, and conversations is now filled with only silence, her sleepless nights clutching tight to his pillow, and her cries. "Why?" she keeps asking herself over and over. "Why me? Why us? Why him? How am I ever to move on? What happiness will I have now without my love, my best friend, and my protector? How am I to ever get through this?" Craig was her everything. Shannon does, however, have this one thing in her very near future. This one beautiful magical dream come true that is happening in just three days that is sure to bring her some happiness and great joy. It is the only reason she took this load and the only reason she is here because in just three days, she will finally meet her favorite stuntman and actor of twelve years, Kenny Kirtzanger, at an upcoming convention. Kenny Kirtzanger is fifty-six years old, Canadian, stands six feet and five inches tall, and weighs about 225 pounds. He has brown eyes, brown hair, and salt-and-pepper facial hair. In 2003, he landed his biggest role to date as a hockey mask-wearing, machete-slinging killer in a slasher movie against a burnt maniac killer who wears a glove with long sharp blades. That's the movie for how she discovered him, and he became her encouragement and inspiration. He began to change her life in more important ways than she ever imagined; and now, with this opportunity to meet him, she hopes to get the chance to tell him how he saved her life. With a twist of fate, Shannon just happens to be delivering to the restaurant that Kenny is at having breakfast this very morning. She is in a surprisingly good mood anticipating her first convention and can hardly contain her excitement at the thoughts of finally meeting her favorite actor. She absolutely adores him. She has only dreamed of this day, when she would finally get to walk up to him, give him a hug, get his autograph picture signed to her, get her picture taken with him, talk to him…aah…memories that she will cherish a lifetime. She pulls up in the parking lot off to the left side of the restaurant and climbs down out of her semi wearing her custom-made shirt with a black and yellow hatchet clasped tight in a man's hand on the front and. "Kenny Kirtzanger is my Rusty Blade" on the back surrounded by chains, black cotton pants, and black lace-up shoes. She walks back to the middle side of the trailer, opens the side door, and pulls out her dolly. She precedes to stack boxes from the trailer onto her dolly not realizing that her life is about to change. After making her delivery, putting the dolly away, and closing the trailer doors, she's standing by her driver's door filling out her paperwork when she notices a tall shadow slowly creeping up behind her. As her heart beats faster out of fear of who this is behind her, he leans in close to her left ear, and with a shift in his voice, he says the four words that make her weak in the knees, "This is Rusty Blade." Shannon almost drops her clipboard and pen in a frozen state because after watching the *Unjoyful Ride 3: Roadkiller* movie a hundred times; and hearing his voice over and over, she knows it is him. She slowly turns to look up seeing his smile that she's only seen in pictures for twelve years and the face that she has only dreamed of meeting. It is him right there in front of her… It is Kenny Kirtzanger, aka Rusty Blade. Along with his goatee, he's wearing a solid cotton black short-sleeved shirt, black pants, black shoes, and a black baseball cap with *CANADA* embroidered across the front in white stitching. As she stands there within just a foot staring up at him, tears start to fall down her face as she can't believe it.

She puts her hands over her mouth, utters, "OMG…it's really you," reaching out to him and finally wrapping an arm around his left side and laying her face against his chest for a second; and she feels his long strong muscular arm gently caress around her, and he lays his head aside the top of hers. For what felt like thirty seconds, she felt the most incredible hug imaginable. The hug she only fantasized about feeling.

"I can't believe this, Kenny. I was meeting you on Saturday. *What!* You are more handsome in person than in your pictures, ha. My name is Shannon Keeler, and I've been your fan for twelve years."

Still shaking inside, she sits down on her bottom semi step, and Kenny walks over and leans against her semi. "Well, hi, Shannon. It's so nice to meet you. I was coming out of the restaurant, and I happened to look over, and I saw the back of your shirt, and I was curious as to who is this girl with my name on her shirt. So I had to walk over. Twelve years and you've never met me? Well, it's about time, then, eh?" he says, laughing.

"It's been time, ha. Thank you for walking over. I didn't even know you were here at this restaurant. I mean, you could have so easily just left, and I would not have known, but you actually walked over. It really is true about how much you love meeting your fans because you just showed it. I only took this load because I was coming here, anyway."

"Absolutely, I do! I appreciate every one of you guys, and I don't miss an opportunity to meet one no matter where I am. So Rusty Blade?"

"Oh yes, Kenny! *Unjoyful Ride 3: Roadkiller* is my most favorite movie of yours. I just love that Rusty Blade"—she laughs—"and I was so happy that you gave him his face because, well, you're so tall, strong, handsome and all… Now I am blushing, ha ha."

"Thank you, that is very kind of you, and I was happy to give him his face as well. I audition for the second one and ended up being a stunt double, but it worked out in the end. I would love to play him again if there is ever a fourth one. So you are coming to the convention?"

"Yes, and it's my first one too. I am superexcited! I don't know what to expect, but it should be fun, and you will be there too. My husband was supposed to be coming with me, but he recently passed away."

"I'm sorry… That's terrible, but I still hope you have fun and enjoy it."

"I am sure I will."

"Well, as much as I've enjoyed meeting and talking with you, I have to run and do some things in preparation for the convention, but I'll be looking for you at my table Saturday."

She stands up with excitement. "I can't wait, Kenny. Wait! You will actually remember me? You will have forgotten about me by the end of the night."

"No, I doubt that. I won't forget you, and, *wow*, are you short." They both laugh. "And you drive that?" Kenny points to her semi. "Really? You barely come up to the door handle. How old are you?"

"Ha ha…yes, I am short. Five feet one to be exact, and I am thirty years old. Kenny, I am so short that I can slump over and walk under the trailer."

"Ha ha, *no way*! That's too funny. You will have to show me one day."

"I'd love to."

"You know, I honestly thought you were much younger."

"Like a kid?"

"Well…maybe early twenties."

"I look like a kid next to you."

"Yeah, this is true…short like a kid but not a kid…an adult kid, and with that being said, I'll see you on Saturday, Kiddo."

"What did you just call me?"

"Kiddo, short stuff. Ha!"

"Too funny! I dig it. I'll be there, Mr. Rusty Blade, he he."

Kenny gives Shannon another side hug and proceeds to walk away. He gets halfway across the parking lot when she yells for him, "Hey, Kenny!"

He stops and turns. "Yeah!"

Shannon runs over to him. "Do you think that sometime after the convention, we can maybe hang out and talk? There're just so many things I've waited so long that I want to tell you…like how you saved my life, how you gave me encouragement and inspiration."

"We will see." He winks at her.

"Okay, bye, Kenny…until Saturday." Shannon smiles.

"Bye for now."

Shannon stands at that very spot until she no longer sees Kenny, and realizing what all just happened, she's overcome with joyful tears and runs back to her semi and pulls out more excited about the weekend than ever. She knew with all her heart that God let that happen. He blessed her with that magical encounter. Not being able to contain her happiness, she puts on her Bluetooth headset and commands, "Call Colleen." Phones rings three times.

"Hello."

"Hey, Colleen."

"What's wrong? Why are you crying?"

"Can you talk?"

"Sure, what's up?"

"You'll never believe what just happened to me this morning."

"No, tell me!"

"He was there, Colleen." She begins to cry. "Kenny was there at the restaurant having breakfast, and I didn't know it at first. I was wearing my Rusty Blade shirt, and when he came out and sneaked up behind me right when I was filling out my paperwork to leave, he said, 'This is Rusty Blade," in Rusty's voice. My heart melted a little. Aw, Colleen… I met my Rusty Blade—I finally met him! You kept telling me since June to be patient and not give up, and I didn't give up and look! This was the most amazing thing to ever happen to me since losing Craig."

"See—I told ya! Way cool! I am so happy for you. Kenny is such a sweetie."

"Oh yes, he is and smells amazing too and so freaking handsome in person. He talked to me and asked me about my shirt and laughed at how short I am, ha." Colleen laughs. "And I got to hug him twice. They were side hugs, but I am totally fine with that. I just can't stop gushing over it. I didn't expect this happening to me. He told me that he'll be looking for me Saturday and called me Kiddo. I asked him if we can talk after the convention. So I am hoping."

"Aw, are you going to tell him how he saved you from that second suicide attempt?"

"Absolutely! I am going to tell him everything."

"Good, and you should, but don't throw too much at him at once. Don't want to overwhelm him and make him feel uneasy."

"Oh no, I wouldn't want to do that. That would suck to make him feel uncomfortable. It's hard when you have waited so long just to talk to someone, and now that you have a chance to say everything, you still can't say it all, but I understand too. I told my dispatcher to map all of my upcoming deliveries around his conventions—and I am going to try and make it to as many as possible."

"Yeah, got to slide into it easy. He doesn't know you, and you don't want him to think you're creepy, but hey, let me know what happens Saturday."

"Totally will! I am telling you, I am going to be friends with that man one day. I am going to make it happen because I refuse to give up."

"Ha, yeah, that would be supercool. Got to jet but talk to you later."

"Okay, bye."

Early Saturday morning, Shannon pulls her semi into a far back parking space next to the hotel where the convention is taking place. She has exactly one hour till doors open at ten, and she's so excited knowing Kenny is in there. She jumps up and changes into her custom-made Rusty Blade shirt; a black fully lined, tiered, triple-layered midleg-length tulle skirt with an elastic waist and embroidered with a circular patchwork around the bottom; and black flats. She grabs her drawing she did for Kenny, her ticket, wallet, and phone and hangs her keys lanyard around her neck and climbs down out of her semi locking her door behind her. She can hardly contain her excitement as she begins to walk to the hotel of the convention. The day has finally arrived. The day she meets Kenny Kirtzanger, again. Having never been to this event, she isn't sure what to expect other than what she had seen in photos and videos on social media. She gets in the long line waiting outside of all sorts of fans and cosplayers—fans dressed in costumes of sorts, like horror characters, dark fairy tale characters, goth, even little girls dressed as dead princess, and some who aren't dressed in any costumes but with shirts of their idols. Some are carrying fake machetes, fake axes, fake swords, glow wands, gloves with fake blades—anything you imagined. Cosplayers are spaced all throughout the parking lot playing reenactments of their favorite scenes. She has never seen anything like it in her life. Other fans waiting to meet Kenny waste no time in coming over to Shannon to adore her shirt, ask about it, and even take a picture. For a minute there, she feels like a star. Even though she met him three days ago, she is still nervous and excited. She wonders to herself if he actually will remember her, and she is about to find out because the doors just opened. Fans scream and cheer as passes are being scanned and paper bands are being placed around each person's wrist. Fans and their fake weapons are being checked, and they run in scattering in every direction. When Shannon finally gets through and goes in, she looks around and is amazed at everything she sees. Fans standing in long lines to by passes, huge banners of horror, advertisements, and floor layouts hanging everywhere, life-size wax figures of horror movie characters, movie props, walls of merchandise, comic books, and clothing. It's like one gigantic human maze to maneuver through. There are sections for movie stars, sections for book and comic writers, sections for illustrators, sections of food, and a bar for drinks. Glass cases with upcoming dolls, toys, and exclusive rare props. Cardboard cutouts of stars and characters for fun photos and cosplayers run around. All throughout the day, Shannon makes her rounds. She stops afar from almost every table making notes in her mind of every detail, and she even meets a few of her other favorite stars who she didn't know were going to be here. She takes pictures of certain things and fans that she thinks look supercool. She even shares conversations with a few. She attends a few celebrity interviews and even watches a costume contest. She is purposely saving Kenny till the very end when there would be less fans around in his line. With only thirty minutes left in the convention, she finally walks over to his table. He has five different photos to choose from. Some wearing his hockey mask and a few from a TV show appearance for fans to choose from to get autograph, but none of him as Rusty Blade. Kenny is with a fan when he looks over and smiles his daydream smile seeing her.

Holy crap! He remembers me, she thinks to herself, and she is overcome with excitement. Once alone, he motions her over to him. He's wearing a black shirt with a white hockey mask detail in red markings and dark-gray newspaper headline about his character, light-blue jeans, and solid-white lace-up shoes.

"Hi, Kenny," she says with a softness in her voice as she walks over to him. "I love your shirt. Probably the coolest one I've seen you wear, and I want it, ha."

"Hello, Kiddo! Thanks! I like your shirt too. So have you enjoyed the convention?"

"Thanks and yes! It's been a lot of fun. I have met some pretty cool people and saw some interesting things. It's been one of the most fun days of my life. I definitely plan to attend more. I hope you don't mind that I waited till now to come over."

"No, not at all, and I am glad that you had fun. Now what would you like me to autograph, or what photo do you want me to sign?"

Shannon picks her photo from his five different choices, and he signs it to her. She pulls out her phone, and they take a few selfies together. It was a dream come true that she didn't want to ever end.

"Thank you for taking a few photos with me Kenny. I know you have a photo opt later in your horror costume, but I don't want my first photo with you to be you behind a mask. I wanted a photo with well...you. I have waited so long for this day. I drew your name back in February and wanted to give it to you, and I wasn't sure if you accept gifts or not, but this is for you. I hope you like it." She hands him a drawing of his name with sorts of different-colored shapes and lines decorating around his name drawn in black.

"Oh, wow, that's fantastic! Thank you, and I do like it. I will definitely take it home with me."

"You're welcome."

Shannon knows this time she wants a full hug, to feel his complete embrace. She wraps her arms around him, giving him no choice, and to her delight, she feels both his strong arms engulf her and press her tight against him. She could hear his beautiful heartbeat as her right ear lay perfectly over his chest. After releasing him and with a soft smile and a hypnotic stare, she says, "Kenny, just forget my name, and call me Kiddo from now on...Mr. Rusty Blade."

"Ha! Sure...okay, and you can call me Rusty Blade anytime you want."

"I already do. This is so awesome! We now share nicknames that we gave each other. I just absolutely adore you. Your wife is one lucky lady, Kenny."

"I don't have a wife, Kiddo."

"Okay, then your girlfriend."

"I don't have a girlfriend either."

"Dear sweet mercy me." They both laugh.

"Do you think that you could ever be friends with a fan Kenny?"

"Hmm, well, I am private in some ways, and trust is something I take very seriously. I've never had a serious friendship with one, but I think it's possible if I get to know the fan well enough."

"Sweet!"

"Are you sticking around for my Q and A at nine?"

"Oh yes, and I have a few questions myself, Mr. Rusty Blade."

"Great! Bring it!"

It's around five in the afternoon; and fans are running around, some leaving, some following their favorite celebrities around or heading to VIP parties. Kenny has an hour and a half till he has to get in costume for photo opts, and Shannon almost is bought to tears at the thoughts of having to leave him after waiting so long to spend time with him. A few minutes just wasn't enough after a twelve-year-long wait. When will she meet him again? When will she get to speak to him again? Will she ever get to tell him everything and maybe build a friendship with him? All of these questions run through her mind as she stands there daydreaming at him.

"Kenny, I know you sometimes hang with your fans afterward, but can we go somewhere and talk? I just really want to tell you some things and tell you how you saved my life."

About that time, a pack of fans yelling his name overtakes Kenny as he was about to tell her "Sure," but Shannon, not hearing him over the loud fans and an unexpected phone call, turns and walks away with a disappointed face. As much as he loves meeting and spending time with his fans, this is one time that he wants to spend time with just one, and it is her. As he pulls himself away from the crowd apologizing, he looks to find she's gone. She has disappeared. Even though he doesn't know her, there is something about Shannon that he enjoys and likes that draws him to her. Maybe it is her soft sweet voice, the way she says his name, or something in her eyes in the way she stares at him; but whatever it is, he just can't put his finger on how curious he already is about her. He runs outside to the side parking lot to see her semi is gone. He feels bad about the whole situation but can't believe that she would just leave like that and before his Q and A. *Why? Where did she go?* Kenny has all of the questions running through his mind now. With another day of meeting fans tomorrow and knowing that she has a weekend pass, he hopes that she will stop by his table again and plans to give her some one-on-one time if she does. He walks back inside to his table and picks up his drawing and goes upstairs to his room before costume change, deciding to skip hanging out downstairs; but she never shows up the next morning. The events that begin to unfold between them next are something neither of them ever expected and changes both of their lives forever.

2

A few weeks have now passed since Kenny and Shannon met, and he still wonders why she left so quick. With him not having social media and no way to contact her, he still wonders about her and even has her drawing in his folder that he keeps in his bag. It's around five twenty on a Friday afternoon, and Kenny has just finished setting his table up for the New Jersey Comic Expo Con that starts at six. He's looking down at his phone when he hears a familiar voice call to him in excitement, "Hi, Kenny!"

He looks up to see Shannon walking fast over to him. He quickly stands up, comes around his table, and greets her with a hug. "Hello, Kiddo, how are you?"

"I am great, Kenny, and you?"

"Just great! Kiddo, where have you been? Why did you leave so fast a few weeks ago? I thought you wanted to talk to me, and after breaking away from my fans, I turned around, and you were gone. What happened?"

"Oh, I've been out there. Up and down the interstates, state to state, shifting gears and hauling freight." She laughs. "It was an unfortunate but unexpected thing to happen. Hey, I don't have time to hang around today. I'm not actually here for the Comic Con. I am just passing through with a load, and I just wanted to see you and say hi. This past Monday made me your fan for thirteen years, Kenny."

"You bought a pass just to see me for a few minutes?"

"Yes! I still hope we get to hang out one day. Will you still give me alone time at your Texas convention next month? I'm just slammed right now."

"That's very kind of you, and absolutely. I'll still give you time. I hope you make it out."

"Yeah, I worked with my dispatcher, and we have my loads mapped out, and I'll explain everything to you, but I have to run to make my load delivery on time. It was great just to see you for a few minutes."

"Thank you. I'm flattered, just to run in here to say hi to me."

"Aw, it was nothing, just the love of a fan—that's all. That's the lengths we will go through to see our favorites. I'll go through any length to see you. I pulled some strings, talked to some people, and they were nice enough to let me come in and see you before your line fills up with fans, mainly because I just delivered a few pallets of water for you all this weekend, ha."

"Nice! I am glad to see you too!"

"Kenny, it was great to see you, but got to run."

Kenny smiles the biggest he has at her and gives her another hug before she walks away. He just stands there watching her until he no longer sees her. A part of him doesn't want her to leave. He's never made such a fast connection with a fan before, and he is starting to like her already without knowing who she is.

The first Thursday of September arrives, and it's a little after noon. It's a bright sunny day in Dallas, Texas, and Kenny just set down at a booth alone in a smokehouse restaurant. Looking out the window that to his left, he sees her climb down from the passenger side of a blue semi while a gentleman climbs down from the driver side, and they make their way to the restaurant. Once inside and seated across the small dining room from him, Kenny loudly whispers to her, "Hi, Kiddo!"

Shannon looks up quickly from the menu at her lunch guest shocked before looking to her right and seeing him.

"Kenny? Hi! Come over here and sit with us." She motions him over to her table. He picks up his cup of soda and walks over to their table and sits beside her. "What are the odds of this happening—ha?"

"I know right! Crazy. How has your week been, Kiddo?"

"Not bad but a mess at the same time. Oh, this is my brother, Jeremy, and this is Kenny. You know, the one I talk about all the time, and now I'm blushing." They all laugh as Kenny, and her brother greets with a handshake.

"Everything okay?"

"Yeah, we teamed up a few days ago after my semi went in the shop for repairs, and we will be working together for about another week. He drives for a different company, but our bosses didn't mind putting us together for my safety. Unfortunately, I am on his schedule and can't make your convention this weekend. I'm sorry Kenny, but how have you been, Mr. Rusty Blade?"

"Just great, Kiddo, and don't apologize. It's okay, and maybe you can make it to my next one."

"I am for sure."

Shannon's brother, feeling like she and Kenny should have some alone time, removes himself from the table and to a different one. Kenny orders a smoked seasoned chicken breast plate with baked beans, French fries, dinner roll, and house salad; and she orders a half rack of smoked barbecue dry rub ribs with baked beans, green beans, and a house salad.

"Can't believe I am having lunch with you, Kenny, so cool. Have you ever had lunch with a fan?"

"Not solo, but I have with a group of fans along with other actors. So this is a first, and it's kind of nice—I must say."

"And I am the lucky fan. I like how we keep running into each other. I promise I'm not stalking you, ha ha."

"Oh no, Kiddo, ha ha. So what happened last month in Chicago?" he asks while they are receiving their food.

"My dispatcher called, and I couldn't hear over everything, so I ran outside. A trucker with a refrigeration trailer broke down about forty-five minutes up the road and I was the closest, and so I left immediately to go hook up to that trailer and keep power going into the freezer so nothing would spoil and delivered it to its destination. I cried the whole way too because I didn't want to leave without getting to talk to you, but I couldn't let all of that food be lost. I mean, of all days!"

"That was nice of you to do that, and, yes, it sucks to have happened on that day, but you did the right thing."

"Yeah. If you don't mind me asking, what are you working on when not attending your conventions?"

"Right now, I am reading a script for my best friend's movie that I am playing a part in."

"Sweet! I can't wait to learn about it and see it."

"It's going to be a good one."

"If you could go back into your past and redo it, would you have rather played football or have your career now?"

"Um…that's tough because I really loved playing football, but honestly, I would keep my career I have now. It has given me a wonderful life, a meaningful purpose, and it has taught me a lot about who I am, where I came from, and what I can offer. It has allowed me to connect with amazing people like my fans. You guys give me so much more than I deserve, and you all never let me down. I know I can always look forward to seeing you all at my events and having a fun time. I truly have the sweetest fans, and I feel so lucky to have been welcomed and given so much support from this fan base."

"I'm so happy you said that because that means you don't regret your career path or us, and that also means you would pick your fans again. We will always love and support you, Kenny. You are so sweet to us and really show us how much you appreciate our support. I mean, how many celebrities out there do you know actually hang out with their fans, parties with their fans, and spends endless hours talking with their fans like you do? Not many at all unless something is in it for them."

"I will never regret you guys or nothing I've done because it's made me who I am today, and spending time with my fans makes everything worth it. It's the least I can for you all for what you all have done for me. I wouldn't be here without you guys. If you can't give your fans just a little free time, then you aren't worthy of their support."

"When did you start your stunt career?"

"Back in 1983."

"Wow…three years before my time, ha."

"Yup! LOL!"

Will you still give me alone time, Kenny, at your next convention?"

"Absolutely, Kiddo! My offer will always stand open for you."

A little over an hour after their lunch began, it has to end as her brother interrupts their laughs and casual conversations about each other to tell her that they have to hit the road. Kenny stands, hugs her tight, and whispers in her ear to please make it to his next con; and she nods in an agreement motion and sneaks his meal ticket while he isn't looking. He shakes her brother's hand again as tells him to keep his fan safe in which her brother assures him that he's very protective over his little sister and watches out for her all the time. Shannon not only pays for her meal but also pays for Kenny's. When he asks his waitress for another ticket, she brings him a blank slip that has a message from her written on it that simply reads, "Have a great weekend at your convention, my Rusty Blade, and thank you for spending your lunch with me. I'll see you soon. Kiddo." He smiles to himself and realizes that he truly has a special fan in her and maybe a little more. He folds the paper and puts it in his pocket and looks over out the window as he hears the roaring engine sounds of her brother's semi pulling away. For a minute, he actually feels a sense of being alone and almost missing her.

It's about four in the evening on the third Sunday of September. Kenny finishes his short day of meeting fans at a Comic Con in San Diego, California. He was a little confused as to why Shannon never showed. Even though she is just a fan who he doesn't know much about, there is also something mysterious and likable about her that he feels drawn too. Not feeling like hanging around this evening, he sneaks outside through the back doors opposite of all the fans, and to his unexpected surprise, she is there, waiting in the parking lot leaning up against her still semi's passenger side with her arms folding and smiling. It's like she somehow knew where he would be and where he would be exiting the building. He stops dead in his tracks in amazement to see her. He just stares at her and slightly smiles.

"Well, hello, Mr. Rusty Blade. How are you?"

"I am doing fine. Just finished the event, and I was leaving. I thought you were coming. I kept looking up for you."

"You were looking for me—really?"

"Yes."

"That's sweet! I finally got my semi out of the shop, but it backed me up, and then my dad got real sick, and I went home to be with him, and he's better now. I was so upset that I couldn't make it in time, and on top of that, the passes sold out before I could buy one, sorry." She looks down disappointed.

"Hey, no hard feelings. I understand, and you can't help that. I'm glad your dad is okay too. I don't feel like hanging around today, so how about that talk?"

"I would like that."

"We can try to sneak back inside the building to a private room…" Shannon tunes his talking out as she looks to her left, noticing a group of eager fans looking their way pointing and mumbling his name. "Um…Kenny…you have been spotted."

"Excuse me!" He looks to now see that fans have begun making their way to him. They both look around frantic, determined not to lose this opportunity again, when he grabs her by her arm and pulls her inside the building. Halfway up the hall, he opens the first unlocked door they come to, and they both dart inside closing and locking the door as they hear the fans come running inside and up the hall. Their giggles and heavy breathing echo in the small dark room. They shh each other and try to compose themselves while trying to be quiet so as not to be heard.

"I've never done anything like that in my life, Kiddo. That was so fun, ha!"

"I know right, totally. Felt like you lived a little, huh, Mr. Rusty Blade? But I don't think we should be in here. What is the room, anyway?" She turns on the light to discover they are standing in the middle of a janitor's room, and they both bust out laughing about it.

"Yeah." He pulls her close him and wraps his arms around her. He whispers softly, "Thanks for paying for my lunch a few weeks back. I'm so happy you're here."

Shannon is almost thrown off by his sweet by unexpected hug and hugs him back. "You're welcome, and don't you know that somethings feels better in the dark, Kenny?" She turns the light back off and lays her head against his chest not even knowing how he may react, but to her surprise, he loosely puts his arms around her, and they stand like that for a few minutes as they listen to the distance chatter up the hall. She can't believe this is happening and wonders, *Why? What made him hold her like this? What is happening between them?* She is lost in a trance listening to his soft breathing and steady heartbeat when he tells her that maybe they should find a more suitable room to hang out in. She slowly opens the door trying to not draw any attention and peeks her head out, looking both directions. The hallway is completely clear at the moment as most fans and guests are at VIP parties. Kenny walks her to an elevator down on the right side of the hall; and they enter, go up, and step out onto the fourth floor. He walks her five doors up the hall, pulls out a room key, unlocks the door, and motions her inside. After stepping inside, she realizes it's his room. They walk over to a small round two-person table in the corner and sit down across from each other. She tries not to let him see her glancing around, taking every little detail in in amazement that she's here, that he actually bought her up to his room to hang out.

"We'll have alone time here, Kiddo." He sits down across from her.

"This is so cool, and it's real nice. Thank you for giving me time with you. Do you know what it's like to wait nearly half of your life to meet someone? It was a forever long enough wait but so worth every minute. You just don't know how much this really means to me. I've only been able to imagine what it would finally feel like to see your face in person after only photos."

"And what does it feel like, Kiddo?"

"Absolutely incredible. We need you on social media, Kenny. You are missing out on all of us, and we are missing out on you. It kills me a little to see other fans getting to interact with their favorites but I can't with you. Sorry if that sounded rude." She looks down.

"Aw, yeah, I've got to get on someday or at least make some kind of fan page so I can communicate with you all, and it didn't sound rude. Tell me, Kiddo, how did I save your life?"

"Kenny, when I first discovered you, I was seventeen, very depressed and suicidal. I even cut my wrist. I laid on my bedroom floor waiting for my life and everything I hated about it and me to be over, but I missed my vein by a hair. After I saw you and discovered you, my whole outlook on my life slowly changed. You not only became my favorite actor that day, but you saved my life—*you*, Kenny. I know that may seem hard to believe, but you kinda have to understand it from a fan's point of view. I had dreams, but I let everyone brainwashed and bullied me into believing that I wasn't good enough and that I could never make any of them happen. I felt worthless, unwanted, and a waste of life. After I found out that you were a stuntman who was crossing over to being an actor with this movie after so many years, it made me realized that I can really be somebody and make something with my life, and have my dreams come true too. It just takes time and effort if I work really hard at it. You stepped into the biggest shoes to fill when you stepped into those villain boots, and you gave it your best shot. You put everything into it that you had not even knowing how you would do, if it would be a success or if the horror fans would accept you, and you made me see that it's okay to try and to go that extra mile. You made me see something in myself that everyone and my depression took from me. You made me see *me*, and you made me want to try. You made me want to defeat my suicidal depression and everybody around me that made me think I couldn't be anybody, and you made me want to live. As the years passed, throughout your career, movies, photos, and interviews, you became my everyday inspiration, my everyday encouragement, and in 2014, you became my Rusty Blade—ha! and now I am blushing. I am a Rusty Blade fanatic, and I love the *Unjoyful Ride* movies. I even have a mini tractor trailer I put together and painted to look just like Rusty Blade's, and I have been saving up to buy my own real one that looks as close to possible as it."

"Wow, Kiddo, that's fantastic! It's nice to know I was such a positive influence for you, and I am glad you turned your life around and I have you as my fan. I must say, though, that it's a little tough to accept so much credit when I've done so little. I hope you also take pride in yourself for all of the hard work you've done to change."

"I do! It was a lot of hard work, and I still battle depression. It doesn't just go away, but I manage it better now. You want to know how you can be such a positive influence with doing so little? Do you know that I discovered you wearing a mask where I couldn't see your face or hear your voice? A masked Kenny and you changed my life. Think about that. It doesn't matter how many shows or movies that you've done stunts for or guest-starred on. It doesn't matter how many movies you've been in or how many awards you have, and it doesn't matter how many fans you have met or how popular you are. It's all in your personality, your character, how you inspire us, how you present yourself, how you treat your fans, how we connect with you and see ourselves in you... I can go on all day, but please don't let me make you feel uncomfortable. If I am saying too much, let me know."

Kenny sits back, folds his arms, and crosses his right leg over his left. "Aw, Kiddo! This is great! You're fine. Keep going. I wanna hear more. Ha!"

"Okay, it's like this! There are famous people that I've been a fan of for a lot longer than you, but did they save my life? Did they make me want to put that razor blade down? Did they make me want to pursue my dreams? *No*, but you did! I've always wanted to meet you and know you more because it doesn't matter how long you have been a fan, Kenny. It's all about the fan connection you have to that person. If you didn't get that role, if you didn't put that hockey mask on, I probably wouldn't be here today, and maybe that is tough for you to accept, but I think over time, you will. Yeah, I did all of the work. I didn't have a therapist to talk to or antidepressants to take. I had to make the change and fight through my depression to survive, but you gave me the push to try."

He just stares at her smiling his proudest smile. "I don't think I have ever met a fan throughout my whole career that has touched me the way you just did. Makes me very proud!"

Shannon tears up. "Thank you so much. That is so sweet, but I am in no means better than your other fans."

"I am so happy we finally met."

"Me too, and enough about me for now. How about you? Where do go after tomorrow?"

"Home for a few weeks, and then I have a convention in Germany in October."

"Wow, Germany! That's so cool! I want to go there one day. Big dream to visit next to Canada. Glad you're getting to go home and rest some. I'll miss running into you."

"It's always fun and beautiful, and I am sure you'll get to go one day. That's sweet, Kiddo."

"If you don't mind me asking, where do you live, Kenny?"

"Vancouver, British Columbia, Canada."

"You mean you don't even live in the same country as me! Well!" They both giggled.

"I'm afraid not. Where do you live?"

"In my semi, ha, but when I want a break, I go visit my parents who still live in my hometown of Loris, South Carolina. I've dreamed of visiting Canada since I was little. It has always been my favorite country to study and learn about. I want to see all of it."

"You should definitely do it, Kiddo. We will welcome you any day."

"Aw, shucks! That's sweet. You have always been a part of my daily happiness, and as my favorite actor, you still keep me happy every day, Kenny."

"How have I affected your happiness without having been in your life? That can't be my responsibility, Kiddo. It has to be yours and yours alone."

"Oh no! Please don't misunderstand me or take that the wrong way. Just being your fan alone makes me happy. It is also watching your movies and your interviews, looking at your pictures, talking about you…how you encourage me every day and how you inspire me every day… That's my daily happiness from you, Kenny."

"That's very kind, and if it helps you, then I am all for it."

"Do you know why I asked you about being friends with the fan? It's because I would love nothing more than to be friends with you. Look, I know that I'm just a fan, and a lot of celebrities have that mentality that if they can't be friends with all their fans, then they aren't going to be friends with just one or they don't think it's ever a good idea, but your career is the only way that I knew about you. It's not like I was born to somebody who knew you or randomly met you on social media or out and about. I had no choice but to be your fan first, and I just don't want me being your fan to cost me the opportunity of getting to know you—the real you, who Kenny Kirtzanger really is. We only have one life…one chance…one opportunity to know someone, and I want to know you. I promise you, Kenny, if you can just step outside of your comfort zone just a little and just give me one chance, just a little bit of trust, and some way to communicate with you, you'll never regret me. I won't meddle into your personal private business. Think of it this way, if I wasn't your fan first and we met, could we be friends? I'm sorry if I'm throwing too much at you at one time."

"Well…oh…whoa, Kiddo! I think I am honestly lost for words right now. Trust is something that I take very seriously, and it's just hard for me to trust people that I just met and don't really know. I've had some awkward incidents with fans in the past, but you are really sweet, and you do seem very genuine. I like you, and so it's something that I will definitely think about and maybe take into consideration."

"And know that I'll never be that type of fan. I'll take it easy with you and be patient. This is amazing! Just the fact that you're even willing to consider it—holy snickers! Thank you so much."

"You're very welcome. So how are you managing being on the road by yourself? Are you doing okay?"

Shannon breaks eye contact and looks down with an unhappy change in her voice. "I'm okay. I mean, it's not easy being a female trucker when you stop at truck stops to shower, to get fuel, or to even rest. I have to stay on high alert for people trying to approach me for money or to hit on me…or even kidnap me. It's a constant fear in the back of my mind as I walk across that pavement and as I lay in my bunk listening to all sorts of voices and sounds from other truckers and their partners, lot lizards, and people knocking on truck doors who are up to no good or just trying to get a dollar, and that's why Craig traveled with me. I just wished I had someone, a guy to talk to. Someone who I can trust and who can trust me. It's scary at times, and sometimes, I am afraid of being out there with no one to protect me. It's lonely. I am lonely now with no one to talk to other than my close family and few friends. I just miss having a man to talk to, to make me feel safe. A man that I can give my troubles to at the end of the day and listens and takes it all away. I just miss Craig! I miss how safe he made me feel and how I could talk to him, and he would just listen. I just feel all of my depression coming back. I feel like that same depressed lonely teen from years ago, but I am much stronger now than I was, and I'll make it. I'm not letting fear or loneliness make me walk away from my career because I'm a woman who gets scared or depressed."

As he takes all of her words in, he thinks of how he can help her to feel safe. There's just something inside of him that makes him want to know her—who she is, why she adores him so much, but after a bad relationship that broke all his trust, can he really trust her? A fan? He doesn't want her feeling scared and depressed. She's his fan whom he has made a connection with, and he would be hurt if anything happens to her.

"Kiddo, I'm going to be honest with you, I've never done this with any fan, and I usually don't get this emotionally involved in someone's personal business, but you are just so inspiring with everything you've been through and overcome. Even without me knowing your full complete background and in ways, you are your own influence without even knowing it, I don't want anything bad to ever happen to you. I know that I live in Vancouver and always somewhere different and busy working on projects all the time and you live here and always on the road and I can't be in your semi with you, but I promise you that I'll do my best to help you feel safe. All I ask that you be patient with me."

Shannon looks up shocked as a tear falls down her cheek, and Kenny moves his chair beside her. "I want you to know that I am here if you ever need someone to talk to or cry to. I'll always listen, and if you're ever in trouble, you can reach out to me immediately no matter the time of day or night."

"That's so sweet of you—like, are you serious? I never ever expected this, but, Kenny, you don't have social media. I would love nothing more than to be able to communicate with you and tell you how my day is going and ask you how your day is going and know how you are from time to time, but how?"

"You want me to trust you, right? And I do feel I can trust you enough to build trust."

"Yes, of course."

"Well, today is going to be a start. I am going to do something with you that I have never done with the fan, and you are probably the only fan that I will ever do this with. I am actually going to give you my email address, and you can write me anytime you want when you need to talk, but don't abuse it. Don't make me regret this, Kiddo. Don't make that mistake!"

Shannon is in disbelief of what she's hearing. Her heart is racing and feels herself becoming emotional. "Your email? Like your actual personal email? I must be dreaming—like, is this real? Oh, don't you worry. Nobody will ever know it or see it. I would never ever do that to you. You won't regret this, I promise."

"I hope not! I am trusting you, and just be careful with it. When you message me, I may not be able to respond immediately, and it may take me some time to get back to you, but I will try and get back to you as soon as I can, okay?"

"Deal, and I don't always expect a reply immediately. I'm a very patient person obviously. Ha! You don't have to give me this chance, but you are, and it's beautifully amazing. I'm not going to screw it up after waiting for so long. This is turning out to be the most amazing day of my life. I just can't believe all this is happening—like you are actually giving me a chance. So incredible, Kenny."

"You're welcome, Kiddo."

They spend a few hours talking about their day, and she tells Kenny about both of her autoimmune diseases—skin lupus and dermatomyositis—and how they affect her in ways by attacking her immune system, her muscles, joints. She mentions how they make her break out in rashes and exhausted all the time. He notices how late it is getting to be and he still has to pack for his early flight and get to bed. He so enjoys his talk with Shannon and is happy he decided to give her one-on-one. She not only met him once but twice and finally got to spend a little fan time with him and exchange email addresses. This night can't get more perfect, and now it's coming to an end.

"Well, Kiddo, I'm sorry to have to do this to you, but I do have an early flight, and I do need to get packed up and get some rest. You can email me tomorrow, and we'll go from there. We will see how this works out, okay? Let's take it slow and slowly build the trust and then work on the friendship."

"I understand! I need to hit the road myself and get some rest too, but you just don't know how much this means me to me and how you just changed my life and my outlook on my future yet again. I can't believe after thirteen years, I'm finally going to get to talk to you, and whenever I want. You truly are such a wonderful human being."

"Too kind, and I am looking forward to seeing what it's like to have a fan in my personal life. This will be fun and interesting." They both stand and embrace each other with a hug.

"Well, Mr. Rusty Blade, I guess this is not only good night, but this is bye until next time we meet again, and I want to thank you for the time that you've given me and for just being who you are and for caring about your fans so much, and thank you for giving me the best day of my life. I really needed this, and I can't wait to message you in the morning. I hope you have a safe flight back home."

"Good night, Kiddo, and you stay safe out there. I, too, have enjoyed this. Come on, and I'll walk you down and out to your truck."

She turns and starts heading to the door in front of him, and that's when he notices it on her upper right arm just barely visible under her shirt sleeve—a light-colored bruise and in the shape of a large hand.

"Hold the heck up a minute! What is that on the back of your arm? Is that a bruise? It looks like a hand, and it's too big to be yours, Kiddo?"

She stops just shy of the doorknob and turns to face him. "Yesterday, I stopped at a truck stop to take a shower, and, well... there is this trucker named Jason that I've been friends with for year now, and he can be a little overfriendly with the female truckers. He's single, and now that Craig is gone, he just feels like maybe he can fulfill my loneliness or something. I don't know, Kenny, but he tried to hit on me in the parking lot, and of course, I kindly turned him down and told him that we're just friends and that's it. I turned to unlock my door, and he grabbed my arm really, really hard— squeezed it. I turned around and slapped his arm and told him to get off me and to never touch me again and that if he can't respect me just wanting us to be friends, then I won't be friends with him any-more. Another male trucker approached him, and I got in my semi and left them in the parking lot. It's okay! I'll be fine. He pretty much knows where we stand now."

"No, Kiddo, it's not fine! A guy like that is not going to leave you alone. Especially not now that you're single. He's always going to think he has a chance with you, and that bruise on your arm is not okay. That bruise on your arm pisses me off, and that guy better be glad he's not out there in that parking lot right now. This guy is the exact type of guy that you said makes you stay on alert when you're walking through a parking lot. This guy is who you need to worried about bothering you and hounding you, trying to get in your bunk or kidnap you, Kiddo. You really shouldn't be friends with him any-more. You have to stay away from him. I know that's not easy with you both being truck drivers, but you're going to have to try and avoid him in any way you possibly can. I don't judge, but I also don't think you can trust him."

"I see your point of view, and maybe in some ways, he is that creepy guy that I now worry about, but he has also been my friend. I don't think he meant to squeeze my arm that hard or bruised me. Besides, that was the first time he has ever reached out and touched me like that. I can't just stop being friends with him. That would be rude, right?"

"Just be careful around him. This definitely makes me happy that you have my email now, and if he ever tries to touch you or force himself on you, you get in your truck and lock the door, or you get somewhere where you're away from him like lock yourself in a bath-room, and you message me immediately. I mean it, Kiddo! I don't care where I'm at or what time it is. You promise?"

"I will…I promise."

Over the next two weeks, Shannon is on cloud nine. She emails Kenny but not too often. She doesn't want to overwhelm him. She tells him good morning or good night, and he checks on her about every two days. They talk about each other's day and where she is that day, where she's going, or where she has been and seen. He hasn't seen much of the States other than when he's in America for a Comic Con or convention, and she even emails him photos of her adventures so he can feel a part of it. He so enjoys seeing what she sees and appreciates that she does that to include him. He even sends her pictures of Canada when he's out and about. Even with their friendship slowly blooming, she still hasn't brought herself to ask him many questions about himself yet. She's waiting till she knows he's comfortable enough and trusts her. Just being able to communicate with him is something she dreamed of, hoped for, and finally has. She has gone from wondering about him and how he is every day to now she can just send an email and ask. She's finally getting to earn his trust and build the friendship with him that she has waited nearly half her life for. She lost her husband and gained the one most amazing person into her life that she never wants to lose. She adores and loves Kenny more with every passing day. He's starting to bring some happiness back into her life that she lost the day Craig died, but she is still careful about how much she talks about. She still hasn't even said those three words to him yet—it just isn't time. What she decides to do next will not only change the way they communicate but open a whole another door into Kenny's world that neither of them ever saw coming.

3

The first Monday morning of October is a bitter cold one in Vancouver. Kenny has just started his day when his phone gets email notifications back to back. What is waiting for him in those messages is something he was not prepared for. He's sitting at his kitchen table when he hears his phone makes sounds from his bedroom. He gets a sinking feeling in his stomach that it's bad. Fully charged and still hooked up the charger, he runs it to grab it. It's one email after another from Shannon.

> Kenny…are you there? I'm saying my last good morning, Kenny… I miss your sweet smile and your warm hug.

> KENNY! I KNOW IT'S EARLY, BUT PLEASE SAY SOMETHING! I just can't do it anymore. I wish I could hear your voice again before it's too late, but I can't. I am trying to fight through this, but I can't. I NEED YOU TO SAY SOMETHING. HELP ME CHANGE MY MIND!

Kenny reads each email twice to make sure he is seeing what he has read and is shocked and feels adrenaline run all through his body. He immediately sends her his cell number and the demands that she calls. He answers after the first ring.

"Kiddo?"

"Hi, Kenny." Shannon has been crying all night, and she sounds exhausted and scared.

"What is wrong? What are all of these emails about, and why are you crying?"

"I can't do it anymore. I just can't be here anymore."

"Can't be where? What are you talking about?"

"This life, Kenny! I can't live it anymore. I'm just so lonely out here and feeling depressed over the past few days. I just…even though I have you, I still feel like I don't have anybody anymore."

"What do you mean by 'you can't live your life'?"

"Being in this semi everyday 24-7 out here on these roads, it just gets to be too much. It's lonesome out here. It's just me and these semi walls, and that's it—nothing else. What I once had for six years is gone. I stop at the truck stops and see the other truckers with their spouses, and it's hard. It's a realization to what I lost and that what I don't have anymore. Why did I have to lose him so soon? What did I do wrong? I miss my husband so much, Kenny. I don't think I will ever find true love again. I'm just ready to end it all and…"

"*No, Kiddo!* You did nothing wrong. None of this is your fault, and you will find someone again. I am sure one of those truckers out there would be happy to have someone as sweet as you. You can't do this! This isn't the answer! You're stronger than this. You survived your depression—remember telling me that?"

"Yeah, but—"

"No buts, Kiddo! You have been so happy, laughing, and full of life over the past months. I'm not understanding how everything has switched so fast. Suicide! Is that what you're telling me?"

"I'm in Seattle, Washington, and I'm not far from a bridge. I'm thinking about driving my semi off it. I'm even wearing the outfit that I met you in at the convention. You remember it, right? My Rusty Blade shirt, black layered skirt, and my flats. That's the outfit that I want to die in because it's the one I met you in. I'm happy to be hearing your voice because I want your voice, your sweet gentle voice, to be the last thing I hear. Don't worry. I'll hang up before I do it. I don't want you to hear the crash, my screams, or any explosions. I can't leave you with that. You have been the one who has been there for me the most in these past months in more ways that I have time to explain. For thirteen years, you have been my happiness, my encouragement, my inspiration, and for the past few months, you've been my friend. You gave me a chance to know you. You gave me a gift that I will always treasure forever. Please don't feel guilty or anything because I've told you that you saved my life once before, and I'm sorry that I'm doing this. I'm sorry that I'm not as strong as I thought I was. I will miss you more than words can say. Just please promise me that you will always remember me and that you won't hate me or be disappointed in me because…I…I adore you, Kenny Kirtzanger, and everything that makes you who you are. To me, I'll always be your Kiddo, and you will always be my Rusty Blade."

Kenny started to feel emotional but fought back from crying. He has to be strong for her. He just can't believe what he is hearing, that she actually wants to end her life. Trying to quickly think of something fast before she reaches that bridge and knowing he saved her life once before without even being in her life, he knows he can save her again, but he wasn't sure if he wanted to get that involved in her problems, but he also didn't want to live with regrets. There is only one way he can save her fast, and even though he wasn't ready for that next step, he knew he had to do it. He won't let her end her life…not on his watch.

"Listen to me, Kiddo. Stop thinking that way. I don't want you to die. I don't want to attend my fan's funeral. Don't do that to me or you. Think about all of your family and friends and how you're going to leave them with that same pain. Did you really wait thirteen years to be in my life just to leave after a few months? You said that you would never hurt me, but don't you think that this will hurt me?"

"No! I don't want to leave you, Kenny, and I don't want to hurt you. You're my Rusty Blade, right?"

"That's right! Do you know that you are only about three hours away from me right now, give or take?"

"Seriously!"

"Yeah! Would you like to come and see me? Like right now? Come out to Vancouver and visit me? It will be your first trip to Canada and to my house. Would you like that, Kiddo?"

"Yes." Shannon is quickly overcome with excitement through her tears. Visiting Kenny at his home is something every fan dreams of, and she has always imagined where he lives, what his house may look like, what kind of lifestyle he has; and now she is getting the opportunity.

"I would so love that more than anything in this world, Kenny... Oh, wow!"

"Good, and I'll be waiting."

She calls her dispatcher and explains she isn't feeling well and needs some rest. He tells her to take a few days off and wishes her well. She punches his home address into her GPS, which causes her to bypasses that bridge as she heads to his house.

Shannon crosses the border into Canada. She can't believe how lovely of a country it really is. From the naked trees that have shed their fall leaves and old big buildings down to the Victorian-style homes and coastlines. Every photo or documentary that she has ever seen never did it the justice that she sees as she makes her way to Vancouver. She is absolutely amazed at how beautifully breathtaking Canada really is. It's approaching one in the afternoon as she turns onto Kenny's road, and with only a half mile to go, she is overcome with the anticipation of seeing him, hearing his voice, and possibly getting a hug. She calls him to make sure she can park at his house with her not having a trailer, and he agrees. His house sets off from the highway secluded by trees in the front and a long gravel drive. It appears to be a huge single-story house built with red brick mixtures with blue shutters and a blue porch. She barely sees him sitting on his porch waving at her as she pulls up past his drive, throws on her turn signal, and backs into his drive as far back up to what appears to be a guesthouse as possible. With a hiss of her air brakes being released, it's a realization to her that he, Kenny Kirtzanger, has once again saved her life. Instead of her lying at the bottom of a bridge broken up, bleeding, burned, mangled, and left for dead, she is now parked in his driveway at his house. She begins to smile and cry happy tears in disbelief. She is still buckled in her seat, tired, exhausted, and with a busting headache when she sees him walking over to her driver's door and opens it.

"Hi, Kiddo, welcome to Vancouver."

She looks at him. "Hey, Kenny, and thank you! Can't believe I am finally in Canada. It's absolutely so stunningly beautiful here."

"Well, are you going to sit here all day or come in because it's pretty chilly out here?" They both snicker.

"Oh, I am definitely coming in. I've waited too long not to."

"Good, come on!"

She climbs down shutting and locking her door. Almost collapsing from exhaustion, Kenny grips onto her tight, and she follows him to his front porch.

"This is all so beautiful! Your house, yard, and you even have a guesthouse—crazy cool! I love it!"

"Thank you."

"You're welcome."

They both make their way up the three steps, and she sees that he has two chairs and a porch swing with two pillows to her right and a long coffee table to her left.

"Kenny, wait! Are you sure you're ready for this? I don't have to go in if you aren't. It's okay—really! I know the emails and that phone call were a lot to handle, but we don't have to do this yet."

He stops shy of his front door, turns to her with a shy smile. "Welcome to my house, Kiddo." And he opens his door and guides her inside. What she sees is everything she has ever dreamed, and she is in pure heaven. She looks around taking everything she can into her memory. To her left is his kitchen, which is open to the living room and other rooms except an open wall providing a small hall across from the guest bathroom. It had all black appliances, white cabinets with glass doors along the top wall, and solid-white floor cabinets with blue-pearl-colored granite countertops and a mini matching island, a large oval kitchen table, and a gray tile floor. Across from the kitchen to her right is his large living room that is also open to the rest of the house with royal mahogany wood floor along the rest of his house. The walls that she could see were a light gray with white baseboards and trimmings, and all of the doors are also white. There is a four-person black couch, two matching black chairs, coffee-bean-colored coffee table, and two matching end tables with small lamps all sitting atop a large white rug. He has a large flat-screen TV mounted above the fireplace, a large bay window with one huge window in the center, and two small glass windows on both sides with a small round table. There is a guest bathroom across from the kitchen, and she counted four closed doors which she was sure to be bedrooms.

"You have one of the most beautiful homes I've ever been in Kenny. I love the whole open floor plan. It's not too big but not too small. It's simple but luxurious in its own way, your way."

"Thanks."

"You don't have to show me around. Just tell me about it—your house that is."

"Well, it's three bedrooms. Off to the kitchen over, there is my guest room, and there next to it is the guest bathroom. The one right there to the right of the bathroom is one that I've converted into my merchandise room—"

"A merchandise room?"

"Yeah, and it has movie props, posters, costumes, awards, a large locked cabinet, and accessories."

"I can only imagine what treasures you have in there."

"Some you will definitely like. There, next to it, as you can see, is my laundry room and the double sliding doors to the backyard. Next is my bedroom, and then over here is another room I turned into my office. I have a connected two-car garage outback beside my room. Come on, I'll show you my backyard."

They walk through the sliding doors into his large backyard with a huge firepit and concrete benches surrounding it. There's a small grilling area next to the firepit. Off to the right is his garage, and off to the left is his guesthouse. It's has two stories with Belmont Blue wood siding and white shutters.

"So beautiful! That is a guesthouse?" She points over in its direction. "I've never seen one or understood why people have them. I'm from the South, and we just pile everybody in our house somewhere, ha."

"Yes! It has two bedrooms upstairs and a large back balcony off from the second floor that looks out through the trees."

"Shoot! I'm living there. Do you have a boat?"

"Yes! Ever been on one?"

"Nope!"

"No?"

"I would love to, though. Can we go back inside, Kenny? It's cold!"

They both walk back inside and over to the kitchen table where they enjoy a cup of hot chocolate with marshmallows at the kitchen table, and she learns that he has a bit of a sweet tooth. Something they certainly have in common.

"Are you okay now, Kiddo? Please don't ever scare me like that again."

"Well, other than feeling like I've been hit by my own semi, ha, yes, I am feeling better now that I am here with you. I just have a headache. I'm so sorry I did that to you. I'm still going to have my moments, but I'll be okay. It's just going to take me some time and a lot of crying to get it all out, but no more suicidal thoughts, I promise."

"Good and know that you can always cry to me. I will do my best to listen. Are you seeing a therapist?"

"I was, but it's been a while. Guess it's time to go back."

"I would feel better if you did. I am concerned about you and definitely recommend it."

"I will as soon as I get home. Is it weird or uncomfortable having me, a fan in your house?"

"Actually, no! Not like I thought! It's actually kinda nice to have company other than family, and it's nice to have female company again."

"I am happy to be your female company too. This right here, Kenny—this!—is all I've wanted for thirteen years. Just sitting at this table across from you having a normal conversation and being the highlight of your day. Nothing more or nothing less—just me and you. Thank you, Kenny, for caring that much about me and for trusting me. You do trust me right?"

"Kiddo, if I didn't trust you, you wouldn't be in my house. So you wanna see something that will make your heart skip a beat?"

"You mean other than seeing you? Ha!" She winks her eye at him. "Yes, I would."

Kenny giggles and maybe even blushes a little as he walks her over to his merchandise room. He punches in a code on the door's keypad, and it unlocks.

"Kiddo, this room is very important to me. It's my life, my career journey. Things in this room can't be reproduced, replaced, or touched unless I tell you, you can touch it, okay?"

"Okay."

"You are the first fan to know about the room and see what lies inside. I am giving you a lot of trust to do this, but there is something in here that I have that I know you will love to see and I want to show you. You deserve it."

"I promise I won't touch anything without your permission."

Shannon's heart begins to beat faster as he turns the knob and pushes the door open. She steps inside and is in complete shock of everything that's within these four walls. One, the wall to her left is framed pictures of him with other actors, actresses, and film workers; and on the wall to her right are movie posters from different horror movies with signatures, and in the corner was a life-size cardboard cutout of himself dressed as his hockey mask wearing killer character. There are two glass cases against the wall. One is about five feet tall with dirt and fake-blood-stained machete enclosed inside, and the other one is about a foot and a half tall with one of his hockey masks from the movie enclosed inside of it. The wall in front of her has two side-by-side windows with a tall wood storage cabinet with two long doors and locks. As soon as Shannon sees the cabinet, she almost senses that something is waiting in there to be seen by her, and she slowly walks up to it. Kenny walks over and unlocks the left door.

"Close your eyes, Kiddo, and hold out both your hands ready for a firm grip."

"Okay...this is fun, he he." Standing there nervously excited, she feels him lay something long, slightly heavy and cold in her hands. "What did you just hand me?" She giggles to herself.

"Open your eyes."

She opens her eyes to see the most amazing thing she has dreamt of seeing in person next to him. It's the hatchet from the *Unjoyful Ride 3: Roadkiller* movie, and she begins to tremble. She just stares at it in jaw-drop shock that he has it, and that she's actually holding it.

"Are you kidding me right now, Kenny? Whoa! I can't believe this! I love that movie so much and your Rusty Blade character, and now I am standing here in the same room with my Rusty Blade holding his hatchet—*what!* Ha! Oh my gosh! Is the real—I mean, it is real!"

She begins to tear up, clutching the black-and-yellow hatchet close to her almost hugging it.

"Ha! Your reaction makes it worth it."

"Thank you so much for this, Kenny—to trust me to let me see it, to let me hold it, and it even still has dirt on it."

"You're welcome. I knew it would make you very happy to see it. I know how much you love the movie, and I felt like you deserved to see it. Now let me see your phone, and I'll take your picture with it just don't post it on social media."

"You're the most wonderful human being ever! I've read about how your fans always describe you as such a sweet, caring gentleman, but this really takes the cake.

"I never realized you guys say that about me."

"That's because you're not on social media to look yourself up and see what all we post and say about you."

Kenny places his hatchet back in the cabinet and locks the door back.

"You should display that in a glass box too."

"Come over here." He walks her over to a small table against the other wall. On the table are passes from his past Comic Cons, tokens from fans, and a small jewelry box. He opens the top lid to reveal the black leather cuff he wore in the *Unjoyful Ride 3: Roadkiller* movie as well. He removes the cuff and hands it to her to hold.

"This day just keeps getting better and better."

She hands it back to him, and after putting it back in the box, they exit the room, and he locks the door behind him. As soon as he turns, she wraps her arms tightly around him. "Aw, Kenny, you're the best!"

"It was my pleasure, Kiddo." He hugs her back.

About that time, his doorbell rings, and he walks over to the door and greets his company inviting him inside. Shannon stands at the edge of the kitchen table hiding in shyness from who was here.

"Kenny, whose semi is...that?" While walking in past Kenny and noticing her standing in the kitchen, he looks back at Kenny.

"Carlos, this is my fan and friend Shannon Keeler, and, Shannon, this is my best friend, Carlos DelValle."

Carlos is of Mexican descent, approximately fifty-one years old, about five feet six inches tall, muscular fit built, with salt-pepper hair, close facial hair, soft brown eyes, and a charming smile that can melt any woman's heart.

"Nice to meet you, Carlos, and that semi belongs to me."

"Nice to meet you, too, Shannon." He looks back at Kenny with a surprised smile. "You've never mentioned her."

Kenny chuckles and clears his throat being caught off guard. "We met back in August at my Chicago convention. She has been my fan for many years, and we just connected."

Shannon intervenes. "We actually met outside a restaurant first...sorry, Kenny."

"You just met two months ago, and she is already here at your house? Well, she must have really made an impression on you."

"Well...um...ha...it's a bit of a story, but anyway, she's the sweetest fan I've ever met. I thought it would be fun to have a personal connection with a fan for once."

"How long have you two been friends?" Shannon asked.

"Twenty-four years, Kiddo."

"Awesome, ha! That's a long time."

"What did you just call her?" Carlos laughs.

"'Kiddo,' it's her nickname I gave her because she's so short next to me, and she looks a lot younger than she really is."

"Ahh, hell! Everybody's short next to you, Kenny." Now they three are all laughing, and Shannon begins to feel comfortable with Kenny's best friend and walks over next to them.

"I call him Rusty Blade because even though I discovered him in his slasher movie, my favorite movie is *Unjoyful Ride 3: Roadkiller*, and, ooh…that Rusty Blade…ha ha…so yeah."

Kenny and Carlos sit in the living room, and Shannon joins.

"So, Shannon, how long have you been a truck driver?" Carlos asks.

"Almost two years."

"You do it alone?" Kenny tries to shush Carlos.

"It's okay, Kenny. My husband was living on the road with me, but he recently passed away, so I am alone right now."

"Oh no, I'm sorry."

"Thanks! I had a major breakdown this morning, and I emailed Kenny, reaching out for help, and that led to him giving me his number, which led to me being here."

"That's Kenny. He is always trying to help others and his fans in any way possible. He loves and appreciates all of you. One reason we have been friends for so long."

Kenny has been staring at Shannon the whole time her, and Carlos has been talking and is completely zoned out until she simply calls his name. "Kenny, if you two have plans or want to hang out, I can head out and crash at a truck stop."

"Oh no, Kiddo! You're fine, and you don't have to leave."

"Good because I don't want to leave." She smiles.

"Are you flirting with him?" Carlos asks.

"Maybe."

Without saying a word, he could already sense the connection between Shannon and Kenny that even they haven't noticed yet, but would anything ever become of it? Only time would tell. He could already see the difference she has made in his best friend. She may be young, but she has a lovely quiet old soul and very mature for her age. It makes it easy for her to fit right in with people much older than her, and Carlos has already grown fond of her. As they both engage in conversation, Shannon watches Kenny talk, taking in every word, every hand movement, the way he laughs… She still can't believe that she's sitting here in his living room across from him. He's just the most beautiful person she has ever seen. A part of her is happy that he's single, and she can just be open and free around him to do and say whatever she wants without offending a girlfriend or wife. Kenny and Carlos talk about shows and movies Carlos is working on and Kenny's upcoming Comic Cons. Carlos works in stunts as a coordinator, and he's a director/producer and actor from what Shannon can tell. She almost still can't believe how much her life has already changed in just these few months. Kenny and Carlos both decide to treat her by taking her out to a nice for dinner. She tries to refuse not wanting them to spend money on her, but with a smile from Kenny that can melt any woman's heart, she agrees. While eating their dinner, they spend a few hours talking and laughing. She learns about Carlos's previous marriages, his fiancée, his three grown kids and how his son has followed in his footsteps, and his sweet granddaughter. He lets it slip that Kenny had a horrible ex-girlfriend who hurt him and broke all his trust for women, and that's why he is shocked to see her but quickly changes the topic after Kenny gives him an evil look. She wasn't ready or in no mood to hear about his ex, anyway. She just wanted to enjoy the night. She didn't talk much about herself. She didn't want to get emotional over her food, but eventually she'll open up more. It was getting late, and they leave, heading back to Kenny's house. Carlos tells them good night; and Shannon, standing in Kenny's living room gives him a hug as she thanks him for dinner. He tells her she's welcome and leaves.

"Thank you for dinner, Kenny. Very sweet of you two to do that. I absolutely enjoyed it and had a great time talking to your friend. He's very sweet like you. I haven't had any kind of fun like this since Craig's passing."

"You're very welcome, and I enjoyed it too. Carlos seems to enjoy talking to you as well."

"I think I am going to go lie down. I've had such a day, and I am still exhausted from it all, and I just need a good cry, I think. Good night, Rusty Blade." She turns and starts heading to the front door, but he stops her. "Where are you going, Kiddo?"

"Out to my semi and crawl into my bunk."

"Uh-uh, you see the door over there past my kitchen?" He points her in the direction.

"Yes."

"That's where you're sleeping tonight, young lady."

She exclaimed in joy, "No way! I get to stay here in your house with you? I wasn't even expecting to ever get to stay in your guest-house, let alone your house."

"Yes, you get to spend the night here in my house with me. After this morning, I don't want you out of my sight right now. If you need to cry, then that is where you can cry."

Shannon goes out to her semi to get a change of clothes for the next day, her pajamas, and shower bag with all of her personal hygiene products. She enters the room where she will be sleeping and sees a full-size bed to her left with white-and-beige bedding, a beautiful carved headboard with matching footboard and nightstands with lamps on both, a white chair in the corner by the window, a dresser with vanity across from the bed, and closet to her right. It's simple but beautiful. She sets her belongings on the chair. After she showers, she sits on the edge of the bed and messages her friend Colleen, who is not only a fan of Kenny's as well but has been her biggest support over him, and tells her a little bit of what happened from her almost suicide attempt to him inviting her out and meeting his best friend Carlos. But she didn't reveal too much to keep some of it for herself. Colleen is so happy for her that she is finally getting to interact with Kenny. She tells her that she will eventually mention her to Kenny and tell him how they met. Colleen thanks her and tells her she's too sweet. Shannon puts her phone on silent and plugs it into the charge and lays it on the nightstand. She lays down in the bed under the covers feeling like she's lying on a cloud after sleeping in her bunk. She's facing the door that she has been slightly left cracked open, and there's nothing but darkness other than the soft glow from the lamp, and she can hear Kenny out in the living room watching TV and chuckling, which makes her giggle under the covers. Oh, how she has long to hear his laugh in person. As she lays there feeling so lucky and blessed, she also knows that it took losing her husband for this to happen. *Sometimes, you have to lose to gain*, she thinks to herself. *But why to this degree? Is there another reasoning for losing my husband? Please, God, why? What lies ahead at the end of my rainbow?* She begins to cry feeling so lost and lonely in the bed as she realizes she hasn't slept in double bed since his passing. She reaches over, picking up her phone, and texts Kenny, "Just want to say good night, Kenny, and I thank you again for such a beautiful day. I just absolutely adore you." Laying her phone on the pillow beside her, she tries to muffle her cries hoping that he won't hear them, but it doesn't work. She begins to hear his footsteps getting louder as they approached the room, and she covers her face under the covers as if she's trying to disappear as she hears him push the door open. He walks over, and she feels him sit down on the side of the bed next to her.

"Kiddo?" He pulls the covers down, exposing her tear-soaked face. "Look at me...hey."

"Hey, Kenny, guess you read my text. I guess it was pretty silly to text you from inside the house."

"No, no, it wasn't. Now talk to me. What's wrong? Tell me what happened. You have got to talk about it and get it out. That's the only way you can move on, and you know that more than anyone."

"I know. It's just so hard, and I hate crying." She wipes her tears away. "Craig was always up before me. He liked greeting me as soon as I woke up, and sometimes he had to make sure I got up. These crazy hauls puts you on flip-flop sleeping hours, and you don't always want to get up when you hear that alarm. I rarely ever rented a motel, but my lower back was already hurting, and I had to head out the next morning for a load, and I just wanted to sleep in an actual bed. So I got us a room in Lenoir, North Carolina. Everything was fine, Kenny. We had a normal day like any other day. Never would have thought anything was wrong. Later that night, he complained that he had a pain in his chest, but we figured it was heartburn or something. When I woke up the next morning, he was still asleep, and I knew something wasn't right. I reached over to wake him, and um..." Shannon tears up.

"It's okay, Kiddo. Take your time." He rubs her arm.

"I reached over, and he was cold and stiff, and I knew he was gone. I jump up screaming and ran out to the office, and the hotel clerk called 911. I didn't want to believe it! I wanted to run back in there and keep trying to wake him, but I called his mom instead.

That was the worst phone call to make. He had an enlarged heart, birth defect. My last memory with my husband will always be waking up beside his lifeless body."

"I am so sorry. I couldn't even begin to imagine, just gives my chills and hurts me that this happen to you. You have to somehow replace that memory with a better one of you two."

"Thank you, Kenny. I do feel a little better. Can that be enough for tonight, please?"

"Kiddo, you don't have to open up all at once. Take your time, and slowly ease into it, and I'll always be here anytime you are ready."

"Thanks for coming in here and checking on me. It means a lot to me that you care."

"You're welcome, and I do care."

"Kenny…um…I have a crazy question, and it's okay if you don't want to answer it, but would you mind staying till I fall asleep?" she asks nervously. "I just don't want to fall asleep alone tonight."

"Sure."

"You're so freaking sweet."

"So are you."

"Are we bonding more, Kenny? Like, are you seeing that you can trust me? I promise I'm not a crazy awkward fan."

He cracks a smile. "Yeah, I think so. Good night, Kiddo."

"Good night, Rusty Blade." Shannon closes her eyes and drifts off into a peaceful sleep. About ten minutes later, Kenny moves her phone from the pillow over to the nightstand, turns off the lamp, and closes the door as he exits the room. He still can't believe that he has a fan sleeping in his house. He doesn't ever let family sleep in his house most of the time, let alone a fan. Someone that he was still getting to know. Has he lost his mind, or does he really just enjoy her company? He doesn't know what he likes about her, but he was sure to find out. They have breakfast together the next morning. She is heading out for a long drive back to the States for a much-needed visit with her therapist. They talk about yesterday, Carlos, and last night. Last night was the first best sleep she has had in a while. She hasn't slept that good since it happened and woke up feeling so rested, energized, and happy.

"Hey, Kenny, do you want to see something in my semi that's pretty cool? Maybe it'll make your heart skip a beat, ha."

"Ha, sure! I was actually wanting to see the inside of your semi."

She gathers up her stuff, and they both walk out together to her semi. She unlocks the passenger door and tells him to climb up in, and she goes around climbing up in on the driver's side. She cranks up her semi so her air brake pressure can build and turns on her heater. She has her curtains pulled closed separating the front cab from the back living space.

"Behind these curtains, Kenny, on the wall between my bunks is my prized possession, and it's one of my most favorite things that I have. I had it made shortly after I started trucking, and I always hoped that one day I would get to show it to you. It is my favorite still shot of you as Rusty Blade that's been burnt into a solid block of wood and hand-painted. I hope you like it."

Shannon opens the curtains and reveals a four-by-three-and-a-half-foot painting of him as Rusty Blade standing in the middle of a highway in front of the black jackknife tractor trailer that's over-heated with smoke and steam all around him and the sun settling in the distance.

Kenny just stares in amazement, almost speechless. "Wow! That is fantastic! I have never seen anything like this of me before. That is really awesome! I love it! Can I touch it?"

"Of course."

He throws his arm around her, pulling her close to him, and she hugs him back. He walks over and sits down on her bottom bunk and rubs his fingers all around the painting, feeling every indentation of the outlines and bumps in the paint. He is truly amazed by it and takes a picture with his phone.

"Can I come back and visit you again sometime, Kenny?"

Kenny gets up and walks back over to her. "You know, Kiddo, I definitely think you can come back and visit me. We both have crazy schedules, but I think we can work it out. I have my Comic Con in Germany in a few weeks, so how about next month for my birthday?"

"I can come spend your birthday with you! I would love to."

"Absolutely."

"Well, if I'm going to make my appointment on time, then I've got to head out. Thank you for saving me yesterday morning, for letting me come and visit you, and thank you for a wonderful evening."

"You're so welcome, anytime."

He tells her that she can keep his number, and they say their goodbyes, and he climbs down out of her semi and walks over to his porch and watches her drive off, disappearing beyond his sights. She is really excited at the thoughts that she can come out and visit him next month for his birthday; but that visit may come sooner and in a way that either of them is prepared, for as trust is tested, a bond is strengthened, and Kenny's past starts to surface.

4

I t's the third Thursday of October, and Kenny had his Germany convention this coming weekend but unfortunately has had to cancel because he is extremely sick. He hasn't spoken to Shannon on the phone in a week but texted her a few days ago telling her he wasn't feeling well and not attending his event. Being very concerned, she has texted him almost every eight hours since to check on him and has even only been making loads out west to stay as close to Canada as possible in case she feels the need to make the drive to his house. Having an intense urge, she decides to call him not knowing if he will even answer, and she's so glad she does. After answering the phone, she is almost bought to tears at how weak just his voice sounds.

"Hi, Kiddo," Kenny answers in a low weak voice.

"I hope you don't mind me calling, but I just need to talk to you. I need to hear your voice. I need to know you're okay. I am driving myself crazy out here worrying about you. I can't focus enough on these loads, and I am barely sleeping."

"That's very sweet that you're concerned, and I appreciate it, but you have to still take care of yourself too. I don't know what's wrong with me. I went out to dinner a few nights ago with Carlos and his fiancée, and then I started feeling sick over the next day and got worse yesterday. I'm only comfortable lying in bed. Hopefully it'll pass soon."

"What are your symptoms?"

"Just your normal stomach bug stuff."

"Kenny just please tell me. It's nothing to feel embarrassed about. We all get sick."

"I am very weak, diarrhea, vomiting, horrible stomach pains, and can't keep anything down. I've never been this sick or felt this pain. It's unbearable at times. I just want it to go away."

"Oh no, Kenny! Sounds like you have food poisoning! Do you have anybody there with you or have you asked anybody to go to the store and get you anything to try to help you?"

"No, unfortunately, I'm alone. Carlos is out working on movies, and my brother and his wife are out of town. Food poisoning?"

"Kenny, listen to me, ever since you told me that you're sick, I've only been staying out west and taking loads out here so that I can stay close to Canada. Right now, I am at a truck stop here in Portland, Oregon, because I'm off today, and then I'm supposed to be heading out tomorrow to Spokane, Washington, to pick up a very important load-probably the biggest load of my career, but you are more important to me, and I rather come and take care of you."

"No, Kiddo! It's okay. Don't miss your load for me."

"Don't you 'No, Kiddo' me, Kenny Kirtzanger! You are far more important to me than any load or any payout. Now I'm calling my dispatcher, and I'm giving my load away. My choice! I'm taking a few days off, and I'm coming out to you. I'll take care of you, and I will heal you if you just trust me. Do you trust me to come and take care of you?"

"Yes, of course, I trust you, and I guess it would be nice to have some company right now. Hey, if you think you can heal me, then please do it. Are you sure you want to give this load away—the biggest one of your career? I don't want you to regret it."

"Absolutely, I am sure! Do you think that I can continue being out here doing this knowing that you're sick as you are? I can't, Kenny! You're my Rusty Blade, and you need help, and I want to be there for you. I want to take care of you. I'll see you in about five, six hours. In the meantime, get some rest."

"You are just too sweet. I don't know what to say. It means a lot to me that you want to do this, and I thank you. I'll see you when you get here."

Shannon hangs up with Kenny and calls her dispatcher and explains everything to him and asks him to give her load away. He is amazed that anyone would want to give a load like this away with its great payout, especially her with her saving for her own black tracker trailer; but at the same time, he knows, too, how much she cares about Kenny and doesn't try to talk her out of it. Instead, he agrees and wishes Kenny well. She makes the six-hour-and-thirty-minute drive up to Vancouver and arrives at a little close to dinner time. She stopped at a store on the way and bought him some stuff to help him. Just hearing the weakness in his voice over the phone made her stomach sink, but she isn't nowhere close to being prepared for what she is about to see once he'd open his front door. He opens his door to greet her wearing long cotton pajama pants, a black pullover shirt, and socks. He is very pale, dehydrated, and can barely stand. Her eyes begin to fill with tears, and she drops the grocery bag in disbelief at how bad he looks and wraps her arms around him—squeezing him tight.

"Aw, Kenny, I am so sorry you are sick. I can't, I didn't realize it was this bad." She releases him, picks up the bag, and motions him inside and over to his couch. They walk inside, and he can barely move around but finally makes it to the couch, and they both sit together. She precedes to empty the grocery bag showing him every-thing she bought to help him. There is antidiarrhea pills, pink liquid stuff for his stomach pains, and four of his favorite hydration drinks to keep him hydrated. He is so touched by her willingness to help him, and he's very thankful to have her.

"Thank you, Shannon"—he only calls her by her name when he's very serious—"for doing this. It means a lot to me that you care this much. You didn't have to do this, give your load away, or buy me this stuff, but you did, and I'm so grateful. I really just want to feel better."

She looks over at Kenny and just goes for it, placing her right hand on top of his hot feverish hand, and he feels sensational chills through his body from her gentle touch but doesn't let it show.

"You're so welcome. You didn't hesitate one bit to invite me out here to your home to save my life. I know that was a huge step for you to trust me in your home, and you did because you care that much for me as your fan and friend. After thirteen years, I will drop anything for you. Now let's start getting you better."

Holding back her emotions, she explains to him how and when to take the pills and when to use the pink liquid. She and Craig both having had food poisoning before, she knows all too well the sickness, pain, and misery he's feeling and knows she can heal him. She's fully prepared to stay with him until he's better, no matter how long it takes. She gives him a dosage of the pink liquid and makes him drink some of the drink to put fluids in him.

"I had to cancel my convention for this coming weekend. I feel bad and hated to do that to my fans. I never want to let you guys down, but I know I can't make it." He looks down, messing with his pajama drawstrings.

"Kenny, you aren't letting anyone down. You can't help that you're sick, and your fans understand that. Yeah, the ones who were meeting you for the first time will be crushed, but they won't hate you. You have nothing to feel bad about. They will be more concerned about you getting better. I bet I can pull up social media right now and find some already wishing you well."

He looks up and smiles at her the best he can. "I don't know how you can get any more sweeter. I guess I kind of needed to hear that, and coming from a fan does make it more believable. I think I am going to lie back down, but make yourself comfortable while your here. You are more than welcome to stay in here and watch TV, whatever you want to do. Help yourself to anything in the fridge, and the guest room is all yours. I only ask that you stay out of my office. I don't like anyone in there without me."

"Thank you, but this couch right here is where I'm staying. I want to be as close to you as possible. I may not hear you in the room. I'll be fine—trust me. Now go lie down and rest, and don't be afraid to yell for me or ask me for something. You can even text me if you have to, and I know that I've never been inside of your room, and I would never go in your room without your consent, but I'm telling you right now, if I feel the need to go in there to check on you, give you something to drink, medicine, anything like that, I will be going in there. Another thing, too, I hope this doesn't sound bad, but when you wake from your nap, we're going to wash your hair."

"Yeah, ha. When you're tall like me, Kiddo, you don't want to fall, especially in the shower, and I've just felt too weak to stand in the shower long. I have been taking quick showers and get too dizzy to wash my hair."

"That's okay, and trust me! After eight months of being on crutches, you learn how to bathe, and I needed help, too, with washing everything, including my hair. So don't feel bad about needing help. It doesn't make you look less than who you are. It will help you feel a little better too. Your hair looks like you just took that hockey mask off." She giggles. "Sorry, that probably sounded rude."

"Ha, no, I believe it, and that's real sweet that you want to do all of this for me. Thank you."

"Hey, it's just the love of a fan who's now becoming your friend, and you saved me twice, and probably somewhere in the future, I may need you to save me again. That's what you do when you care about someone. Can I give you a hug?"

"I'd like that."

She curls up in his extended arms and hugs him tightly. "I just adore you, my Rusty Blade, and I'll get you through this, I promise."

Kenny has never in his life felt a hug as warm, as inviting, as sincere, or as magical as her hug. He almost wanted to keep hugging her and not let go, but he begins to shiver in cold chills, and she sends him to bed. Throughout the rest of the evening, she makes a few trips into his room taking him his hydration drinks and to check on him. At one point, she just stares from his doorway at how peacefully beautiful he looks sleeping. He has a large master bedroom with the same-color walls and hardwood floor as the rest of his house. His king-size bed sets in the middle of the back wall with the head looking out to the door and a large ceiling fan. The opposite wall is a large flat-screen TV hanging on the wall above his dark cherry oak long dresser. In the corner between it and his double windows on the sidewall is a tall full-length mirror on a stand. Dark curtains hang over his windows that match his dark bedding. He has a nightstand on both sides of his bed that matches his dresser with small lamps on them and a huge walk-in closet next to his bathroom. Once he wakes from his nap, Shannon goes into his bathroom to set up to wash his wash. It's a lavish bathroom, even for him. Once stepping in, she sees the whole bathroom is an off-white cream tile. On the wall to her left are several towel racks. To her right is a long double sink with gold and crystal knobs and faucets to her right all dressed in with crystal knobs on the cabinet doors and gold knobs on the drawers, off-white marble countertop, and a mirror that reaches both ends. Next to the sink is his toilet, and built into the corner is a large square shower made of dark-gray tile mixtures adored with all glass walls and a glass door with gold trim. Next to the shower is a beautiful round garden tub of a soft cream color that appears to be almost two feet deep with two small steps. It sets close to the wall with the same gray tile as the shower built around it with space and shelves to set stuff. She fills his tub with about six inches of warm water and gets his shampoo and conditioner from his shower and goes back into his kitchen and gets a cup. Back in the bathroom, she calls for him and has him set on the side of his garden tub facing her. He is still wearing his same pajama bottoms but changed into a plan white tank top. She has him lean his back so she can wet his hair and squeezes some of his shampoo onto the middle of his hand and begins lathering it up throughout his very short hair.

"How about a little scalp massage, Kenny?" she says while scratching and massaging his scalp.

"Whatever you want to do, Kiddo."

"So cool that you have a garden tub. I have always wanted one. Do you use it?"

"No, not really. I think I've been in it twice years ago, but you are more than welcome to use it. It takes about an hour to fill it."

"Aww, thank you."

"This feels so nice, Kiddo."

"I'm glad, and I don't mind at all, Kenny. Whatever makes you happy."

She rinses the shampoo from his hair and adds the conditioner and rinses that after it sets for a minute. Then she takes a towel and gently rubs it all over his hair trying to absorb as much of the water as possible before blow-drying his hair dry. He was so touched by her and her willingness to try and help him feel better. He believed a little more that she truly does care for him. He lies back down after thanking her with a hug, and she cleans up his bathroom. Around midnight, she is awoken from the sounds of him in his bathroom, and she jumps up running in to find him on the floor leaning back up against the wall. Seeing her come in, Kenny says with a shaky voice, "Oh, Kiddo, did I wake you?"

"Don't you worry about waking me. That's why I am sleeping on the couch."

She gives him some more medicine and softly caresses his shoulders and tells him to slowly try and stand up. In an angry tone out of not feeling good, he pushes her hands off his shoulders. "No, Kiddo! Just go away and leave me alone! Get out of my room! Go…! Now!"

Shannon looks at him with a calm voice. "I'm not going anywhere, Kenny Kirtzanger. I'm here to help you, and that's what I am doing rather you want it right now or not. I know how miserable you are. I've had this stuff once myself, and it's not fun. Now we're going to get you up off this bathroom floor and back in your bed, understood?"

Surprised by her soft tone and patience with him, he stands, and she helps him get back in bed and goes back in his bathroom, wets a washcloth with cold water, and sets on the side of his bed gently rubbing around his face with it until he falls back asleep. She is starting to love him more now than she ever imagined, and she would do anything to help him feel better. The cycle repeats itself when she wakes again around two thirty in the morning to the sounds of him and once again is by his side. This time the medicine helps him sleep through the rest of the night. While he's lost in peaceful dreams, she whispers to him softly that she loves him. It's the first time she has said it to him. She hasn't been able to get the courage to actually say it to him. He wakes in the morning around eight and still weak but already feeling better. He walks in the living room to find the TV playing in low volume and her asleep on the couch with nothing but a throw pillow under her head, no cover, and her cell phone revealing her wallpaper which is a picture of him and her from the August

Comic Con. He stands there looking down at her smiling. He can't believe how she truly stood by his side all through the night and never thought he would ever make this kind of a connection with another woman, but he has no regrets, and he wouldn't let her go now for nothing in this world.

He leans down over the back of the couch and gently shakes her. "Kiddo? Hey, Kiddo, wake up."

Shannon wakes to his handsome face staring back down at her. "Good morning, Kenny!" she says, sitting up quickly. "How do you feel?"

"Good morning, and better, thanks to you. I think I would like to try and eat something. How about you?"

"Sure, but you're not making nothing. You just had a rough night! So go sit at the table, and I'll make you something."

"You're so thoughtful, but you're my guest."

"And I'm making my host breakfast," she says, winking her eye at him.

Shannon keeps breakfast simple so as not to upset his stomach. After eating, she gets him another cup of coffee and sits back down at the table with him.

"Kiddo, I'm sorry I got angry at you last night. Anybody else probably would have walked out or mouth back off, but you...you stayed, and you didn't get mad or anything. You were so sensitive and gentle, thanks."

"I knew you said it out of not feeling good. Being miserable like that can make anybody angry. Can't hold it against you. I wasn't walking away from you. Not when you needed me the most. That would have been the wrong thing for me to have done."

"Well, I know I can always count on you and even during my weakest moments."

"Absolutely! Hey, out of curiosity, why don't you have any pictures displayed or hanging up?"

Kenny shifts in his chair while holding onto the rim of his cup and clears his throat. "My ex-girlfriend had them everywhere. Everywhere you looked, there were frames of photos—"

"You mean, she lived here with you?"

"Yes, and since we've broken up, I've enjoyed not seeing them everywhere."

"What was her name?"

"Kimberly."

"How long did you guys date?"

"Three years but broke up two years ago."

"I'm sorry, I feel like I am meddling into your personal business. You don't have to talk about her if you don't want to."

"It's fine, Kiddo! You opened up to me, and so I don't mind opening up to you. She was a model and an actress. We met on the set of my slasher movie and became friends. We started dating later down the road, and everything was perfect for the first few years into our relationship, but then she got where she wouldn't do anything with me that I wanted to do. It was all about her and what she wanted. She didn't like going to my conventions with me, and when she did, she was jealous over my fans. She just made me feel lonelier than in a relationship. She tried to control everything including, what friends I had, who I talked to, communication with my fans, my money, and even me, and I wasn't having that. She became very distant when I wouldn't give into her, and I eventually found out that she was seeing someone else. I blamed myself at first for not giving her, her way. But she hurt me, used me, cheated on me, and broke my trust for women. You, Kiddo, are the first woman I've trusted like this since her."

She is burning with furry inside at this Kimberly woman and tries not to overreact and show him how much it has affected her.

"I can't even say anything because she has me mad, and I would love to slap her right across her face! Blamed yourself? Why? Because you didn't let her walk all over you! That's all her fault! I mean, she was lucky enough to have you...to be with you. Lucky enough to be loved by you, and she used you and cheated on you! I'm sorry, Kenny."

She breaks eye contact and stares off, shaking her head in disbelief.

"Yeah, she wasn't a good girlfriend, and she never would have done for me what you did last night, but it's over, and I haven't seen or spoken to her since and don't care to."

"So you haven't dated since the breakup?"

"No, and I'm happy being single. It just really ruined relationships for me. Carlos keeps trying to set me up on blind dates with actresses he works with, but I kindly refuse."

"Blind dates don't hurt, Kenny, and you never know, you might just find the right one that you have been waiting for your whole life. I can also guarantee you that she will be who you never expected."

"Maybe you're right to a point, but I don't know if I can trust enough again to fall in love. Kimberly just hurt me so deep."

"Uh…that woman! I would kill to have been her for one minute…one minute to have you love me."

Shannon, just realizing what she said, quickly gets up and starts cleaning up after breakfast hoping he didn't hear her. She can't believe she let that slip. Even though she does care deeply for him, she doesn't want to say anything to hurt their friendship. Throughout the rest of the day, he still has moments of being sick, and she is right there to help him through it. By dinnertime, he seems to be completely better. He enjoyed his first real meal in three days that she prepared—Southern style. She is still not letting him do much, but he insists and helps her clean up afterward. As it approaches seven, he goes in the living room, sits on the couch, and starts surfing through the TV channels; and she joins him.

"I am just wondering, where did you put your drawing I gave you?"

"Oh, it's hanging on the wall in my office above my desk so I can see it when I'm in there working. Carlos saw it and thought it was really neat."

"Sweet! He seems really cool. I hope to see him again, maybe hang out or something."

"You definitely will. We may do something for my birthday."

"I've already got you a birthday gift."

"You bought me a present? You didn't have to do that," he says, smiling at her.

"Nobody ever has to do anything for anybody, Kenny, but we do because we want to, and I wanted to buy you a gift. I've waited thirteen years to give you something and to share your birthday with you."

"When is your birthday?"

"February twenty-third. Kenny, I hope this doesn't make you uncomfortable by saying this, but you are absolutely so…handsome. Wow! You have the most beautiful brown eyes I've ever seen, and that smile…ah…a girl can get lost in there somewhere and never want to be found."

Kenny grins and tries not to blush. "Aw…such kind words, Kiddo."

"I am really enjoying our bonding time, and even though you're doing better, I hope I don't have to leave yet. You couldn't make it to your convention, but you can at least spend the weekend with a fan, right?"

He chuckles. "I'm enjoying it, too, Kiddo, and, no, you don't have to leave yet. You can stay through the weekend."

"Perfect."

Shannon spends the next day with Kenny. She watches his favorite TV shows with him and listens to him talk about his past stunt roles, him breaking bones in his back from a stunt gone wrong, where he grew up, and how he and Carlos met. They talk about their hobbies and interests. She is in pure heaven finally getting to learn about him and share some of her own background with him. She tells him about ripping her ACL and shredding her meniscus in her left knee while jumping on a trampoline and undergoing two surgeries to repair it and a year of physical therapy. She learns about his six other siblings and that most of his family still lives in Saskatchewan, Canada, his parents passing, and how his brother Daniel played professional football. He learns about her two brothers, parents, and her spoiled dog, Newbie. Deep down inside, he is starting to really care for her. He enjoys her company and their talks because for once, he can talk about himself where he couldn't with his ex. Sunday morning awakes Shannon, and she realizes she has to head back over to the States, but she knows, too, she'll be back in less than two weeks for his birthday. They said their goodbyes in his living room because she doesn't want him outside in the cold.

She looks up after hugging him. "It gets a little harder to leave with every visit, but as soon as I pull out of that drive, I get to count down to the next one. I've so enjoyed this time with you, and I can leave in peace knowing that you're feeling better. I won't have to worry about you, and I can go back to texting you normal stuff every day and sending you pictures of my journeys."

"I've enjoyed your company too and being able to tell you a little bit about my past and learning some about you. You keep me smiling and laughing the whole time you're here, and that's something I haven't had in a while. You help me to feel normal. You keep those texts and pictures coming, and I'll call you tomorrow and check on you. You are welcome to come back anytime I'm home and not busy."

"I'd love that very much."

"Me too."

"Sweet! Other than Carlos texting you, I can't believe no one has called to check on you since I've been here. That's not cool at all."

"I had you, Kiddo."

"Oh, stop it before I change my mind on leaving," she says, giggling and blushing.

"Ha!"

"Until next time, my Rusty Blade…like next month for your birthday."

"I'm looking forward to it, Kiddo," he says, raising his left eyebrow for the first time while calling her, her nickname.

"Wait…did you just…you raised your eyebrow? I've seen you do it in pictures, and oh, I love it when a man can do that."

"I'll do it more often, then."

"Oh, let me get out of here, Kenny."

They both laugh as she walks down his porch steps. Once she's gone, he begins to miss her and wishes she was still there with him.

5

It's the day of November fourth, and it's a cold bitter day in Vancouver, British Columbia, with snow in the late evening's forecast. Shannon arrives at Kenny's a little after three and backs her semi up his drive, ecstatic as it is the day of his fifty-seventh birthday and her first with him. She is tired from driving through most of late night and early morning hours to make it in time due to high-demand holiday deliveries and taking road conditions into consideration but would not have missed this day for nothing. She is feeling excited and happy that he invited her out to share it with him, and she can hardly wait to give him his gift and see Carlos again. He invites her in but not without greeting her with a warm hug first. Cold, she sits on the far end of the couch by his burning fireplace to warm up. She watches the colors and shadows from the flames dance on his wood floor before looking over at him standing by his kitchen table looking through his birthday cards he recently received. She pats the couch seat cushion beside her, and he walks over and sits beside her. She reaches in her bag and pulls out a small box beautifully wrapped in black wrapping paper with a white-and-blood-red-splattered ribbon and bow.

With a smile, she hands it to him. "Happy birthday, Kenny!"

"Thank you, Kiddo." He removes the bow and ribbon, rips the paper off, opens the box, and is stunned at what he sees.

"I hope you like it."

"This is the coolest thing I've ever seen." He placed his hand midway on her back. "Thank you, Kiddo, I love it!"

"You're welcome."

He pulls out a custom-designed sterling silver ring of the hockey mask like the one he wore in his movie's battle scene. He moves the ring around in between his fingers and sees the inside band engraved description that simply says, "Love, Kiddo," with a heart on both sides. He slips the ring onto his right ring finger and hugs her tightly.

"So sweet of you, Kiddo."

A knock comes on his door, and he opens it inviting Carlos and his fiancée in. "Hey, guys, come on in."

Carlos hands Kenny a gift bag and wishes him a happy birthday, and then Camilla hugs him. "Happy birthday, Kenny!"

"Thanks, guys."

Shannon walks over and greets Carlos with a hug. "So nice to see you again, Carlos."

"Yeah, you, too, Shorty."

Kenny looks over at him with a smirk on his face. "What did you just call her?"

"Shorty! That's my nickname for her now."

"Sweet! I love it, Carlos."

Kenny reaches over and gently grabs Shannon's arm, pulling her closer to him. "Camilla, meet Kiddo, I mean Shannon, ha."

"So you're the fan he was telling me about a few weeks ago. He talked about you more than anything over dinner."

"Oh, really?" Shannon looks to Kenny trilled as he stands there smiling, blushing, and can barely get his words out.

"Well…um…yeah…I told her about you, ha."

"Honey, he talked a lot about you. Said the nicest things I think I've ever heard him say about anyone."

Shannon just stares over at him smiling, and he smiles back winking his eye at her before they all walk over into the living room. He opens his gifts from Carlos and Camilla and shows them what Shannon gave him. Shannon gives Carlos a name drawing she did for him, and he thanks her with excitement. They catch up from their last visit, about her holiday deliveries and plans, and she talks to Camilla. She is a French Canadian actress and stunt performer, appears to be African American, and has average height with a toughness about her but is absolutely beautiful. She's very sweet and makes Shannon feel very comfortable and welcome around her. Around five, Carlos goes into the kitchen and starts to prepare dinner. He enjoys cooking, and after Kenny getting sick from a restaurant a few weeks ago, he wants to cook him a safe and healthy birthday dinner. Kenny goes outside and fires up his grill, and Shannon is dumbfounded.

"Wait a minute, you guys grill in this cold weather?" she asks with a confused laugh after Kenny returns.

"Oh yeah, Kiddo, we are just used to it."

"Oh, snap! I'm from the South, and, honey, when it's cold outside, our tails cook inside."

They all bust out laughing, and Kenny just shakes his head at her. "You're a mess, Kiddo," she mumbles under his breath heading back outside. "Never in my life, ha."

He and Carlos go out and throw the steaks on the grill. Camilla goes into the kitchen to make the salad, green beans, and baked potatoes; and Shannon follows offering to help. She learns how Camilla and Carlos met and starting to date, about her kids, and career. She is staring out the sliding glass door from the kitchen out at Kenny and Carlos now sitting by the firepit that is now burning with a bright crackling fire, talking, laughing, and drinking a beer. She falls into a daydream haze for a minute before Camilla snaps her out of it.

"Shannon…Shannon!"

She jumps back to reality. "Huh? Sorry, zoned out I guess."

"More like daydreaming, sweetie."

"So what all did he say about me?" Shannon asks, curious.

"He told me about how you two met, you losing your husband, how you always stay so in touch with him and send him pictures of things you see and places you go, and told us about your first visit. He praised you for how you gave away your load and came out and took care of him. He said that you always say such kind words to him, and you are probably the sweetest fan he's ever met. He said that he's happy he decided to give you a chance and connect with a fan on a personal level, and it's been fun so far. He really seems to enjoy having you in his life. Carlos and I have actually noticed that he does seem happier now. I haven't seen him smile or laugh this much in a while. He is a private person, especially with his emotions and feelings, but I really think he likes you even without him saying it. His face really glows talking about you. He seems attached to you already."

"Aw, I really hope I can get him to see that it's okay to open up just a little. Feel free some. I am so happy to finally be a part of his life. I've wanted it for thirteen years. Waited and never gave up, and he's everything and more than I ever imagined. You know how fans say we have celebrity crushes, well, that's mine out there, and he's absolutely the most beautiful man in the world to me."

"Aw, that's sweet! Does he know?"

"Know what?"

"That he's your crush?"

"Oh, heavens no! I don't want to make him uncomfortable around me. Carlos doesn't know either. It won't matter, anyway. I think I am far from being the woman of his dreams, and besides, he's not looking."

"Oh, I wouldn't say that. You're sweet and really seem to make him happy. From what I know about him, he doesn't care about looks or body and doesn't judge."

"Really! I mean, I am only five feet one, and I'm not exactly skinny neither, but I am losing weight. Plus, I have these autoimmune diseases that limit me and keeps me covered in rashes…uh… so embarrassing."

"That's great, and don't be. I think you are beautiful just the way you are, and I just met you. So you love him in a way that you would date him?"

"Thanks! That's very sweet of you, and, oh yes, definitely if given the chance, but I doubt he would ever fall in love with me. I think our twenty-six-year age gap would stop him. His ex ruined that for the rest of us. So why embarrass myself and risk hurting our friendship?" Shannon turns away trying to hide her emotional pain. "Excuse me…I need some fresh air…claustrophobia," she says, stepping outside onto the front porch.

Kenny walks back inside to see she isn't nowhere in sight. "Where's Kiddo?"

"Your porch! She needed some fresh air after our girl talk."

He walks out to see her looking out at the clouds. "You okay, Kiddo?"

She turns to see him walking up behind her, and she nods that she is.

"It's so beautiful out here, Kenny. All of the pictures and videos that I've ever seen of Canada can't compare to seeing it in real time. I can't wait for it to snow. I love snow, and it doesn't snow where I live. I only get to see it on the road while I'm traveling. It will be nice to actually enjoy seeing it fall."

"I'll play in some snow with you, too, and I can throw a mean snowball. I like seeing your excitement for it too. I hope you get to see plenty over the next few days while you're here."

"Me too, and I've never built a snowman or made a snow angel. Do you think we can if it snows enough?"

"Of course, and I'll be happy to help you build your first one."

"This is going to be so fun. I'm not looking forward to putting them heavy snow chairs on my tires to get out of here, but, hey, got to take the bad with the good."

"Yeah, hey, is Jason still bothering you?"

Shannon looks around trying to avoid answering, but Kenny doesn't let her off that easy. "Kiddo?"

"He sends me little texts here and there asking me where I am hauling to or how my day is going. He asked me a few weeks ago if I was talking to anybody yet and stuff."

"Stuff? Like what?"

"Kenny, can we not talk about him right now? It's your birthday, and I just want to enjoy this day with you," she says, while rubbing down his coat sleeve.

He smiles. "Okay but later!"

They both walk back inside and sit down at his kitchen table that Camilla has already set with plates, silverware, napkins, drinking glasses, green beans, baked potatoes, salad, and condiments. Carlos brings the steaks in, and they all enjoy spending the next few hours eating and talking. This is the happiest Kenny has been in a good while. While having cake, Shannon keeps glancing over at him and Carlos and Camilla notices, elbowing each other to look. Kenny even glances back a few times, but Shannon looks away hoping not to get caught, but on the last glance, they lock eyes and smile at each other for a few seconds, and she can't help herself. "Happy birthday, my Rusty Blade, and thank you for letting me share this day with you. It's been absolutely incredible, and I hope to spend more birthdays with you, Carlos, and Camilla. Aw."

"I hope so, too, Kiddo."

After dinner and cake, she and Camilla help each other clean while Kenny and Carlos go out to add more fire to the firepit, for it isn't snowing yet but dark now enough to enjoy the beautiful flames and sparks.

"That's one sweet fan you have there, Kenny."

"Yeah, she's fantastic. I didn't expect us to bond this much so soon, but the whole suicidal thing and then me being sick really made us close. Her coming out and staying with me like she did and never leaving my side really built my trust for her."

"I bet she was there every time you made a sound."

"She came in every few hours to check on me and had me drink something. She even slept on my couch just so she could be across from my room, and she was up and in my room every time I threw up or moaned in discomfort faster than you can blink an eye, giving me medicine and put my tail back in bed." They both laugh.

"That's great! She's definitely a keeper, Kenny."

"Oh yeah, I even told her—out of discomfort, of course, felt bad about it—to get away from me and to get out of my room. But she was so calm about it and told me she wasn't going anywhere. She even refused phone calls the whole time. Told her friends when they called that her Rusty Blade was sick and she didn't have time to talk."

"She definitely seems to care about you. I can't imagine what she pays in fuel and travel just to come out here to visit you. I mean, to give up the time with her family and friends that she does to drive into a different country and go through that border just to see you, that's true right there."

"Her company pays for her fuel from what she has told me before."

"They pay for her fuel when she's working, not when she's off the clock driving out here to see you. She pays for that, and I know because I've already asked some of the truckers on set how that works, and that's what they have all said. She pays for everything to come see you, but to her, it's nothing to be here with you, I'm sure."

"I didn't realize that. That is pretty sweet that she is willing to do that to see me. I know she's saving to buy her own truck on top of everything and mapping her loads around my conventions."

"She kept glancing over at you over dinner. It was too cute, Kenny. I am very happy for you that you have a great female friend again and one that you know you can trust and that isn't self-centered like Kimberly was. You two do seem to have fun when you are together. I haven't seen you this happy in a while."

"Yes, she's just great, but I'm not happy about this Jason friend of hers."

"Jason? Who's Jason?"

"A truck driver that she has been friends with for a while. Now that her husband is gone, he's been hitting on her. She had a bruise on her arm from him where he grabbed her and squeezed her arm too hard back when I saw her again in September. Now I just found out he's texting her stuff, and I don't like it, Carlos. He just gives me a bad feeling, and she even seems uneasy talking about him. I've told her to be careful around him and that she probably shouldn't be friends with him anymore."

"A bruise! That's not good. Sounds like he's a little into her too much. Maybe he's in love with her or obsessed with her. She needs to be careful and avoid him as much as possible. Good thing she has you protecting her."

"Yes, and she knows she can call me anytime. That guy doesn't want to meet me for the wrong reasons. He hurts my Kiddo, and he's going to have a very bad day. I can promise you that."

"Ha! You called her your Kiddo."

"Ha! I did, didn't I? Well, she's special to me, and I care deeply for her as well."

Shannon and Camilla walk out, and Camilla sits beside Carlos, and he wraps his arm around her, cuddling her close to him, and

Shannon sits by Kenny but not too close out of fear of making him feel uncomfortable. It's a still cold night with snow clouds hiding the stars in secrecy. As they talk and laugh the night away, Shannon, not being used to this degree of cold, begins to shiver even with her heavy jacket and goes to her semi to retrieve her double-layer full-size fleece blanket and makes her way back over by Kenny.

"Cold, Shorty?"

"A little, I'm just not used to being outside in this low of a temperature."

"Have some tequila. That'll warm you up."

"I don't drink much since getting my commercial driver's license, but thank you for the offer."

"Smart girl."

"I've actually never had tequila, whiskey, or any type of hard liquor. I only drink wine and daiquiris, and I have never been drunk."

"Shoot, Shorty, really? You've got to get drunk at least once in your life."

"Maybe one day."

"Well, as long as you let me be there and Kenny too."

It finally begins a light steady snowfall, and Carlos and Camilla says their goodbyes and heads home because he has a long day of work tomorrow, and Shannon goes inside while Kenny puts out the fire in his firepit before heading back in. After walking in and locking his sliding glass door, he notices she or her blanket is anywhere and catches a glimpse of her shadow in his porch light glow outside on his porch swing. He steps outside, and to his left, she is siting up against the side of the swing closest facing out his porch, wrapped up in her blanket watching it snow in his front yard. He walks over and sits beside her on the swing. "You've been waiting for this, Kiddo."

"Yes, and I am going to enjoy it too."

"Can I enjoy it with you?"

She turns back to face him with a smile. "Oh yes, and you can some blanket, too, Mr. Rusty Blade. I don't bite, ha."

"Ah, darn, ha! Just kidding and thanks," he says, pulling some blanket over himself.

"Did you have a great birthday?"

"Fantastic birthday! The best I have had in a while. My brother is coming by tomorrow and wants to meet you."

"No way, that's cool! Daniel, who played football?"

"Yeah."

She turns back to watch the snow leaning against the side of the swing, and she feels sensations run through her body as he wraps his warm hands around her waist, pulling her back into a side cuddle, and she sits perfectly wrapped in his long strong arm that's around her now. She doesn't ask why or wonder why he makes such a move as to cuddle with her. Instead, she just lies there leaning against him and wanting to enjoy every moment of it.

"I absolutely…just so adore you, Kenny Kirtzanger."

He squeezes her tight and in silence, and they continue to swing and watch the snow fall for few minutes longer.

"I'll always be there for you. Maybe I'll get snow in to where my chain tires won't even help me out."

"I'll always keep you safe, too, Kiddo. Even from that Jason guy."

"Let's just freeze this moment and have it forever."

"Let's get some sleep and get up and build that snowman."

Shannon sits up, turning to him; and without hesitation and before realizing what she did, she leans in and gently kisses him on his left cheek, sending tingles through her body as well as his. With her lips still inches from his ear, she whispers, "I've always wanted to do that." She pulls back with a nervous smile to see him smiling back at her.

"Kiddo?"

"Sorry."

"Don't be."

6

The next morning, there are two feet of snow, frosted trees, and frozen ponds and lakes. Overnight, Vancouver, British Columbia, became a beautiful white winter wonderland. Shannon wakes around seven and can see her semi from the guest bedroom window, and the tires all the way around her semi are half hidden behind a beautiful white bank of snow that's glistening in the sun's light. "Crap! Now I'll have to dig out from around them to put on my snow chains," she thinks out loud to herself. She gets dressed and walks out into the kitchen, stopping in her tracks as she see Kenny standing at his kitchen counter with his back facing her, making coffee. He's wearing long dark-green-and-black cotton pajama pants, socks but no shirt. He turns and sees her. "Good morning, Kiddo."

"Good morning, Kenny," she says as she stares at him up and down. "Sweet mercy me, Rusty Blade."

"Like what you see, Kiddo?"

"Love is more the word I am thinking."

He turns back blushing and starts the coffee. "I'll go put a shirt on."

"Oh no! Don't you dare! I've waited for this since seeing you without one on in that *X-Case Files* episode."

He chuckles as he pours them both a cup of coffee.

"I remembered that episode. I wasn't too sure about being shirtless at first, but it turned out all right."

"Oh yes, it did, but on the real side, just be comfortable around me. If you want to be shirtless, be shirtless. This is your home, and I want you to be comfortable even while I'm here, and you're not going to offend me, and besides, I don't mind. I'll try not to stare so much."

"Oh, Kiddo, ha!"

After they have breakfast prepared by Shannon, he scoots his chair closer to her, puts his arm across her back, leans in close to her left ear, and speaks softly. "So, Kiddo, tell me again, what's your favorite Rusty Blade line?"

Shannon giggles. "An eye for an eye!"

"And why did Rusty Blade do an eye for an eye?"

"To do unto others the same as they did to him."

"That's exactly right, and so eye for an eye, Kiddo." He kisses her on her left cheek and gives her that Rusty Blade chuckle before getting up to go shower. Too shocked to cry, she just sits there with her fingertips placed over her cheek in disbelief as to what just happened. He really just kissed her cheek, and what made him do that? As she continues to replay him kissing her over and over in her mind, she gets up and goes outside to examine the snow ready to build her first ever snowman and with his help.

She's walking around carefully sticking close to the porch so as not to fall in the snow when a car pulls up in his drive and stops a car length in front of her semi. An older gentleman gets out and walks around heading her way carrying a wrapped package that she's sure is a birthday gift for Kenny. She knows it has to be his brother Daniel, because he favors Kenny. He looks about the same height but more built from his past football career. He walks up to her, extending his hand. "Hello, I am Daniel."

"Hi, Daniel, I am Shannon! Nice to meet you. Kenny told me about you."

"He told me about you too. Just said the kindest things about you. I really appreciate you coming out to him last month and taking care of him. That was very sweet of you. Makes me feel better knowing he has a great friend like you that will be here for him when I'm not around."

"Well, that's what you do when you truly care about someone, and I would do it again. He will always have me, I can promise you that. There's nothing out there more important to me than him. Anyway, he was in his room taking a shower, and I stepped out to give him complete privacy, and the snow was calling me. He's probably out now."

"You are definitely a special kind of fan that would make anybody proud to have you. I'll go in and see if he's out. You better come in, too, sweetheart. Wouldn't want you to freeze your toes off."

"Nope! I kind of need those, ha," he says, following him inside.

Kenny opens his birthday gift from his brother; and Shannon and Daniel talk about her, her semi, and what it's like being a trucker versus him being a football player. Daniel seems to like her sweet Southern charm and how she keeps his brother smiling and laughing so much. It made him feel real happy in knowing that Kenny has such a sweet caring friend in his life. After Daniel leaves, she drags Kenny outside in anticipation and excitement to play in the snow and with him. They are running around laughing, ducking behind trees, and throwing snowballs at each other and seeing how big they both can make their next one. He throws one that makes her lie her on her back. She is lying there just laughing. Feeling bad, he lies in the snow next to her, and they both make snow angels. He helps her stand up, and they both can't contain their laughter at the difference in the lengths of their snow angels. He helps her build her first snowman. He wanted it to be the biggest and best for her, and thanks to his height at six feet five inches tall, he does just that. She goes and breaks some limbs off a nearby tree for the arms, and he takes his scarf off and wraps it around the base of the snowman's head. He runs inside and comes back out with raisins for the eyes and mouth and a carrot for the nose. Once complete, they both step back and examine their snowman, and she immediately wraps her arms around him, thanking him and telling him how perfect and beautiful their snowman is. She can hardly contain her excitement as she pulls out her phone and begins snapping photos of their snowman and snow angels. He takes one of her beside the snowman as well. They head back inside where they enjoy hot chocolate by the fireplace. Kenny curiously watches her as she filled out her logbook and learns about her career that he once pretended to have when he played as Rusty Blade and what all she does and the ropes to being a trucker. She tells him about the truck that she's saving to buy and that she wants it to look as close as possible as the one from the movie. It was more perfect of a day than she ever imagined. She had so much fun and truly felt lucky to have spent that time with him. It's memories that she will carry with her for the rest of her life.

As night falls, it begins a steady heavy snow pour with strong winds howling. Shannon is in the guest room gathering her things to leave tomorrow when the power goes out. She grabs her phone and turns on the flashlight as Kenny yells to her asking her if she's okay and to come out into the living room. She finds him layering blankets on the floor in front of the fireplace and adding pillows for extra comfort. It's pitch-black with the exception of the glow from the fireplace, and she turns her flashlight off.

"Does this happen a lot?"

"Sometimes, and it can be off for a few hours or all night. That's why I'm doing this."

She sits down on the makeshift lounge in front of the fireplace, and he joins. "It can get pretty cold, and I just want to make sure you stay warm, Kiddo."

"Thanks, and I want you warm too. Can't have my Rusty Blade freezing, especially with you just getting over that food poisoning."

"You're sweet, Kiddo."

"You are too," she says, swaying over and shoulder bumping him.

"You know, I never thought back when we met that here we would be just three months later. I never thought I would connect with a fan like I have with you, but there's just something in you I see. I guess it was your determination and survival or maybe how zealous of a fan you are to me in never giving up on meeting me and trying so hard to be in my life and how you are so sweet and make me laugh, but whatever it is, I truly do like you."

"Aw, I almost don't know what to say. I'm just happy that you gave me a chance to prove myself to you. I know that with your career, you have to be careful with who you trust and let into your life, but you can't keep everyone away because you never know who you'll miss out on, and you couldn't just compare me to every other fan. I knew from the moment you saved my life, I wanted to know you. I've given up on some much in my life, and I've missed out on people because I was too shy or scared to try, but I never thought once about giving up on you."

"Trust is tough in this business. You never know who is being real and who isn't. So many go after the wrong reasons with us."

She starts shivering, and he puts his arm around her. She cuddles up next to him. She thinks back to last night when Camilla was cuddling with Carlos and how she wished that she could had so easily done that with Kenny and now she is. She closes her eyes and just feels the moment while listening to his soft breathing.

"Getting to share this personal intimate alone time with you makes me happy that you are single," she says, looking up at him.

"I so agree, Kiddo. Do you think you will be leaving tomorrow with all of this new snow? I don't want you out in dangerous conditions and risk getting in a wreck or hurt."

"I hate driving in the snow sometimes. It can be pretty scary, especially when you feel your trailer sliding on the icy roads. Good thing for side ramps to stop us if we lose control and need to run off the road. It will depend on how deep the snow will be. I will have to dig from around all of my tires and put my chains on them just so I can get out of your drive."

"I can help you."

"That would be great because they are superheavy. As much as I am enjoying this and don't want it to end yet, I think I am going to go lie down. My back hurts a little, and I should get some sleep with it getting late."

"Kiddo, you will freeze back there. Just lay down here so you can stay warm. I will stay out here with you." Kenny wasn't ready for their time to be over either.

She lies down on her left side with her back facing the fire, facing him. He's still setting up, and he covers her with her blanket from her truck. She stares at his ring still on his finger that she gave him for his birthday shinning in the fire glow before closing her eyes and drifting off. Feeling tired himself, he lies down next to her, covering up with his own blanket. He watches her sleep in the soft glow of the fire burning behind her for a few minutes before dozing off. She wakes around two in the morning, noticing that the power is still out and cold. She cuddles herself right against his warm body who's lying on his back. The feel of someone against him, and her shivers awake him. She apologizes if she made him feel uncomfortable in any way doing that, but he assures her that it's okay and puts more wood on the fire that's barely burning now. They both lie back down on their sides, facing each other.

"I am curious about something."

"And what would that be?"

"What is a celebrity crush?"

"Ha! How can I answer this and without blushing? A celebrity crush can mean many things to different fans depending on their intensity and desires. You were once a fan of a pretty celebrity back in your day that I am sure you had the hots for, ha. Lucky whoever she was."

"Maybe." Kenny laughs.

"For me, it just means that I absolutely adorably love that celebrity. I would like to maybe experience what a romantic dinner date would be like or holding their hand while on a walk. Maybe lying in their arms while falling asleep and maybe even a kiss. Yeah, just a lot of fantasizing."

"Am I your celebrity crush, Kiddo?"

"Why do you ask?" she says, giggling.

"I overheard Camilla saying something to Carlos about you having one."

"Oops! Ha, you weren't supposed to find that out. I am just surprised that you actually want to know with you being private and all."

"I do."

"Yes…yes, you are."

"That's sweet, and I'm flattered. You are blushing, Kiddo."

"Stop it!" she says, snickering and pulling her blanket up over her face and back down.

While rubbing around her industrial piercing in her right ear with his fingertips, they stare at each for a moment before they both simultaneously kiss each other on the lips, sending tingles throughout their bodies.

"I'm sorry, Kenny, I shouldn't have."

"Don't apologize. I kissed you too. Come here," he says, pulling her back into a cuddle.

They both fall back asleep and wake in the morning around to power restored and a total of five feet of snow. She looks out the guest room window to see that from her driver's door and down of her semi is completely buried. She feels him walk up behind her. "Doesn't look like you're leaving today, Kiddo."

"Nope."

"I'm fine with that."

"Me too, Kenny, I didn't want to leave, anyway."

"I didn't want you, too, either. Come on."

While at the table having breakfast, she keeps staring over at him and thinking about last night. "Thanks for keeping me warm and for staying out there with me all night," she says, avoiding bringing up the whole kiss thing. "I didn't even think about it, but we could have also slept in my semi. It has a pretty mean heater that will roast you out the door, but I much liked last night's sleeping arrangements," she says, winking her eye at him.

"Me, too, because that would have meant getting out in that weather to get in your semi and digging our way back out."

"My first wedding anniversary without Craig is coming up next month, and I am not looking forward to it, but I think I'll be okay."

"I'm sorry, Kiddo, and if you will need a shoulder, I'm only a phone call away."

"Thanks! Did you ever want to get married at any time in your life?"

"Not really! I just never fell in love with the right one to that degree, I guess. I never saw myself as a husband and or a father. I am too much of a big kid myself."

"Hey, I am a big kid, too, but I still dream of being a mom one day. I'm not going to lie, I wish you at least had a son. Oh, sorry, shouldn't have said that."

"It's okay, but why a son?"

She gets a text, and he sees the uneasiness in her stare as she reads it.

"Something wrong?"

"It's nothing," she says, shaking her head and forcefully laying her phone back down on the table.

"Kiddo, don't tell me nothing. What was that?"

"Jason!"

He shifts in his chair with a sign of annoyance, crossing his legs and leaning back. "What did it say? Tell me! I can tell you didn't like it."

"He asked me how I am holding up out in this weather and if I would meet him for lunch or dinner the next time we are in the same area. I'll reply later."

"Lunch or dinner?"

"He is always inviting me, but I kindly refuse every time. I guess, I may as well go and get it over with."

"You don't have to do nothing to get nothing over with except tell him no and enough is enough. Don't make yourself uncomfortable for him, and you don't want to give him any wrong signs. Plus, you may not be safe alone with him. I just don't know about this guy. Just something about him makes me feel uneasy, and I really wish you would stop talking to him. I have come to be very protective over you, and he just better watch it."

"I guess you're right, but he is so nice to me. I just hate being rude to people. I'm being careful with him, and besides, my brother has all of his trucker friends keeping an eye on me if they are around me."

"You can go about it without being rude, and not doing something you aren't sure about isn't being rude, Kiddo. It's being cautious."

"Yeah, my best friend Tammy told me the same thing. She doesn't like him either."

"Sounds like a caring friend."

"She is! We've been friends since high school, and she was once married to my brother, who you met, and they have three kids together. She's also a truck driver, and I love her so much. I have to finish my logbook today, and so I may not be as much company today."

"I also need to look over my script lines and do a few other things as well."

The sun melts the snow enough that Shannon is able to pull out the next morning. She hugs Kenny tight before leaving and tells him she'll see him at his upcoming convention in Lexington, Kentucky, that's happening in a little under four weeks away during the first weekend of December. With every visit, the leaving gets harder, and Kenny misses her as soon as she's gone. She turns his usual quiet house into laughter and fun conversations the whole time she's there. She gives him the company he has lone for. An hour up the road, she pulls off into a truck stop and breaks down in tears. Knowing she needs to talk to someone, she calls the only friend who truly understands her feelings for him with being a fan herself. She calls Colleen, but she doesn't answer, and so she sends her a private message through their social media.

Hey, Colleen, I know you're busy, but I am just in a crush-depressed mood, if that makes sense. It's not easy when you feel yourself falling in love with someone who isn't looking for love because his ex ruined it for everyone else. Every time I walk through Kenny's door and feel his warm embrace while laying my head against his strong chest and listening to his beautiful heartbeat, I just want to look up at those beautiful brown eyes of his and say, "I love you." But I get scared and chicken out in fear of it hurting our friendship or something, and let's face it, I know I won't ever compare to her—her beauty. I guess I shouldn't think that way or let myself feel less than her, but I do, and I can't help it. I can't even bring myself to simply tell him I love him. That's depression for you, ha. It keeps you living in fear of always saying something wrong and losing everything and everyone that keeps you going in life. Plus, I always think the negative thoughts first, like maybe it's because I feel like maybe he won't think I am good enough for him or maybe it's because I don't compare to her. I mean, what can I offer him? I am just an interstate trucker with a semi, or maybe it's because having him as a friend is better than not having him at all when I didn't have him three months ago. Sorry to be bothering you with this, but I feel like you are the only one I can talk about him without judging me. I know it sounds crazy that I can fall in love with a man who's still so secretive about his past and everyday life and who's twenty-six years older than me, but I am, Colleen. I am starting to hopelessly fall in love with Kenny Kirtzanger, my Rusty Blade.

A few minutes later, Colleen replies,

OMG, that's so cute! Kenny is such a wonderful man. I think you should just go for it and tell him, but ease into it. What his ex did to him is not your fault, and he shouldn't make you pay for it, and stop putting yourself under her. Make him realize that you two are perfect for each, and you'll know when it's the right time to say those three words to him. You are probably the sweetest most adorable female friend in his life right now. I would think that he would be happy to know how much he means to you. I mean, after all, you gave away a load worth over a million dollars, and it's nice payout and put saving for your own truck on the back burner to care for him. Don't let your depression keep you from happiness. That's not fair to you, and I don't think he will cut off the friendship just because you have feelings for him, and what does the age difference has to do with the price of rice in China? You loving him with him being fifty-seven is no different than if he was thirty-seven. Stop thinking you aren't good enough, because you are. Don't be sad, and chin up. Love ya, girly.

It's been a hard two and half weeks. Shannon has been steady hauling one load after another and is extremely exhausted. The only few days she had to rest was going home for Thanksgiving, and then she was back at it. She has texted Kenny "Good morning" every morning, and he has called her every single night just to check on her, and during their last phone conversation, he told her he misses her for the first time. What beautiful words those were to her ear. Every time she looks over at her passenger seat, she wishes he was in it, riding the roads with her and being her road buddy. She's often thought about inviting him out on the road with her but too nervous. A week before his convention, she calls him just needing to talk. She finally agreed to meet up with Jason for dinner as a friendly get-together. She tells him a little bit of what happened. She met Jason at a steakhouse in Amarillo, Texas. He was waiting for her by his semi to walk her inside once she parked next to him. Dressed in slacks and a dress shirt, he handed her a small bouquet of flowers, which she accepted out of not wanting to be rude. After walking inside and being seated, he told her to order whatever she wanted, his treat. She refused at first to let him pay for her, but after constant persistence on his part, she agreed. Over their food, they talked about the usual trucker's life and the crazy holiday deliveries. He thanked her for finally meeting him and that's he had been wanting this day for a long time. He confessed how he has always thought she was a beautiful person and developed feelings for her after Craig passed away. He asked her if she was talking to anybody new, in which she mentioned that she wasn't comfortable talking about that. She laid down boundaries to what their friendship will be and how he has to understand that she isn't interested in him that way. Not wanting to believe it right away, he told her she can always grow to love him, making her super uncomfortable to the point that she ended their dinner early, and she assured Kenny that he didn't touch her in any way. He was not too happy about learning that this guy has a crush on his Kiddo, especially because of the bruise he left on her arm or him not wanting to accept just being friends. He knows now that he has to protect her in every way possible and that he has to somehow convince her to finally kick Jason out of her life. Even though he has only known her for four months, he has grown to care deeply for her and knows that if this guy ever puts another bruise on her, he'll hunt him down. A few days before his convention, she surprises Kenny by telling him that not only will she be at the convention all day Sunday but that she is also staying in the same hotel both Saturday and Sunday night. He calls her back to ask if she would like to skip exploring the convention floor and instead be his sidekick at his table and help him all day as his handler, which she accepts with excitement. The night before the event, she checks in around six that evening. She is so looking forward to sharing his table with him all Sunday and even more excited knowing that they are on the same floor and across the hall from each other. She makes it up to her single-bed hotel room on the second floor and props her door open with her bag and wanting to have some fun. Not knowing if Kenny is even in his room, she knocks on his door before running in her room, grabbing her bag, and shutting her door before he opens his. He opens his door to find no one there but can hear the low sounds of her laughter coming from within her room. He knocks on her door and steps aside, and once she opens it seeing no one, he pushes her inside and shuts the door with them both laughing.

"You want to play games, don't you, Kiddo?"

"Oh yeah, Mr. Rusty Blade, and what are you going to do about it? Eye for an eye me?"

"Ha ha, maybe." He leans down and softly kisses her lips. "Not going to lie, I've been wanting to do that again."

"Me too, and way before you ever knew about me."

They are both so ecstatic to see each other and immediately embrace with a long tight hug before she walks him over to a small love sofa setting to the side of her full-size bed where they both sit together.

"Kenny, I hope you are okay with me staying across from you."

"Not at all, Kiddo. You can't help that this happened to be the room that they gave you when you checked in."

"Actually, it is! I made sure I got a room near you. Look, normally I would just sleep in my semi, but I found out that Jason will be passing through late Sunday night, and I am pulling out Monday morning. He doesn't know I am here, but if he spots my semi, he may be tempted to hang around if I am in my semi. That's really the only reason why I am still friends with him, just so I can keep tabs on him and know where he's going. I'll feel safer with you across the hall from me."

"I am totally fine with you being across the hall, and I can keep an eye on you. You will be with me all day tomorrow, and I don't want you out of my sight. Stick close to me okay. I promise I won't let this guy bother you, and I can have him thrown out if he comes in showing his tail. Just let him try something. I can't stand knowing he makes you feel this way."

"Thank you. I am so happy I have you to protect me, Kenny. He's on thin ice with me."

"Well, I hope it breaks soon."

"Kenny? Um...I just want to say that I hope me coming to all of your events doesn't make you feel like I am following you or stalking you. It's just...I mean, if it does, I won't mind cutting back some."

"Oh, not at all. I am happy to see you here, and I'll never tell you or any fan that you can't come meet me."

Shannon, out of no longer being able to contain the words anymore and wanting to finally tell him, blurts out, "I love you, Kenny!" Then she mumbles to herself, "I love you... Ha, I said it." She looks over at him for his reaction.

He stares at her for a few seconds before cracking a side smile. "Aw, Kiddo, I think that's sweet."

"I hope I didn't say it too soon, but I couldn't keep it in any longer, ha."

"No, I'm surprised you haven't said it before now."

Kenny explains a little more to Shannon on what she can expect tomorrow and how she will be helping him. Early Sunday morning before the convention, he shows her the ropes on being his handler and what all she will be doing. She is superexcited to spend the whole day with him at his table, helping him out. All throughout the day, she was happy to be able to talk to him in between fans coming over and they even went to lunch together. She got to learn some behind the scenes of the convention and what all takes place and goes into making them happen, but what she really enjoyed was taking care of Kenny by getting him water or whatever he needed. Once the event ends, she excuses herself and heads to her room because she doesn't want him to feel like she's living in his shadow as he hangs and mingles with his fans, and she doesn't want to see all of the hot beautiful women throw themselves at him. She is a natural and doesn't believe in the need to wear makeup or fix her hair every day just to be accepted or to feel beautiful. She just wants to be loved and accepted for who she truly is from the inside out. No amount of makeup, fake nails, or done-up hair should ever be what defines beauty; and she only wears makeup and gets her hair done for special occasions and paints her nails herself, and she loves to dye her hair a different color depending on her mood. He comes knocking on her door around seven and invites her to join him and five other guests who are friends of his to dinner, which she accepts. Over dinner, she gets acquainted with everyone as she and Kenny tell a bit about their story and her career. Eventually, they make it up to Kenny's room, and he invites her inside. He has a large lavish room with two full-size beds, a small round table with two chairs, a desk built into the dresser, and a large TV. He thanks her for helping him and told her that she did super and he would definitely have her again. He so enjoyed having someone at his table that didn't feel awkward or silent. Around ten thirty, she tells him good night and heads across the hall to her room where she goes to bed. Shortly after midnight, she calls Kenny, and knowing he's asleep, she feels terrible.

"Kiddo?"

"Kenny, I am so sorry to wake you, but Jason just spotted my semi in the back far-in parking lot, and he texted me asking if I am awake and if I am in my semi. He's parked beside mine."

"Are you kidding me? Tell him you are trying to sleep and leave you alone."

"I can't make him leave. He has every right to be parked out there. I am scared!"

"Come to my room."

"What?"

"Come to my room, Kiddo. You're sleeping in here with me tonight in the other bed, and I'll walk you out in the morning."

Monday morning, she wakes early and notices he is still sleeping. She sneaks out of his room, and seeing that Jason is gone, she checks out and leaves. It's around nine that morning, and Kenny checks his plane ticket only to realize he's in trouble. He calls the one person that he knows he can count on, hoping she's still in town.

"Hello."

"Kiddo, where are you? Have you already left or still in your room?"

"Yeah, I left this morning. I didn't want to wake you. You needed your rest. I am about two hours away. What's up?"

"I am going to miss my flight because I read my departure time wrong, and I checked and can't get another flight, yet that doesn't have major layovers. I'm stuck here at the hotel with about an hour till checkout."

"Oh no, you aren't! I am turning around and coming after you. I have spare time."

"Thank you! You are a lifesaver."

She turns around at the next available opportunity and heads back to the hotel. As she driving to him, she wonders how he could have made this mistake for someone who flies a lot, but for whatever reason, she doesn't care because that just means she gets to spend more time with him and he gets to ride around in her semi with her. She pulls up in front of the hotel, and he's waiting outside with his luggage. She climbs around her gearshift leaver, opening the passenger door and motioning him over. He sets his bag on her foot board, and she moves it to the back where her bunks are, setting it on her bottom bunk.

He climbs up in and greets her with a hug. "Thank you for coming after me. So very kind of you to back track here two hours out of your way to come after me."

"It was nothing, and I'm not just going to keep going about my travels knowing you're stuck here for God-only-knows-how-long. Not a chance, and besides, I would rather have you on my truck with me. You can give me company and see what it's really like to be Rusty Blade, just without the killing, ha."

"Well, Jason better stay away, then," he says, giggling.

"Were you flying back home, Kenny?"

"Yes, until after the New Year. I need to call Carlos and tell him not to bother picking me up from the airport."

"I can't get you home as fast as that flight was going to, but I can get you home in about—"

"Kiddo," he cut her off—"I am in no hurry to get home. I'm actually kind of looking forward to this adventure with you and get a glimpse into your career. I know you have been wanting this. Just take me across these states with you."

She gets back on the road heading back in the direction in which she came from. She's happy she took the day off to allow herself to make up time. Kenny stares out his window, amazed at how everything looks from her semi. He curiously asks her where they are heading, in which she tells him Lancaster, Ohio. She has an early morning pickup. It is about a three-hour drive. As they travel, she tells him about her truck wanting him to feel safe and comfortable just like she is when at his house for her semi is her home.

"You don't have to sit there buckled in the whole time. You are welcome to go in the back and stretch out on any bunk anytime you want. You can pull my blackout curtains close to give yourself some privacy or if you want a nap. I also have a TV with built-in DVD player that you can watch whenever you want. You can find something to listen to on the radio. Do whatever you want, Kenny. I just want you to be as comfortable as possible while riding with me, because your life is going to be a bit different out here. You can also help yourself to my fridge and snack cabinet."

"Thank you, and that's all very kind, and I'll keep all of that in mind, but for now, I am riding up here with you and sightseeing."

About two hours up the road, they stop off at a roadside diner that she knows well, and she treats him to a late lunch. They sit with her facing the window looking outside at her truck. She goes over with him what all he can expect being out on the road with her from showering to what happens at truck stop parking lots to weighing stations and other expectations. They talk about the simple things and laugh over the senseless silly stuff. It was a trip down her memory lane of when she and Craig shared these moments every day, and now she's sharing them with her Rusty Blade. She couldn't be happier finally having someone back out on the road with her and keeping her company on her semi to help get her through the long drives. She knows he will keep her safe. She is having such an amazing time listening to him talk about how excited he is to be out here with her and what he hopes to see when she looks up and sees the one person parking next to her that she doesn't want to see. With uncomfortable emotions showing on her face, she blurts out that Jason just arrived.

7

Shocked and displeased, Kenny turns to finally get a look at this guy who makes his fan so uncomfortable. Jason steps down out of his semi and begins to walk around it, inspecting his tires. He appears to be late forties, stands about five feet ten inches tall, and weighs approximately 190 pounds. He's clean-shaven, bald, and has a roughness about him. Shannon doesn't want Jason to see her here or approach her or Kenny, so they both dodge out of the other side door of the diner and hides. Once Jason is inside the diner, he enters the men's restroom, and both she and Kenny make a beeline for her semi where they quickly climb in, and she pulls back out onto the road.

"He reminds me a lot of my slasher character I played in the way of that he never goes away—just appears out of nowhere, and they even share the same name. Do you think he is following you?"

"I don't think so! We drive for the same company and a lot of times we get sent out in the same direction or meet in the same area. This has been going on since I started. I have thought about trying to get hired on with the company my brother drives for. Maybe it will help us not run into each other so much."

"If you do get hired on and he still pops up everywhere you are, then you will know for sure that he's following you, and you don't have to worry about him bothering you while I'm out here with you. Do you haul in and out of Canada?"

"Not at the moment, but I will be next year."

They finally reach Lancaster, Ohio. Kenny has enjoyed just getting to relax and see parts of the states that he hadn't yet seen. Even with the light snow and cold temperatures, they spend the rest of the afternoon riding through and touring places such as a brewery, glass museum, another museum, and finally ending their adventures with a tour of the Rising Park taking in the breathtaking views and learning about its history. While walking along a trail, he learns about her love for waterfalls, castles, bridges—all of the things that she always makes time to see during her drives. Somewhere between clouds and sitting out under a starry night sky, he reaches over and grabs her hand while they exit the park and head back to her semi holding hands. She was shocked but happy to be holding hands with him. It's something she has desired and longed for since meeting him. Feeling his fingers intertwine with hers and his large palm pressed tightly against hers is the most incredible sensation next to their kiss. After dinner, they stop off at a gas station to satisfy their sweet tooth before parking at a rest stop for semis only. Her alarm buzzes at five the next morning, and she quickly turns it off so as not to wake him sleeping up above her in the top bunk. She quietly gets up, stepping through her curtains that are pulled closed, and dresses. She turns her engine over, and her semi fires up. She has forty minutes of travel time ahead of her to make in order to reach her destination to pick up her assigned trailer, which contains quits, comforters, sheets, and curtains. She pulls out and onto the road carefully for fear of ice, and the motion of the semi and the hissing of break pressure waken Kenny. He hops down from his bunk wearing long pajama pants and a long-sleeved shirt and opens the curtains to the cab and joins her up front in the passenger seat.

"Oh, good morning, Kenny, how did you sleep?"

"I slept just fine, Kiddo."

"Good! I was worried you wouldn't be comfortable. I hope I had it warm enough for you too. I left the heater on all night."

"I was warm enough."

"Did you get enough sleep? You didn't have to get up yet if you weren't ready."

"I'm fine, and besides, this is my first time experiencing this, and I want to see how you work."

She arrives at her destination and drives around to and up past the loading dock. She pulls up, centering her semi with the only trailer there, and slowly begins to back. The reverse warning beep echoes through the early morning air. With a slight bump from her semi's fifth wheel latching around the trailer's traction pin, she and Kenny both climb down. Once she matches the trailer's paperwork to hers, he follows her as she walks around the trailer and making a per-trip inspection. She raises the landing gear, and she explains the three cables attached to the back of her semi and how and where they connect to the trailer. Once back on the road, he asks about their next destination and learns they are headed to a bedding-and-bath store in Springfield, Illinois. It's about a seven-hour drive with traffic, and she has plenty of time to get there. During breakfast, she shows him a map of the route that they will be taking. He is super thrilled to learn that he'll get to travel across the whole state of Indiana to get there. With Christmas coming in less than three weeks, she is booked soiled with back-to-back loads for the upcoming week with very little free time for. She hates that she's too busy to stop at places for him to see, but he assures her it's okay and he understands. He is just enjoying the sights. They manage to avoid running into Jason as they travel through Iowa, Nebraska, South Dakota, Montana, Idaho, and Washington before crossing into Canada and making their way up to Vancouver, British Columbia, to Kenny's house and dropping him off just a week before Christmas. He hugs her tight and thanks her for the trip. They joke about how their adventures will make great memories and conversations to come. She's in a rush to make her next few deliveries along the way of heading home to see her family as well for Christmas. He watches her pull away until he no longer sees her before heading inside. Later that day, Carlos stops by for a visit and to see how Kenny's adventure went. He invites him inside, and they sit at the kitchen table.

"So how was it being out there in her semi with her?"

"It was great, and I had a fantastic time. She was busy, and we couldn't adventure out much except for the first day, but it was overall a wonderful experience, and I am happy to have done it."

"Great!"

"Yeah, she really is such a sweet person. So easy to talk to and just makes you feel so welcome. She has such a big heart and a kind soul. I saw Jason, and I can see how he intimidates her. He's a big guy with a toughness about him. He could really be a problem for her in the sense that she wouldn't be able to defend herself against him."

"Oh, that's not good, Kenny. You don't have to tell me everything, but just curious about what all happened."

"In Ohio, we went to a few places, but my favorite was touring Rising Park. It is beautiful and huge. It has a playground, a fishing pond, and breathtaking hilltop views. I have pictures I can show you. We walked this trail, and I learned a lot about her, too, from personal things to her silly little loves. I don't know what made me do it, but I even grabbed her hand at one point, and we walked hand in hand."

"Say what? Ha! That's sweet, man. Keep going. This is getting interesting."

"We travel through several states like Illinois, Iowa, Nebraska, South Dakota, Montana, Idaho, and Washington before crosses into Canada. We were able to stop in Iowa, but we had a little free time in Nebraska City and did a few things. The most fun was visiting the Arbor Day Farm, and it was supercool. It had a fifty-foot-tall treehouse, a greenhouse, hiking trails, and interactive exhibits. We drove through Sturgis, South Dakota, and I got to see that huge biker bar from the road."

"No way! Lucky you!"

"It's big. We drove through most of the other states without being able to stop and do much, but I am happy for what I did see, and it was a beautiful fun experience. We were like big kids on a big road adventure and eating all of the junk food we want. She even told me at one point that she didn't care if I gained a little weight, that I would still be handsome in her eyes."

"Sounds like you two had a lot of fun, especially her. I am happy for you. You needed this and to get out, explore, and do things aside from your conventions. There is so much out there to see. How was it living on the road in her semi?"

"It was different. We stopped at truck stops to shower, and that was something new for me, and even though the showers were always clean, she made me wear flip-flops in them, highly recommended it. Sometimes, we went to a restaurant for dinner, and she loved stopping at her favorite little roadside diners for lunch. She tried to take me to all of her favorites, but a lot of times, we would run in the store while she was getting fuel and buy snacks. She pulled into rest stops often if she felt claustrophobic, and she never hesitated to stop if I needed to go. Just all of the patience in the world, Carlos. It took forever to fill her tanks up, and the weighing stations were a bit insane. She didn't really talk on her CB much. She isn't crazy about using it, but I had fun playing my Rusty Blade character with the other truckers, ha! I met a few of her trucker friends including her best friend, Tammy. Most of her friends are actually fans of me, and so I signed a few autographs and even took a few photos. They were just the nicest people."

"You're making me want to go out on the road with her now."

"Go for it. You won't regret it."

"She just talked and talked about her close bond with her mom, her best friend Britney, who's dating her brother, and goes out on the road with him. She also told me about her best friend, Colleen, who lives in Edmonton, Alberta, Canada, who is also my fan. Colleen and I met back in June at a horror con here in Canada, and she posted her pictures with me on her social media. When Kiddo was looking through recent photos of me, she came across hers and thought Colleen looked supercool with her crazy hair, tattoos, and piercings, and she had to talk to her. So she started commenting on her picture, and they just kept talking about me and became instant friends. They haven't met in person yet, but they are planning to soon. She said Colleen has been there for her the most when it comes to talking about me and has given her so much support. Crazy, eh? And I actually remembered Colleen once I saw the picture of us together."

"It's wonderful at how fans are bought together and sometimes become friends just through their favorite celebrities."

"Yeah! A lot of nights, we would just sit together on her bunk, and she would go on her social media and show me past photos from conventions with my fans. She asked me about my childhood and growing up and how my life was before my career, and you know, it was so nice to just talk about normal stuff and about me and what I enjoy doing in my spare time without my career being the only center of the conversation. At times, I don't even see her as my fan but more and more as my friend. She has shown me that it's okay to step outside of my comfort zone a little and allow myself to be more opened and carefree."

"That's great and sounds like you two are getting closer, and she does seem to truly care about you, Kenny, which makes me almost not want to bring this up."

"I care for her too. She's the best thing to happen to me in a long time, ha. Can't believe I just said that, but it's true. Wait, bring what up?"

"Your old stunt friend Jaylen from back in the day."

"Yeah, What about her?"

"Well, Camilla and I are going to a Christmas party on the twenty-fourth, and she's going to be there and asked me if you would be there. She just ended her six-year relationship and wants to see you."

Kenny shifts in his chair and signs. "Me! Why does she want to see me?"

"Well, I think she is still interested in you. You know you two almost hooked up right before you and Kimberly got together. You were into her too. Look, I know you aren't looking. Just come, have fun, and mingle. There's no harm in that, and it'll be good for you to see some of your old buddies that will be there."

"I don't know, Carlos. I mean, what about Kiddo?"

"What about her? She encourages you to get out and do stuff like this and go on blind dates. You've told me that yourself. I am sure she likes you a lot more than she's letting show, but you can't let how this may affect her also affect your life and happiness. This is one mingle that you should look into. You and Jaylen go way back and you never know."

"It's not that easy. She and I have gotten so close lately, and she loves me, and I believe her."

"Really? Exactly how close?"

"I think it was the third night of being on the road, and she was lying in her bunk under her heavy blanket, and she was shivering uncontrollably because her autoimmune diseases had her feeling like she was freezing, and with me being on the road with her, I, of course, was using her extra blanket. So I kind of felt like I needed to make her warm, ha. I got down and lay in her bunk beside her, and I covered both of us up with the extra blanket, and I cradled her in my arms because she was shivering pretty good. She kept apologizing to me that she was shivering so bad and that she hated it because it makes her body ache. I told her not to apologize, that she couldn't help it."

"That was very sweet of you."

"She shivered for about a good five to ten minutes before I notice that she was starting to relax a little, and she told me that she hoped even after she stopped shivering that I wouldn't go back up in the top bunk. I kind of squeeze her a little bit, and I told her that I was pretty comfy right there next to her. I was rubbing my fingers along her rashes on her hands that had turned purple from her cold spell, and she looked up at me with a little smile and her sweet brown eyes, and he said, 'I love you, Kenny Kirtzanger, and everything that makes you who you—all fifty-seven amazing years of you. I'll always be your Kiddo, and you'll always be my Rusty Blade, and you'll always be the most beautiful man in the world to me.' Just gave me the chills."

"Wow!"

"Just the sweetest, most kind words anyone has ever said to me, Carlos, and I believe her. I know she genuinely loves me for me and not just the actor I am. She stared at me for a moment, and I reached up and gently rubbed the side of her face."

"Stop blushing, ha ha. Do you love her, Kenny?"

"I care deeply for her."

"Yes, but do you love her?"

"Carlos, you know I don't say those words anymore. Love is a very big deep personal word, and I don't say it but to certain people. It's hard for me to use it freely after my past relationship. Kim just ruined love for me."

"True, but don't you think that's a little unfair, Kenny? Yes, Kim hurt you, but is that really fair to you to not explore and see what's out there? Hey, I'm not saying that Shannon is the one, and I'm not saying that Jaylen is the one either, but you cannot let your past seal your present or your future. The one for you can be right under your nose, and you won't even know it, because you're letting that pain keep you from seeing that. Look, I've been married twice, and now I'm engaged again because I didn't let that first failed relationship blind me from love, and you should not let one bad apple ruin the whole bushel for you either. You're never too old to still find love even if it is with someone is twenty-six years younger than you or an old friend. I want to see you a happy man and with someone who truly loves you. Just think about it."

"There's truth in there somewhere, I suppose. Okay, I'll come to the party, but I'm talking to Kiddo about it."

"Great! I'll let Jaylen know."

It's the day before Christmas Eve, and Shannon just dropped her last trailer for the holiday season and is on her way to her parents' house for Christmas when Kenny calls her.

"Hello, Kenny."

"How's Kiddo today?"

"Exhausted, tired, and ready to get out of this semi for a few days."

"How's Rusty Blade?"

"Just fine! Where are you today?"

"Driving through Charlotte, NC, on my way home till after New Year's."

"Good! I'm happy that you are taking a minivacation and spending time with your family. I worry about how much and how hard you work, especially with your health. You need some rest."

"Aw, thanks! I am looking forward to it too. Both my brothers will be home too. My parents are so excited about having all of us under one roof together."

"That's great! Hey, can you talk right now? I want to talk to you about something."

"Sure, I'm wearing my headset. What's up?"

"Carlos came over after you dropped me off, asking about my adventures with you, ha, and mentioned this Christmas party happening tomorrow and invented me—"

"I think that's great, and you should go and have fun instead of spending the whole Christmas week alone."

"There will be a lot of our old stunt friends there and old of my old stunt friends from back in the day named Jaylen. She wants to hang out with me."

Shannon becomes nervous and feels as her heart beats faster at the sound of hearing Kenny mention another woman's name.

"Jaylen? Who's she?"

"We met way back in the early stages of my stunt career, and we've been friends for almost my whole career. We almost hooked up before I got with Kim, but we didn't want to mix friendship with pleasure. I haven't seen her in a while. Carlos really thinks it would be a good idea for me to go and see her. What do you think?"

"I think you should go see your old friends. It will be good for you but only if you are comfortable with it. You shouldn't do it for anyone else but yourself. You two almost dated once? Is that what she wants now? Sorry, I shouldn't ask that."

"It's okay! There were feelings, but our friendship was more important to us, and Kim and I were already talking and going on dates by the time Jaylen told me about her feelings for me. I don't know what she's up to, and I told Carlos I'll go, but I wanted to run it by you first. I trust your opinion, and we have gotten really close, and I know how much I mean to you."

"You mean the world to me, Kenny. Just be careful, and don't let her pressure you into anything. Thanks for telling me."

"You mean a great deal to me, too, Kiddo. Are you okay? Don't worry about this whole Jaylen thing," he says, sensing sadness in her voice.

"I am fine, really. Hey, you should be getting a package from me today. It's your Christmas present, and you can open it anytime you want. I had it marked for delivery today and—"

"You got me a Christmas present, Kiddo?"

"Of course…well, actually I made it. I've been working on it for a while."

"But I didn't get you anything."

"And you don't have to. I don't expect you to ever get me anything just because I give you something. I did this out of the goodness of my heart and because I love you. Hope you enjoy it, Mr. Rusty Blade."

"I am sure I will. You're just the sweetest."

"I hope you enjoy the party and hanging out with Jaylen. Let me know how it goes. It was great talking to you, and I'll text you when I am home."

"Please do, and I will tell you all about it. Bye-bye, Kiddo."

"Until next time."

Later that day, Kenny gets a package at his door from Shannon, and feeling excited and being curious, he quickly opens it. He pulls out a postcard from North Myrtle Beach, South Carolina; and in her handwriting, it simply says,

> Merry Christmas, Kenny K...my Rusty Blade, from our beautiful sunny sandy beaches
> Love, Kiddo

Then he pulls out a crocheted afghan blanket of the Canadian flag with double Ks for his initials stitched in black in the bottom-right corner. He wraps it around him to feel its warmth and texts her, thanking her for it and that he loves it. She tells him that she has always wanted to crochet him something and that she had worked on it for several months and thought it would look great on his crouch, in which he agrees. He notices that she mailed it from her parents and decides to keep the address for future needs. A little while later, his brother, Daniel, stops by. They both sit out on the porch, and Kenny tells him about the party and about Jaylen possibly still being interest in him. Daniel has never been crazy about her because of her nitpicking and controlling issues in the past, but Kenny makes it clear that they are just friends. Getting chilly, they both head inside.

"Whoa...where did you get that?" he says, pointing at his blanket that is stretched out over his crouch.

"Kiddo made it and sent it to me for Christmas. I just got it today. Isn't it neat?"

"It's beautiful! She is so sweet to you. That's the girl you need in your life. She is so good to you, loves you, appreciates you, and doesn't put anything above you. I mean, look at how she takes care of you while she is here. She's cooks for you, cleans your house—everything without you asking because she loves you that much. She's almost like a wife to you without being your wife, ha."

"Yeah, I used to try and stop her in the beginning, but she told me she enjoyed taking care of her husband when they were off the road and she misses it. She's happy to do it for me, and if it makes her happy, then I told her I won't stop her, but I don't expect her to do it. Do you know there was one day in the beginning she was here, and I left for a few hours and went and picked Carlos up from a movie set he was working on and took him to lunch. She decided to do some of my laundry, and she automatically emptied out my pockets because her husband was always bad for not doing that, and so she just made a habit to do it. Everything that was in my pockets was lying on my kitchen table when I walked back through my door—money, business cards, you name it. I knew, too, from that moment on I can trust her."

"That's just sweet right there. Women like that hard to find these days. You can tell she was raised good ole Southern belle to always love, respect, and take care of hers, and that accent of hers."

"I know right!"

"Just so cute listening to her talk sometimes, ha."

"She is so silly too. Just makes you laugh. She would play these silly songs and sing along in a different tone and bounce around in her seat. I got an inside look into her music interest, and it ranges from classical all the way to heavy metal. She's so simple, Daniel. Just loves the little things in life, and to see her excitement over the smallest things is beautiful."

"Like what?"

"I learned that she loves all shades of purple. She loves clouds and takes pictures of them often. She will drive her semi miles out of her way and hike to see a waterfall. She gets excited over high bridges and beautiful sunsets that color the sky. She sometimes likes to sit under a starry night sky and imagine her future and jokes about putting a sunroof in her semi so she can see the stars while lying in her bunk. She even had star-shaped lights put in the cab of her truck. She's amazing! So easygoing and carefree. She's very open about herself, where I am private, and it's a balanced mixture. While I was out with her, she always made sure I was comfortable and fine with wherever we ate or stopped at to explore."

"She wanted you to feel a part of it."

"Included...yes...you're exactly right, and I think sometimes after being in this business for as long as I have, you kind of forget a lot of the outside world from the business world—the normal world and what is really out there and what I've missed out on, and you get used to having fans and just going where you're invited and needed and don't ever think to just get out and go where you want to go and meet the people out there instead of them coming to meet you. You almost forget being a normal person, and I know when she calls, it won't be just another movie idea or a convention invite or nothing to do with anything within my career. It's just going to be a normal conversation about our days, and those are phone calls I look forward to. She has really just opened my eyes to everything that I've been missing out on. She makes my crazy busy days feel normal for a while. I really do enjoy her company."

"Sounds like it, and she enjoys you, too, I'm sure. Well, Kenny, if you ever decide to love again, I hope you will love her because she's just great. I'll see you around. I've got to go into town. Have fun at the party tomorrow."

It's Christmas Eve and the evening of the party, and Kenny is anxious about going and still uncertain if it's a good idea. He texts Shannon again, and she assures him that it'll be good for him to go and see his friends and have a fun night out. He tells her he almost wishes she was there to go with him, and she happily agrees with honor that he would even consider her. He even tells her that she slept under his blanket from her last night just to feel like she was close. Carlos and Camilla pick him up around five, and they make the twenty-minute drive to the venue, and there is already a crowd of about forty people. Most are old stuntmen and stuntwomen around Kenny and Carlos's age, with their spouses and a few others with their adult children who have followed in their footsteps. The party is being held under a white close-in tent with heaters to provide warmth with the weather not being too cold. There are three huge triple-layered chandeliers adorned with beautiful sparkling crystals in different lengths hanging in sections of the tent with strands of mini clear Christmas lights lining the tent's walls, and Kenny can't help but think how Shannon would love these and snaps a few photos and sends to her. She thanks him and tells him that he can text her anytime throughout the night if he needs to. On one side of the very large tent is a seven-foot Christmas tree in multicolored lights and traditional ornaments with emptied wrapped boxes for show under it and three long tables lined up together with Christmas-themed cloths that contain a buffet of various meats, breads, sides, desserts, and drinks of both alcohol and nonalcohol—champagne, eggnog, punch, coffee, hot tea, and hot chocolate. Most of everything was bought by guests. Round tables with white tablecloths and chairs take up most of the tent's center with enough walking around room. The opposite side of the tent contains speakers and a device playing music with a small dance floor. Outside of the tent all around are trees decorated with colorful Christmas lights, huge yard decorations, and a gazebo with clear stands of lights wrapped around and throughout its posts, giving it a soft glow of light. Over the next few hours, some guests come, eat, mingle, and leave for most have other gatherings to attend. Kenny and Carlos talk to friends they haven't seen in a while and catch up on how everyone has been doing and or working on. Carlos's son and his girlfriend also attend. They, along with Carlos and Camilla, hit the dance floor for a little fun while Kenny watches from his table and laughs at them. Around eight, Jaylen shows up and sits down at the table across from him. She's just as beautiful as he remembered with her golden blonde hair, piercing green eyes, and tiny frame. She greets him and thanks him for coming. She hasn't seen him since he and Kim parted ways. He tells her that she can thank Carlos and his fan for him coming because he really didn't want to. She curiously asks about her, and he tells her that he now has a fan in his life—more like a very good friend, and she encouraged him to come and have fun. He tells her how Shannon drives a semi in the United States, how they met four months ago, and who comes to his conventions and drives out to visit him every month. Jaylen, on the other hand, is not interested in hearing him talk about another woman. She has her eyes set on him and tells him they should have dinner sometime. He surprisingly accepts under the condition that she understands it's just a friendly date, in which she only agrees just to get him to go. They plan their date for after New Year's because he is hoping to see Shannon first. Carlos drops him back off at his house around ten that night. He texts Shannon and tells her he had a great time and he is happy he went. He will call her tomorrow for Christmas and tell her all about it and that he wants to talk to her about a few things. She replies that she's glad he had a great time. After hanging up and feeling sad, she texts him, "Merry Christmas Eve, my Rusty Blade. I love you, and have a good night." He replies back, "Thank you, Kiddo! You have a good night, and Merry Christmas Eve to you too."

The rest of the night Kenny and Shannon lay in their beds with a three-hour time difference and over three thousand miles between them wishing they were only rooms apart. She wanted this to be her first Christmas with him, and for the first time in over three years, he didn't want to wake up Christmas morning alone. Kenny just wanted her company.

8

Christmas morning silence awakens Kenny, and he forces himself up out of bed. Noticing that it's only a little after six, his time, he knows Shannon is already up for it being after nine, her time. After checking his phone, he finds a text she sent just fifteen minutes ago wishing him a very Merry Christmas and that she misses him. He feels a warmth of happiness come over him that makes his morning of being alone just a little better. After sleeping under his crocheted blanket again, he grabs it off his bed, wrapping it around him as he heads out into his living room to notice the light snow fall happening right now. He thinks of her and how she would be so in love with waking up to a white Christmas instead of the rain she woke up to. After having a small breakfast and coffee, he showers, dresses for the day, and gives her a call.

"Well, hello, my Rusty Blade."

"Hi, Kiddo, how has your Christmas morning been so far?"

"Oh, just great except for the rain. I love rain but not today."

"I know—that sucks. It's snowing here, and I thought of you as soon as I saw."

"Send me some, ha. What are you doing today?"

"Probably going to my brother's in a few hours for most of the day. He loves the blanket you made me, and so do I, Kiddo. I've been sleeping under it, and I have it wrapped around me right now. It's so warm."

"I am so happy you love it, and that's why I made it for you. So how was the party and Jaylen? What a fancy name!"

"Better than I expected, and I enjoyed catching up with some old friends."

"That tent was beautiful, and I could picture us sitting at the gazebo all night talking. Sorry if I shouldn't have said that."

"Don't apologize. I agree, and maybe we will...one starry night."

"Aw...no way...you remember—so cool."

"Of course!"

"Jaylen is so beautiful, Kenny, from what I could see in the picture you sent me. I'm almost a little jealous."

"Don't be, Kiddo. Her beauty will fade, where yours won't."

"Oh my gosh, that's so sweet—especially coming from you, thank you."

"Well, it's true."

"Kenny, does it ever make you uncomfortable when I tell you I love you? I won't say it if it does."

There's a little pause. "No, Kiddo—not at all. How soon do you think you can come out?"

"Really?"

"Yes!"

"I can fly out as soon as Tuesday. I would love to spend New Year's with you."

"You would get on a plane? You are scared to fly."

"To see you, Kenny Kirtzanger, yes—yes, I would. There's a first time for everything, right?"

"Kiddo, you fly out as soon as you can, and bring enough to stay with me till after the first. I'll pick you up from the airport. Don't be scared to fly. It will be just fine. You will be fine. Don't even think about it... Just think of me."

"Okay, I will." She pauses. "I love you, Kenny, and I will let you know when I am coming. I hope you enjoy the rest of your Christmas and say hi to Daniel for me."

"I will, and I'll see you in a few days. Bye-bye for now, and you can text me later."

"I will... Until next time."

Kenny is growing fonder of Shannon with every passing day, and now with Jaylen in the picture, it really has his thoughts and feelings all over the place. On one hand, he has this sweet, lovely, but very young fan who truly cares for him and will do anything for him. She makes him laugh and makes him happy; and then, on the other hand, he has his friend of twenty-some years that at one point he almost hooked up with who is beautiful, successful, and a talented stunt actress who is closer to his age. The thoughts of actually feeling something for either of them scare him. He's just not sure about being in another relationship.

The following Friday afternoon, he is waiting at the airport for her plane to land. Still shaking from her first flight, she greets him with a tight hug, excited to see him. He grabs her luggage, and they start making their way through the large airport. He asks how her first flight was, and she tells him "not as bad as she had always feared but it was still nerve-racking" with a laugh and the best part were the clouds. He tells her he knew she would love that. That's about as close as she can get to them. Exiting the airport, she is thrilled to see there is still snow. Later that night, he is sitting on his couch under his blanket, and he calls her over to join him.

"I made you a Christmas present. Open it!" he says, handing her a small gift bag.

She digs through the tissue paper and pulls out a see-through oval locket pendant hanging on a gold chain, and enclosed inside is something that she has always wanted from him…a locket of his hair. She's almost bought to tears as she puts it around her neck.

"I can't believe you actually did this for me. You actually gave me a locket of your hair. Something very personal from you—a part of you that I'll always have no matter where I am in this world and even after you're gone. I love it so much, Kenny. Wow! Thank you!"

"You're very welcome. I remember you telling me one time about wanting it, and at first, I thought it was weird, but I actually think it's sweet that you want my hair to wear around your neck. That's love, Kiddo."

She hugs him tight, and he offers to share his blanket with her, and she scoots as close to him as possible, and they watch a few movies before she falls asleep with her head laying on his shoulder. Feeling sleepy himself, he very carefully gets up while gently laying her down so not to wake her. He covers her with the blanket she made him before going to bed. He was so happy having her back in his house.

He is thrilled to be ringing in the New Year with her tomorrow night and couldn't wait to tell her news in the morning that is sure to make her superexcited. He awakes to the aroma of maple syrup, coffee, and Canadian bacon in the air. He walks out into his kitchen to find her making pancakes for breakfast. She loves taking care of him and surprising him with the littlest things. As they have breakfast together, he surprises her by telling her that they will be spending the evening at Carlos and Camilla's house for dinner and fireworks. Just the four of them. She is feeling ecstatic. Being invited to Carlos's house is something she has wanted since Kenny's birthday party, and she can hardly contain her excitement over the thoughts of seeing where he lives and what his house looks like. She's really looking forward to seeing both his martial arts awards, as well as awards he has won throughout his career in the acting business and tequila bottle display. She absolutely adores Carlos and almost as much as she does her Rusty Blade. Carlos is funny, spontaneous, outgoing, intelligent, loves his career, but also tough and serious when he needs to be. He is very hardworking and never misses an opportunity to do something great. Next to Kenny, he is the sweetest man she has met. Around five that evening, they make the short drive to Carlos's. He lives in a small two-story soft-gray house built with siding and a two-car garage and very close neighbors. Camilla greets them at the door which leads straight into the living room, and she gets a smell of pasta and garlic. She walks into the living room, which has a light-brown wood floor and cream-colored walls which lands throughout the rest of their house. Their living room is an average size with a couch sit lining the wall in front of the double windows, black coffee table, and an end table with a floor lamp next to it. On the opposite wall is a fireplace with a flat-screen TV attached to the wall above it. To her right of the living room is a wall adorned with family photos and friends with a small round table with beautiful flowers. She walks into the kitchen where she finds Carlos at the stove checking on his lasagna he made. It's a large open kitchen with a prep island in the center with a sink, cabinets, and drawers. White marble tile lines the floor with cabinets lining two of the walls with the light-brown wood and galaxy-black countertops and black appliances. Shannon greets Carlos and thanks him for inviting her to his home. She learns that there is a guest room and bathroom on the main floor and a master bedroom with a full bath and two bedrooms and guest bathroom upstairs. He walks her outside through the kitchen sliding door where and shows her his deck he just built. It's a brownstone color and lays low to the ground. There is also a matching bench and table he built as well.

She is amazed at how skilled Carlos is and joked with him that he can build Kenny one too. His backyard is completely fenced in with various trees, flowers, and bushes all around. Camilla has a green thumb and loves flowers. Carlos takes her into a small office room. The walls are white with brown baseboards and brown window frames and a chandelier hanging in the middle putting off a soft glow. He walks her over to show her his tequila bottle collection that he has collected over the years. Four long glass shelves built into the wall are packed from end to end with various bottles in different sizes, shapes, and colors. Some are old bottles, some are emptied, and some are still sealed and limited editions. She also learns he is a hot sauce lover too. On the other side of the room are various sizes of trophies he has won at martial arts tournaments, and hanging above on the wall are framed certificates and medals. They all four sit down to a nice but special New Year's Eve dinner that consists of Carlos's famous homemade lasagna along with garlic French bread, salad, and Nanaimo bars for dessert and conversations. It was her first time trying them, and Kenny's favorite and now hers too. She enjoys trying the different foods of Canada. After dinner, Camilla and Carlos, both refusing to let Kenny or Shannon help clean up, shoo them out of the kitchen; and they go outside and sit on the bench. With only three and a half hours till midnight and a New Year, fireworks can already be heard as they light up the calm, pleasant dark sky.

"Great weather for tonight."

"Yes! Even with the patches of snow still lying in places. I'm happy to be here with you, Kenny, thank you."

"Me, too, Kiddo, and thank you for giving up family time and flying out," he says while rubbing his hand along her back.

"Oh, I wouldn't have missed this. We all have to break our fears at some point. This is a memory I'll have for the rest of my life, and

I won't have to regret that I didn't do it. My family was totally okay with it. They know how much you mean to me and how much I enjoy visiting you."

"That's right! Don't ever let your fears hold you back, Kiddo, because that is when you will miss out on the best thing."

"You are letting your fears hold you back from love, ha. You know, Kenny, losing Craig so soon has shown me just how precious and short life is, and it has taught me that you shouldn't leave this world with any regrets and what-ifs…what could have been. You just go for it and give it a try, and if it doesn't work, at least you tried, and I don't want to leave this world with any more regrets. I don't want to leave world without knowing you. That's why I have fought so hard to be in your life. That's why I make the sacrifices I do to come visit you every month. Just setting here next to you in this close, private personal matter is more to me than any piece of jewelry or flower you could buy me or any fancy dinner date you could take me on. Just give me priceless memories with my Rusty Blade. That's all I want from you."

"Very powerful statement. I still don't fully understand how or why I mean so much to you like I have over these years, but I'm starting to see. You really are such a lovely person with a big heart and someone I am happy to know."

"Can I get very open and deep with you about something?"

"Sure! You can tell me anything."

"Do you know why I tell you I love you so much? It because I don't think you can ever say it enough. When Craig and I first got married, he used to say it to me like all the time. Probably every hour and at first it drove me crazy, ha, but then I would hear other women talk about how their man would almost never say it or only said it when they were wanting something or if she said it first or trying to make up for an argument. Made me realize that I was lucky that my man actually wanted to tell me, and from then on, I loved hearing him say it as much as he wanted, and I know that he loved me more than he did anyone else and now," she says with a break in her voice and then clears her throat. "Now with him gone, I'm glad I have all of those 'I love yous' to last me for the rest of my life. I just want to know that if something ever happens to me, I can leave you with enough too."

"Aw…come here, Kiddo," he says, wrapping his arm around her and cuddling and hugging her. "That is so freaking sweet, and nothing is going to happen to you."

"I never thought nothing would happen to Craig, but he's gone, and we never know. I could wreck my semi, one of my incurable autoimmune diseases alone with something like the flu or pneumonia could kill me. Someone out there could kidnap and kill me. We just never know what lies in our tomorrows."

"Stop thinking like that, Kiddo. You have to keep those negative thoughts and worries as far away from your mind as possible."

"I will try. Carlos and Camilla need to be out here because they are missing these fireworks."

"They will be out closer to midnight. Carlos is probably having some tequila and feeling good right about now, ha. I'm just glad it isn't too cold for this."

"Aren't you going to have a beer or something?"

"Maybe."

"Go on and get drunk if you want. I'm not getting drunk. I can drive us back to your house if you trust me to drive your car. Have fun! It's New Year's—I got you!"

Forty minutes remain in the year before a new year starts when Carlos and Camilla come outside. Carlos brings out him and Kenny a few drinks, and Shannon tries champagne for the first time with Camilla. They all spend the last part of the year talking about memories from the year that is about to be gone forever. The three of them talk about their goals and New Year's resolutions before Carlos asks Shannon what her resolutions are. She tells them that she plans to continue to lose weight and get as healthy as possible and she has always wanted to write a book and be a published author since she was ten years old. She has been writing in a journal and hopes to publish it within the next few years. They are all surprised to hear as she has never mentioned it before and give her full support and encouragement that she can make it happen. Camilla curiously asks what her book is about, but she prefers not to say right now and apologizes but promises to tell them all eventually. The last two minutes of the year begin to tick away, and Carlos wraps his arms tight around Camilla, who is standing beside Shannon, kissing her on her cheek. She is watching the fireworks color the sky when she feels Kenny approaching her from behind. He loosely puts his arms around her, and she leans back lying against him. Carlos tells them that they look so cute next to each other with their major height difference, avoiding mentioning that he thinks they could make a great couple. Midnight arrives along with a New Year, and there's no one else that Shannon or Kenny wanted to celebrate it with but each other. She wouldn't have been happier anywhere else but standing there leaning against her Rusty Blade. He leans down and whispers, "Happy New Year, Kiddo," in her right ear; and she softly says it back to him. It was one of the best New Year's of her life, and she hopes this new year will be the best year of her life, and she is looking forward to having all of her new friends here in Vancouver a part of it. They both leave around twelve thirty and head back to Kenny's.

9

S hannon flies back home the next day with having to return back to work in two days, and it's back to work on Carlos's movie, for Kenny is acting in it and will be on set every day until he has to fly out for a convention in Stockholm, Sweden, in less than two weeks. With the long hours and retakes, there isn't much time for her and Kenny to call each other, but they still make time to text. She worries about him working twelve to fourteen hours a day with little rest, but that's the life of an actor. She learned about the movie while at Carlos's the other night and is excited to see it when it's finally released. She even joked around with Kenny that he got to come out on the road and see how she works and how awesome it would be if she could go and see him work one day, too; and to her surprise, he and Carlos chuckled and told her maybe. She couldn't be happier being friends with Kenny, and now she's becoming friends with everyone close to him. In some ways, losing Craig was a blessing in disguise. She knows none of this, getting to be so close to Kenny, spending nights with him—none of it would have ever happened. She still misses her husband dearly and still has her moments of crying and asking why, but with having Kenny in her life now, it gets a little easier with each passing day. He has help to fill the emptiness in her heart and reduce the loneliness in her life. She loves him more than she ever imagined and almost to the point it scares her. As his fan, she has adored him for thirteen years, and now she longs to love him and have him love her. Those three words are something she dreams of hearing him say to her and hopes it will happen. He was someone who is private, emotionless at times, and not looking for love; so she still doesn't understand his affection toward her—the cuddles, hugs, touching, smiles, eye winks. But she loves them all and doesn't plan on taking advantage of it for whatever cost there is behind it. She just hopes he never stops. Even though he claims to not be looking for love, she still fears him falling for someone one day and her losing him and everything that she has worked hard to have. She has been nervous since this Jaylen has popped back up, and at times, she feels a little jealous about their upcoming dinner date that he told her about at Carlos's. She's always wanted to go out on a date with him but has been too nervous to ask. What if she is after Kenny? What if Kenny falls for her? What if they start dating? What will that mean for Shannon? All Shannon cares about is his happiness, and she isn't one of those jealous girls who think that if she can't have him, then no one else can, and if he was ever to decide to pursue a relationship with this or any lucky beautiful woman, she knows she won't interfere. Just as long as he still makes time for her. As long as this girl will be good to Kenny and treat him right and love him the way he deserves to be loved, makes him feel the way he has always wanted to feel, and says everything he has always wanted to hear—she'll be happy for him because she loves him enough to let him go. The first time any woman hurts him, though, it will be on. She wasn't in his life the last time he was hurt, but she is now and very protective of his feelings, and she won't put up with no woman hurting him again. No woman better ever make that mistake of her having driven her semi out to anywhere because they hurt him.

It's around midnight in California and eight in the morning on Friday in Stockholm, Sweden, and the morning of Kenny's convention, which doesn't start till four that evening. She texts him, and to her surprise, he calls her happy she's still awake.

"Hi, Kenny, good morning."

"Hello, Kiddo, and good night."

"How are you? First time we have spoken over the phone since New Year's."

"I am doing great, and it is, and it's good to hear your voice."

"It's good to hear your voice as well. I can literary talk to you for hours and never get tired of hearing your voice or hearing you laugh."

"Thank you, Kiddo."

"You're welcome."

"What was your text about that you sent me a few hours ago where you said that this man is driving you crazy?"

"Jason! He keeps asking me out to dinner again. He is also telling all of his trucker friends, some who are mutual friends of mine, and my brother that he really likes me a lot and wishes I would spend as much time with him as I do with you. Ugh, Kenny! My brother isn't happy about it either. He told Jason to stop or our friendship will be over. Sometimes I am scared."

Feeling himself become furious inside, he says, "Are you kidding me, Kiddo? He can't seem to take no for an answer. Don't you do it! Don't go on any more dates with him. He's getting way too attached to you."

"I won't! The only reason I haven't cut the friendship completely off is because I am afraid that that will hurt him so bad to the point of stalking me, or worse—"

"What do you mean by 'worse'?"

"I don't trust him anymore. I wish I never became friends with him, but I give everybody a chance. He was friends with my brother first and then became friends with Craig, and now…oh, Kenny."

"Kiddo, listen to me. I know that I'm not with you out there, but I won't let this guy hurt you, I promise. I'll get to wherever you are faster than a bullet if he touches you. Just promise me that you will keep staying as far away from him as you can and if he ever touches you that you will press charges. Don't let him get by with anything."

"I promise I will. I am so grateful for you and you being here for me. Means so much to me. I couldn't imagine going through this without you. I love you, my Rusty Blade."

"You will always have me, and I will always be your Rusty Blade. He's going to meet 'Rusty Blade' too, if he doesn't leave you alone."

"Are you ready for your friendly dinner date with Jaylen?"

"As ready as I will ever be, and it will be nice to catch up."

Shannon is silent for a moment, and Kenny senses her worries. "Don't worry, Kiddo. I'll be fine. You and I will go out for dinner sometime."

"Really? I can go on a dinner date with you?"

"Of course! I need to go down to the main floor and finish setting up. I will text you when I have a free minute and when I go to lunch, if you will be awake, but don't put off rest just for talking to me. I want you to get your sleep. Good night, Kiddo."

"Thank you, Kenny, and I hope you have a fun time, meet the most fans, and have the best time. You deserve it."

Kenny calls Shannon on the last Saturday of January. He just got back home from his friendly dinner date with Jaylen and wanted to tell her about it. He trusts her with his feelings enough to comfortably open up to her. He tells her that he met Jaylen at a fancy restaurant of her choosing where she made reservations, like the one you walk into, and it just screams money as you hear the person playing piano from somewhere in the middle of the room. They were seated at a square four-person table with an elegant white tablecloth trimmed in gold, fancy white-and-gold china, silverware, and wine glasses. Totally had her written over it just like his ex. Kenny has never been a fancy person or into the fancy things in life. He is more like Shannon, simple and low-key. Jaylen took it upon herself to order their meals ahead of time. She ordered him filet mignon and her leg of lamb. The date started out with them talking about old times and catching up on what they have been doing since last seeing each other two years ago. Jaylen just got out of a six-year relationship due to differences in the relationship and tells him that she still after all of these years is interested in him. He was already expecting it to come out but just wasn't prepared for hearing the words and felt a lump in his throat. He has always cared for Jaylen. She was his first on-screen stunt partner, and she has been one of his good friends for over twenty years. Seeing her again and being in her presence actually made him nervous and made him think back to some of those old feelings. Jaylen still having his number told him that she never called due to not knowing if he was in a relationship but she will now with him being single. After parting ways, he drove around for a little trying to clear his head. Shannon fighting back emotions from hearing about his date that he seemed to really enjoy and about his old feelings for Jaylen makes it hard for her to speak without sounding scared or heartbroken but tells him she is happy he had a great time and decides to make a brave bold move by asking him if he will be her Valentine, and to her amazement, he says yes and told her that he was already thinking about asking her and taking her on a dinner date on Valentine's Day. After hanging up, she jumps up out of her bunk and breaks out into a happy dance being so happy and super-excited that her Rusty Blade is actually going to be her Valentine. It may be a friendly dinner date, but it's something she's hoped for and something that every fan fantasizes about. She's so happy she had the courage to ask him and before Jaylen had a chance. She calls her mom with happy tears streaming down her face and tells her. Even growing up old-school, her mom knows how much Kenny means to her daughter, and even with a huge age gap, she accepts Shannon's love and desire for him. She has always seen her mom as her closest best friend and trusts her with everything. She can tell her mom anything and knows that her mom will always give her the best advice and support. They are alike in a lot of ways, and to her mom, Shannon is her "mini me." She is always a natural, but after waiting so many years for this date, Shannon knows she wants to look as pretty as she feels and has a few weeks to find the perfect dress to wear, and she knows that getting her hair and makeup done, too, will be in the cards.

10

I t's been a long anticipating few weeks for Shannon, and the wait for her dinner date with Kenny is closing in as she backs her semi up his drive the day before Valentine's Day. She has already bought the perfect dress, and Camilla insists on doing her makeup and fixing her shoulder-length brown hair tomorrow. She even went as far as to get her nails professionally done, which now shine in a deep rich red color with added sparkly glitter. Knowing ahead of time that Kenny would be out with Carlos for lunch, she patiently waits for him on his porch swing taking in the beautiful weather. Later that evening as the sky begins to change colors, she asks him if she could watch the sunset from his back guesthouse deck that overlooks a mountain. He walks her to the back side and up a set of stairs, and she asks him if he will join her. The deck is a chocolate color with a large round table and six chairs. She leans up against the side of the deck overlooking and waiting. He walks up next to her. "This is so beautiful, Kenny. I mean absolutely breathtaking."

"Yes, it is."

"Do you sit out here often?"

"Only when I have company staying over out here. I guess, I do tend to forget how peaceful it is. Glad you wanted to come out here."

"Well, you know me and sunsets, ha, and this is one view I haven't seen yet."

After the sun sets, and she adores it, they both sit down at the table, and he smiles and takes joy in watching her stargaze. Just seeing her love for the simplest things that people never think about makes him adore her.

"Are you ready for tomorrow, Kenny? Me...you...Valentine's Day...oh yeah, ha! and our first solo dinner date."

"Kiddo, you are a mess. Yes, and I am looking forward to it. I haven't had a Valentine in over four years."

"Well, you will tomorrow, Mr. Rusty Blade. Thank you for being my Valentine, Kenny."

"You're welcome, Kiddo, and it's going to be special."

"You know, out there driving up and down the roads, you see sunsets every evening that stretches for miles and miles, bursting with different colors and the same big starry sky night after night, and it still never gets old looking up and seeing the twinkling stars that shine over us. It's just so beautifully amazing. Takes your imagination to a whole different world and lets you daydream about what you wish you had."

"So sweet, Kiddo. I wish I could be out there seeing that with you," he says, looking out over the sky.

"You are, Kenny." She looks over at him and he back at her. "You are out there in my truck with me every second of every day. When I am watching the sunset, the sun rising, and when I am stargazing, you're there. You were before we met, and you always will be."

"I'm almost speechless. Touching! You know, Kiddo, I don't have many regrets in life, but if I do have to regret one thing, it would be social media because for all of these years, I had a fan like you out there that I didn't know about. That I've missed out on, and that's a regret because you're simply amazing, and I wish I could've known you sooner."

Shannon tears up overhearing Kenny say that. "Can I hug you?"

"Yes, I would love a hug."

On Valentine's Day, Camilla picks up Shannon around one. She won't see Kenny again until he picks her up from Carlos's for dinner around five. She tells Camilla that she is surprisingly nervous, and Camilla tells her not to be. She reminds Shannon of that time in Kenny's kitchen telling her that he is her celebrity crush and that maybe tonight, she should tell him a little bit of how she feels, especially with Jaylen around. They sit at the kitchen table and have a light lunch. Carlos is out for a few hours, and so they have plenty of girl talk before it's time to start getting ready. Camilla does her own makeup and fixes her hair first. She invites Shannon upstairs, and after changing into her dress for the date, she sits down at Camilla's makeup vanity, and she wraps a towel around Shannon to protect her dress. Camilla, being a makeup expert, has already picked out a foundation shade, eyeliner and eye shadows, blush, and lipstick for Shannon's pale tone. After Camilla finishes Shannon's makeup, she still refuses to let her see until her hair is done. After Camilla is done with Shannon's hair, she made her go see herself in a full-length mirror hanging on the inside closet door, and she is almost bought to tears when she sees herself.

"Oh, wow! Sorry, trying not to cry. I haven't seen myself like this since my wedding day. I feel...so pretty."

"That's because you are pretty, sweetie. Even without the glam. It just enhanced you, and now you're beautiful."

"Thank you so much."

"You're so welcome, and I will be glad to do your hair and makeup any day. I just can't wait for Kenny to see you. So glad I get to see his reaction too."

Carlos arrives home around four, and Camilla calls him up to see Shannon. He freezes in the doorway of their bedroom stunned by seeing her.

"Shorty? Dang! You look amazing—wow!"

"Thank you, Carlos."

Kenny arrives around four fifty, and Carlos greets him. Shannon told him he didn't have to dress up for her; but he's wearing black dress shoes, black dress slacks; and a white button-down dress shirt. Camilla comes down dress in a beautiful long black evening dress, diamond earrings, a necklace; and her hair in an updo of bouncy curls. She asks Kenny if he's ready to see his Valentine and he says yes. Camilla calls to her, and Shannon begins to make her way down the stairs slowly so as not to trip. He doesn't see her till about half-way; and when he finally does, his eyes widen, his heart races, he gets flutters in his stomach, and he's almost too stunned to smile at seeing her. She is wearing a red knee-length strapless dress with a crystal beaded bodice and black-and-red heels. Her makeup is a natural look with red lipstick, soft red-and-pink eye shadows, soft pink blush, and black eyeliner. She has a loose French braid and rings of curls all around. Carlos and Camilla are all smiles and giggles at Kenny's reaction as Shannon approaches him.

"Kiddo…you look…wow!" he says, looking her over.

"You look very handsome, too, Kenny. It's amazing what makeup, a pretty dress, and different hair can do, huh?"

"Trust me, you don't need it. Let's go, Kiddo." Shannon blushes and giggles.

Kenny drives to the location of last year's Christmas Eve party minus a white tent and Christmas decorations. As they got close, he tells her to close her eyes. Once parked and her eyes still closed, he walks over to the passenger side and helps her out. He walks her carefully, telling her when to step up. When he tells her to open her eyes, she is amazed and touched by what she sees. It's the big gazebo from the picture he sent her except this time there is a small round table with a red cloth and two chairs in the middle of it and about ten pink and red balloons tied to the posts going around it. Shannon thinks back to telling him on her truck one night how she loves balloons, and she is thrilled that he remembered and did this for her. In the middle of the table is a vase of red, pink, and white roses. There is two champagne glasses, a bucket of ice with a bottle of champagne, silverware, napkins, and two dinner plates with trays over them locking in the heat. Hanging inside the middle of the gazebo is a big crystal chandelier, and next to Kenny's plate is a small wrapper box. She almost wants to cry at the sight of what he has done for her. Everything here is things that she has told him she loves. To go to this length with them not even being a couple only makes her imagine how amazing of a loving boyfriend he would be, and she almost feels herself wanting to tell him right now. He seats her and sets across from her.

"This is all so beautiful, Kenny! Words can't express how beautiful this is—from the balloons to the chandelier, the flowers, and… you. Happy Valentine's Day, Kenny Kirtzanger."

"You deserve it, Kiddo. You deserve a special day after everything you have been through. Happy Valentine's Day, Shannon Keeler."

"You really are romantic."

"I can be."

"Don't blush, Kenny."

As they enjoy their dinner together, they talk about each other, and he tells her more about the movie he's starring in. No mention of Jason, Jaylen, or Kim as they just talk about each other. He can't remember the last time he had a dinner that he enjoyed as much as this one, even if it was just between two friends. She always makes him smile, and she always makes him feel appreciated. After their meals, she hands him a small red gift bag adorned with pink hearts, apologizing for it being so girly. He giggles, telling her it's okay. He pulls out a long box and opens it to reveal something he's been wanting for years. Something rare, expensive, and very hard to find. It's a sterling silver and Italian calf leather fountain pen in a deep shine chocolate with a limited circulation. She had to pull a lot of strings to get it, but seeing him happy with it made it priceless. He looks up at her, now smiling at him. "Kiddo...where? How?"

"Don't underestimate me when it comes to somebody I love wanting something. I'll spend hours and go to the next level to find it and being a trucker with connections helps."

"I almost want to cry, and I don't cry, Kiddo. I have been wanting and hunting for this pen for years. Thank you so much."

"You're truly welcome, Kenny. I love you!"

"This is for you, Kiddo," he says, handing her a red velvet box with a white bow on the lid.

She opens it, and her face lights up as she pulls it out. It's a sterling silver necklace with a silver bar that says "Rusty's Girl" engraved deep, and a tiny purple gem dangles from its corner. Kenny quickly goes over and hooks it around her neck.

"Thank you, Kenny. I love it so much."

"You're welcome, Kiddo, and you are my girl. Hey, let's get out of here."

They ride up to a strip mall where they walk, window shop, and dive into sweets. It is the best night of Shannon's life, and she didn't want it to end. If just this night was this amazing with Kenny, then how would every night be?

Back at his house, sitting on the couch, she turns to him. "I love you, Kenny, and thank you for being my Valentine and for letting me be yours. This is a night I'll treasure for the rest of my life."

Kenny just looks at her with a soft smile. "You really do love me, don't you, Kiddo?"

"Yes, I do! You mean more to me than you will ever know. You are worth every mile that I drive and every penny that I put in my fuel tank. Every sacrifice I make from family time to loads to even my own semi."

"Sacrifice your semi?" he says, looking at her with a questionable look. "You sacrifice buying your own semi for me?"

"Of course! Sometimes, it takes me four to eight days to travel out here to see you depending on my location, and that sometimes costs me loads if there aren't any going in my direction. The loads that I've turned down or given away over the past six months have been worth every memory I have with you. I won't ever be too busy for you. I'll always have time for you."

"But, Kiddo—"

"Don't you 'but, Kiddo' me, Kenny!" she says, smiling at him. "Someday in the future, Kenny, you are going to leave me here alone just like my husband did, and all I will have is my Rusty Blade semi and all of the time in the world to enjoy it—just to drive by your house and cry because I can no longer back in your drive or come back in this house…" Shannon pauses as she tears up with a break in her voice, and Kenny wipes a tear from her cheek with his left thumb.

"Aw, Kiddo."

"Because you won't be here. So for now, I rather enjoy you and whatever time you're willing to give me. Now I'll never take you for granted, but I am certainly going to take advantage of whatever time I can spend with you. Having that semi is my dream, but you were my dream long before it, and you're certainly a lot better than that semi." They both chuckle.

"I don't know what to say, Kiddo. I never knew I could mean that much to someone."

"You just haven't had the right person to tell you, to show you, to appreciate you like I do. I'll never hurt you or turn my back on you, and I thank you for every second of your life that you have let me be a part of, and I will love you every day for the rest of my life. Now I know I can't share your golden years with you, obviously, but I want to be a part of yours. I want to be in your future because I didn't get your past, and I'll park that truck any day of the week and come to you if you're sick, hurt, or just want some company. If you ever want to pack up and get the heck away from here, I'll put you on my truck and take you across the States again with me. I'd take care of you, Kenny, I promise. You are such a dream, Kenny. You're so handsome. Your smile was probably the first thing I noticed about you, and I think I fell for it more than anything else at first. That smile—your smile, it's made of daydreams, and you have those beautiful brown eyes for daydreaming. I scan everything, Kenny, as if I am recording all of you in my memory. From every freckle to every blemish and every inch of your skin. I love the glimmer in your eyes when you smile and the way your Adam's apple dances when you laugh. I love how you can make the side of your smile go back a little higher and how you stand with that slight bend in your left knee. I love your salt-and-pepper beard, your laugh, your touch, your hugs. Even your flaws, Kenny. If I could make you younger, I would only so I could have you a lot longer or I would make me closer to your age so I wouldn't have to be here too long without you. Sorry, I am rambling and probably making you uncomfortable."

"It's not things I am used to hearing, but it isn't making me uncomfortable. You have a way with words, Kiddo. I can see why he loved you so much."

She tells him good night with a hug and just as she reaches the bedroom door of the guest room she sleeps in. "Hey, Kiddo?"

"Yes," he says, turning to look at him.

"For what it's worth, you really looked beautiful tonight. I definitely like seeing you dressed up."

"Thank you, Kenny. That means a lot coming from you. I may just have to more often."

She comes out of the bedroom the next morning with her purse and overnight bags. Kenny is already on the phone telling Carlos about some of last night and his gift she gave him. He looks over and sees her standing there waiting but not wanting to interrupt him.

"Hey, Carlos, I will call you back." He ends their phone conversation. "Hi, Kiddo, what's up?"

"I wasn't sure if I was going to be leaving today or tomorrow, but it's today. My dispatcher asked me if I would be willing to take a new driver on board and train her over the next six weeks."

"Oh, that's cool! You will show her what to do?"

"Sorta! She learned most in trucking school. I will take her out and let her drive and make deliveries to make sure she can operate the semi properly and do her pretrip inspections. I will have to take notes and log her performance, and she has to complete a certain amount of hours with rest."

"Neat! Well, good luck!"

"Thanks! It shouldn't be too hard. My brother trained me, and I remember a lot of what we did. I will be steady focusing on her, and so I may not get to call you often, but I will text you every chance I get."

"That's okay, Kiddo."

"I will miss you till my next visit in April. Enjoy any conventions you may have coming, and be safe working on that movie."

"I am going to miss you, Kiddo. My house will be so quiet. You be safe out that with her. Hopefully she doesn't cause any problems. Introduce her to Jason, ha."

"Oh no! Ha!"

After saying their goodbyes, she stops at his glass door and looks over at him still sitting on his couch.

"Kenny, I want to know something. I need to know this, and you don't have to say the words, because I know you don't say them. Just a simple yes or no will be good enough.

"What, Kiddo?"

"As your fan, friend, and someone that you care about, do you feel any love for me? Like do you love me?"

He walks over wrapping his arms around her and whispers yes in her ear. She gasps in shock, and as she turns heading out, he hears her mumble to herself. "He said yes. He actually said yes. My Rusty Blade loves me. Oh, wow."

He feels a sense of relief as he watches her leave, and knowing she won't be back for over a month makes him miss her already, but with a busy schedule ahead of him, he is sure the days will pass quickly.

11

O ver the next six weeks, Shannon stays focused on her student, so she only gets to call Kenny once a week but texts him daily. He even made sure to call her and wish her a happy thirty-first birthday. She told him about her young female student and that they had gotten along well and have quickly become friends, which wasn't hard for her with her kind, sweet personality. She actually enjoyed training her and told her dispatcher that she will be happy to do it again and turned in a positive report for her student who was hired by the same company. Kenny stayed busy on Carlos's movie set and had two conventions. About once or twice a week, Jaylen stopped by the set to hang out and watch the movie come to life from behind the cameras. She and Kenny began hanging out more and more and going to lunch and even dinner sometimes. Though she has been his friend for many years and at one time a crush, he is being careful around her. Missing Shannon made him want to spend time with Jaylen but still not inviting her to his house. Shannon being so emotional, loving, and open has made him start to feel feelings that he has been trying to get locked away since the day he broke up with Kim. As much as he tries to fight it and not wanting to express it, he's starting to feel love again. She decides to take a week off the road to rest up and spend time with her family and plans to visit Kenny after the first of April. With him and Jaylen getting close again during these past weeks and scared of losing him to her, she has been feeling depressed about it thinking it may be time to be fully open with him about her feelings. Around the second week of April, she is about ten minutes from Carlos's when she calls him asking if Camilla is home. She trusts her and so loves their girl talks. She is in desperate need of one before getting to Kenny's. Telling her that, unfortunately, she is out, Carlos invites her out anyway, assuring her that she can talk to him and he will try and help her. She parks her semi on the street in front of his house, turns on her hazard lights, and places her warning cones in front of and behind her truck to alert drivers in advance of approaching her semi. She walks around the back of his house through the gate like he told her. He is sitting in a black metal chair on his patio, and she sits down across from him.

"Hey, Shorty, what's up? What did you want to talk about?"

Shannon looks up at Carlos with a tear in her eye and an uncontrollable shake inside. "Carlos, I know that Kenny and Jaylen have been getting close, and with a long friendship, it's understandable, and now they have been spending so much time together. I know she wants him, but I just honestly don't know how to handle it. I mean, I want him happy even if it is with her."

"Why?"

"Well, because there's something that neither of you two know yet, and that is that I am absolutely magically beautifully in love with him. I am in love with my best friend, my Rusty Blade. I love him with my entire heart and soul. I am absolutely crazy about him. I knew it would happen after getting to finally be in his life after waiting all these years. He is the only reason I still get up every morning, the only reason the wheels on my semi keep rolling, the only reason I didn't drive my semi off that bridge that morning."

"I knew it! You are actually in love with him, and finally it's out. I had a feeling for a while now. It's all over your face, and I see it in your eyes. I almost wished I didn't push them two back together."

"That's not your fault. In all honesty, why should I ever think I had a chance with him? I mean, look at me. I was scared to tell him because I didn't want to hurt our friendship that I've waited nearly half my life for."

Shannon breaks down in tears, and Carlos moves over to the bench beside her and holds her. "Hey...Shorty...look at me." She looks up at him. "You know what I think?"

"What?"

"I think that you are probably one of the sweetest, most gentle kindhearted girls I know to walk into his life. He has been a total different person since you have been around, and I know that you truly love him, and I think you should tell him."

"Carlos—no! I...I can't! I can't risk our friendship. I can't lose him."

"You won't lose the friendship over your feelings. He won't do that to you. You mean too much to him, and you never know, he might feel the same way, but you won't know if you don't try. No regrets, right? He needs to know. Trust me on this!"

"Really? How amazing would that be? I guess I should tell him. I have never given up on him, and I'm not about to now. He's worth fighting for, and this Jaylen better watch out because I am his Kiddo, and she won't ever be to him what I am. Thank you for the talk."

"You're so welcome, and glad I could help, and in all honesty, I would much rather see you and him together, but that's not my decision to make. I know you will be good to him."

Shannon hugs Carlos, walks over to the edge of his house, and turns back to him. "Thank you, Carlos, and you can tell Ms. Jaylen that she better buckle down and not keep relying on just her pretty looks, fake nails, done-up hair, and fancy dresses, because this isn't a beauty competition. It's war." She winks her eye. "I'll talk to you later. Love you!"

"Oh, snap! Ha! Go get him, Shorty."

She arrives at Kenny's and finds him in his backyard cleaning his grill. He had already told her in a text that he wants to talk to her about something, and she just knows it is about Jaylen. She greets him, and seeing that he has grown out his Rusty Blade beard makes it a little easy for her to hide her fears and worries with smiles and excitement.

"You grew your beard, Kenny...whoa."

"You like, Kiddo? Ha! I had to for the part in this movie, and I've been waiting to surprise you with it. Let's go in and sit down so we can talk."

"Sure."

"Let's sit here on the couch."

"What's on your mind?"

"You know I trust your opinions and with my feelings, and I know that you will always give me straight honesty with what you think is best for me if I can't figure it out. You're the only one next to Carlos and my brother, Daniel, that I can open up to. As you know, Jaylen and I have been talking for a few months and even went on a few dates and have been spending time together. I can tell that she really wants to be in a relationship with me."

"Do you?" she says, looking down, sad.

"It's hard, Kiddo, because I feel myself starting to go back to all those years ago when she and I were close, and at one point, I did have feelings for her, but I don't know if I can do it. I mean, she just got out of a six-year marriage, and I just keep thinking back to what if everything with Kim repeats itself? I don't know if I am ready to put myself in a relationship and open up again just for it to be the same thing, but then I think about Carlos and you saying if I don't, then what if I miss out on the one who's the one for me? I know you and Jaylen haven't met yet, and you two will while you are here, and maybe you guys can be friends. So I just…what do you think? Like help me out here, Kiddo."

Shannon feels nauseous and devastated at hearing him actually considering Jaylen and just knows she has lost him because she waited too long.

"Kenny, she does not like me at all. She does not like the fact that I come out here and I spend time with you. She does not like the fact that we talk on the phone every day, and she definitely doesn't like how close we are. There will never be a friendship between her and me, and she has made that perfectly clear to me."

"Hold up! Are you serious?"

"Yes, and she even told me that you would pick her over me. She told me that if she and you were to hook up, there will be no more me coming out here spending nights with you and talking on the phone with you will be reduced and that I will never be to you what she is and what she can be."

"When did she tell you this?"

"Social media, Kenny. She sent me a private message. She told me I am just an old trucker girl who didn't compare to her talent and beauty."

"Wait! Do you still have it?"

"Of course." She pulls out her phone and allows him to read the message for himself. "She said that she can take you from me, and another weird thing that I have noticed, too, is that since she has been back in your life, Jason now has his friends list private and unenviable."

Kenny isn't happy with this new discovery and finding out that Jaylen is being mean to his fan.

"No one will ever take me away from you, Kiddo, and why didn't you ever tell me about this so I could have confronted her? She has no right to talk to you like that, and she will never control who comes here or who I talk to."

"Yes, but I...I couldn't, Kenny. I just couldn't do that to you. I love you enough that I can get out of the way for you to be happy." Shannon begins to tear up.

Kenny slides closer to her and gently grabs both her hands. "What do you mean? Talk to me, Kiddo. Tell me what's going through your mind."

Shaking her head in refusal, she becomes more emotional. "I won't hurt your happiness, Kenny, or our friendship. I can't risk it! I've wanted this for too long, and I care more about your feelings than I do my own. I love you and probably more than she ever will, but I can't do this to you. I'm sorry! I need to step outside." She pulls her hands out of his, standing up and trying to walk away but he stands up and stops her by grabbing her from behind and spinning her around so quick till she falls on him, causing him to fall back on the couch and her landing on top of him; and they both giggle. She's staring him right in his eyes, and he has his arms tightly wrapped around her.

"The truth is, is I love you, Kenny. I've loved you for nearly half of my life, and I'll love you every day for the rest of my life. Just promise me that if you do decide that she is the love of your life, you won't let her come in between you and me. You won't let her take you away from me." Shannon lays her head on his chest and begins to cry. He softly rubs along her back.

"Kiddo, look at me."

"Yeah."

"No one and I mean *no one* will ever come in between us. I have a connection with you that no woman will ever come in between. I wish you would help me understand what you are hiding from me. I've been opening up to you to the point that I am now learning to feel again, and so it kind of hurts me that you're hiding from me."

"Do you love her, Kenny?"

"I care for her as a friend."

"No, are you in love with her?"

"No."

"You can't date someone if you aren't in love with them, and do you think she's truly in love with you, the real you?"

"Now that I can't honestly answer. I don't know her true love for me. Maybe I'm just a rebound to her, or maybe she has wanted to be with me all these years, but after what Kim did to me, I don't know if I can ever believe a woman when she tells me she truly loves me for me and only me. She does have some ways about her that make me wonder if she would be fair."

"Well, whether you choose to believe me or not, Mr. Rusty Blade, I can look you right in those beautiful brown eyes of yours right now without blinking and tell you that I love you. I'm in love with you, Kenny Kirtzanger! There, I said it."

"What did you just say?"

"I'm in love with you. I'm absolutely crazy about you."

Staring at her, he can't believe what she just said to him. She's really in love with him? What makes her love him so much? This bombshell totally changes everything and sends his mind in different directions. He does have love for Shannon, and in some ways, maybe he saw it coming. She lays her head back down on his shoulder gently pressing her forehead against his cheek, feeling a sense of relief that's finally out and he now knows. She can now be completely open around him. They have been lying there in that very spot for a few minutes when she kisses him on his earlobe and begins moving her fingertips along his chest, sending tingles through his body and causing him to twitch. He turns his face to her and kisses her between her eyes, and they giggle, though his silence scares her. What is he thinking? Did she just make a mistake by telling him? Would it be enough to get her in his sights too? With so much more she wants to tell him, she decides it would be best to give him so time and heads out to her semi to retrieve her logbook.

The next day brings sunny weather, which is good for Kenny's backyard cookout he has planned. Around two that afternoon, Carlos and Camilla arrive, followed by Daniel and his wife, Paula. She and Shannon meet for the first time but have heard some much about her already she feels as though she already knows Shannon, and they instantly click. Shannon just has a way about her that makes anyone comfortable with her. An hour later, Jaylen arrives. It's her first time at Kenny's house in over five years. They all sit around the firepit, and Kenny sits between Shannon and Jaylen and moves closer to Kiddo. Shannon can't help but feel uncomfortable and less pretty next to Jaylen. Kenny excuses both himself and Jaylen for a talk, and as they walk around his house, Carlos takes advantage of the opportunity and right there in front of everyone.

"So, Shorty, did you tell Kenny?"

"Yes."

"How did it go? What did he say?"

"I think it went okay. He seemed shocked and was silent for most of the night."

"What did you tell my brother?" Daniel asks.

"Um…um…ha."

"You may as well tell him, Shorty."

"Well, Daniel, I am in love with your brother, and I told him yesterday."

"Jaylen and now you too. Just love him for the right reasons, and you're good with me."

"She doesn't like me, though. She made it her mission to find me on social media and sent me a message. I don't how she managed to find me so quickly."

"What!" Carlos blurts out.

While Shannon proceeds to bring up the message so she can read it to everyone, Kenny takes Jaylen to his porch to confront her about it.

"Jaylen, now you and I have been friends for many years, and I've always respected your other friends and never passed judgment, and what you said to my Kiddo really upset me as well as her."

"What did I say?"

"The message you sent her on social media."

"Oh, that."

"You really didn't think she was not going to show me? That was very rude of you to talk to her that way and also include me as in making decisions. That assuming and controlling are some of the things that turned me against Kim."

"I didn't mean it that way."

"Well, then what way did you mean it, Jaylen? You insulted her and her career and then going to sit out there and joke with her about her semi. That girl has been through enough already in the past year without you, my longtime friend, being mean to her and harassing her online. She had been nice to you this little time that you have been here, and yet you have been avoiding her."

"I know, and I'm sorry, Kenny."

"Well, don't let it happen again, and you owe her an apology as well. You two are both my friends, and you're not the only one interested in me, but she is, too, and I'm not going to have you two hating each other over me."

"She's in love with you? Yeah, we'll see about that."

"Excuse you? Leave her alone! Let's just go join everybody and have a nice little cookout."

They head back over, and everyone gives Jaylen the cold shoulder for a while before the alcohol comes out, loosening them all up. Kenny throws pork chops, burgers, corn on the cob, and shrimp kabobs on the grill. He is still hurt by his longtime friend but doesn't ignore her when she comes around, and he doesn't let her take time away from Shannon neither. Later that night, after everyone has left and it's all quiet, he gets to looking for Shannon and finds her lying on a blanket in the middle of his backyard—stargazing, for it is a clear night, and millions of stars have filled the sky.

"Can I join you?" he says, lying down beside her.

"Absolutely! Great evening, Kenny, and food. You're such a good cook like my Craig was."

"Thank you, Kiddo. I noticed you took your rings off."

"Yeah, it was time. It was hard, and I cried like a baby, but it's part of moving on. I'll always love him and miss him, but I can't wear my wedding rings forever."

"I'm sorry."

"For years and years, we lay under the same millions of stars, Kenny, and I wanted nothing more than to believe that I could be in your mind at that exact moment, but, of course, I wasn't because you didn't know about me. I used to think about you every day and wondered at that very moment where you were, what you were doing, if you were happy when I barely knew anything about you, and I've missed you every day when you didn't even know about me. Ha, crazy, huh?"

Kenny rolls to face her as she has rolls to face him too. "You know, Kiddo, you have the most beautiful soul of any woman I have ever met."

"Thank you, and you are absolutely the most beautiful man in the world to me. Kenny?"

"Yeah."

"Can I rub my fingertips through your beard? I've been dying to since seeing you with it as 'Rusty Blade.'"

"Ha...sure."

"Close your eyes. I want you to only feel it."

"Okay," he says, closing his eyes and feeling sensations run through his body from her running her fingertips gently through his beard.

"Feels like I am in the movie with my Rusty Blade."

"Ha, I still look like him to you?"

"Oh yes!"

"Just a more aged 'Rusty Blade'—eh?"

"Oh no, Kenny! You're still as handsome as you were the day you played him."

"I wish you didn't have to leave tomorrow."

"I know, but I'll be back in two weeks for four days."

What's about to happen during the following week will forever change Shannon's present life and Kenny's future.

12

It's somewhere between five and six in the morning. Shannon is traveling a long highway heading for Charlotte, North Carolina. It's a dark lonely road with only a few cars passing by. It's been eight days since she left Kenny's, and she's making a loop to head back and arrive in about seven days. She is pulling an empty six-foot-three trailer to a bedding factory to will be filled for her to deliver to a store when all of a sudden there is a flash of headlights, horns blowing, tires squealing, air brakes locking up, and a semi rolling down a road embankment. Smoke, dirt, and the smell of burnt rubber fills the air, and a car sits down the other side of the road embankment with its passenger side smashed against a tree. A witness who was traveling at a safe distance behind the semi calls in the accident and reports that the oncoming car was seen swerving in and out of its opposite lane, causing the semi to be forced off the road. Around eleven in the morning Vancouver time, Kenny is sitting at his kitchen table when a number that he doesn't recognize calls him. He answers it; and what the caller on the other line tells him is devastating, heartbreaking, scares him, and the worst news he could have ever received. After hanging up, he's shaking and fighting back tears as he calls Carlos, and with a quiver in his voice, Carlos knows something is wrong and it's bad, for Kenny doesn't cry often to or around people.

"Carlos, are you busy right now?"

"No, what's wrong?"

"Can you come over?"

"Sure."

"Please—now!"

Carlos pulls up to find him on his porch swing with teary eyes and nervously bouncing his leg.

"Kenny…buddy…what's wrong?"

"My Kiddo, Carlos, my Kiddo," he says, fighting back tears.

"What's wrong with Shorty?"

"I got a phone call," he says, clearing his throat, "from her dispatcher. She gave him my phone number a while back so that if anything ever happened to her, he can call me, and that's what he did. That's what I got."

"What!"

"She was driving down a highway this morning, and a guy was driving in the opposite lane. He was drunk and swerved in her lane. She slammed her brakes and ran off the road to avoid hitting him head-on, which is what she was taught to do, and she lost control."

"No, you're kidding me!"

"She rolled her semi three times. It's completely totaled. She was pulling an empty trailer, and it's heavily damaged too. She was airlifted to a local hospital. Her driver's side window shattered, and a piece of glass went through her left side and into her left lung, causing it to collapse, and her left collarbone is fractured from her seat belt. She was going in and out of consciousness and barely holding on. At the hospital, because of her weak immune system and blood loss, she was fighting really hard to breathe, and her blood pressure was too high, and her heart was beating too fast. The doctor said the safest way to try and heal her lung and save her was to put her in ICU." Kenny finally breaks down crying and can hardly speak. "Now…in a medically induced coma, and she's on a ventilator. It doesn't look good, Carlos. They aren't sure if she'll pull through."

"I can't believe this. OMG! I am about to cry."

"I'm scared, Carlos! I am scared for her, and I am scared of losing her. That's my Kiddo, man. That girl means so much to me." Breaking down, he covers his face with his hands.

"Kenny, we just have to stay positive for her because right now, she can't. We have to think that she will be okay. She is a tough trooper, and she needs us right now, and we have to be there for her."

"I have never had someone in my life other than my close family and friends that I never wanted to lose more than that girl. I can't imagine my life without her now. What she brings to it and the happiness she gives me. I can't handle this, Carlos."

"I know. She's the best thing to walk through your front door in a long time. What about the drunk driver?"

"He was taken to the hospital for treatment, and he's facing charges. He just better hope she doesn't die. She could be in that coma for at least a week."

"This is just unbelievable. That poor girl has been through so much, and now this."

"Her dispatcher gave me the hospital's info and I am probably flying out as soon as possible."

"That's great! She needs you there. She needs to hear your voice and to feel you touch her because she can. Even though she's in that coma, she can hear everything happening around her, and she can feel people, and you know she isn't going to leave you, Kenny. She's going to fight to come out of this coma to you. Right now, she's just lying there not even knowing if she's in the world. She's just in this big long dream, and I'm pretty sure you're there too."

"I need to be there. She took care of me when I was too weak and sick to take care of myself, and now I want to be there for her. I'm just not ready to see her lying there hooked up to all of those tubes and machines. I don't know how I will handle it."

"It is going to be hard. Well, I care about her, too, and if you don't want to go alone, I will be more than glad to go out there with you. Would you like that?"

Kenny stares off into space. "Yeah, I would. Don't think I'll be able to handle this alone."

"Okay, go pack for probably a week, and I'll go home, fill Camilla in, and book our tickets. You just focus on her and getting ready."

"Got to make sure I take my blanket too."

"The one she crocheted for you?"

"Yeah. I love it and it reminds me of her."

"I think that's a wonderful idea, and everyone can still work on the movie and their scenes while we are away."

"I've already canceled my luncheon with Jaylen for tomorrow, too, and I don't think she was thrilled even though she told me I was doing the right thing and wished Shannon a speedy recovery."

"She probably wasn't. She probably feels that because you two have been friends longer, you should pick her first and wait till after to fly out."

"Well, that's not going to happen. One thing Kiddo told me back when we first met that I've found to be true is that it doesn't matter how long you've known somebody or how long they have been in your life, all that matters is the bond you have with them, the connection you have with them, and what they mean to you. Right now, Shannon definitely means more to me, and she's of the most importance right now. Jaylen and I have been friends for over twenty years, but Kiddo has been the one there for me for these past eight months."

"Exactly! I'll call you once I book everything."

"Thanks, and I'll call Daniel. He's going to be busy all week, but I always tell him when I am going out of town."

Paula, Daniel, and Camilla are all saddened by the news of what has happened to Shannon; and Camilla even breaks down, causing Carlos to break down as well. She books Kenny and Carlos plane tickets for their flight, a hotel room near the hospital, and a rental car. The next morning, she drops them off at the airport. Kenny called Shannon's dispatcher back yesterday and got her mom's phone number. He called her to inform her he was coming and found out she and Shannon's brother, whom he met a while back, are there with her. Her father isn't in the health to make the trip, and he's home with Shannon's older brother who stayed with their dad. He barely slept through the night and was silent the whole flight. Every time he would stare out of the plane's window at the clouds flying by, he thought of Shannon and her love for them and almost broke down. He just didn't want this to be real. He wanted it to be a bad dream and to wake up and everything be fine.

The next morning, they arrive at the hospital. Kenny texts Shannon's mom to let her know that they are there and waits for her to come down. Meeting for the first time in the lobby, they both greet her mom with a hug. She thanks them both from coming to be there for Shannon. It makes her so happy to know her daughter means that much to them.

"How is she? Just prepare me for what we're going to see," Kenny asks.

"You will never be prepared for what you're going to see. She is stable and resting peacefully right now. Her doctor came by this morning, and all of her vital signs are good for now, and her lung is holding up the best it can. They have her on pain medications, antibiotics, and supplements to help keep her immune system up. She has a tube running up her right nostril and straight into her stomach that is supplying her vitamins, minerals, and proteins because they had to give her blood. It is like a feeding tube. She is hooked up to a vitals machine and the ventilator. She has an IV in her right hand and, of course, a urine catheter. ICU is on the second floor, so come on—I'll take you guys up."

Carlos and Shannon's mom chatted during the walk to the elevator and up to the second floor, but Kenny was silent the whole time with so much running through his mind and trying to mentally prepare himself for walking in her room and seeing her. As they walk the ICU hall and rounded the corner, he feels an uneasiness in his stomach. They reach room number nine, and the door is locked and can only be unlocked from the nurses' station. On the wall next to her room is a small camera, push call button, and a speaker. She explains to them that anytime they want to enter her room, they have to push the button and give them her name and they will unlock the door. She tells them her brother, Jeremy, is in there with her right now. They just knock on the door, and he opens it. Kenny is still not prepared for what he is about to see as he enters the room last, behind Carlos. Seeing her makes his knees buckle, and he stumbles, trying to catch himself with the wall, but falls into Carlos, pushing him against the wall. He turns away from her in the corner of her room, trying to collect his composure.

"Carlos...I can't handle this. I can't see her like that. Look at her," he says, speaking softly.

"You have to, man. She needs you right now and to know you're here. You can do this for her. Come on."

They walk over to her bed to see she's peacefully sleeping. Her arms are propped up on pillows to try and reduce the puffiness from excess fluid. She is covered in cuts and brushes from broken glass and her seat belt, and both her eyes are swollen. There is a big machine next to the left side of her bed that is reading her heartbeat, breathing, pulse, and blood pressure. A smaller machine is next to it, that is for her ventilator, that is also reading how many breaths she is taking on her own. She is wearing a thick strap around her face that is supporting the tube that is now breathing for her. It is connected to the two long big blue tubes running from the smaller machine. She has a small tube coming out of her left side that is connected to a round cylinder pump hanging behind her bed. It is pumping blood and fluid out of her lung. To the right of her bed is her IV fluid bag and the sedation medicine, that is keeping her deep into her coma. Her room is chilly to help keep her machines from overheating. Staring down at her, Kenny wipes a tear from his eye. Her brother tells them that a while ago, she was trying to wake up and caused her blood pressure and heart to shoot up and they had to sedate her more and that she will have periods of doing that. Carlos and Kenny also learn that she was driving another semi during the accident because hers is in the shop for repairs. Her brother brings up pictures on his phone of the wrecked semi and shows them both. He tells them that the doctor said she is lucky to have survived it. The top is completely caved in. Kenny almost feels weak at seeing the semi. He asked if he could have a few minutes alone with her, and they all three step out. He pulls up a chair that's in her room and sits right up against her bed rail. While staring at her hand, still not wanting to look at her and all of the tubes hooked to her, he softly rubs the top of her warm hand.

"I am here, Kiddo," he whispers and looks over to her. "Your Rusty Blade is here, and I am not leaving you, I promise. I am so sorry this happened to you, and I want you to know that I will be here with you every single day until you open your lovely brown eyes. You're going to make it. I just know it because you are a trooper, and

I know you aren't ready to leave me. Carlos is also here too. I just keep thinking back to the New Year's party. Everything bad that you said that could happen to you, and it did. I'm so scared right now, but I'll be your strength."

He lays his head on her bed rail while still rubbing her hand, closes his eyes, and begins to tear up. He was just about to speak to her again when a nurse walks in, and he quickly stands.

"Hello! Oh, you don't have to get up."

"Hi."

"I'm Candy, and I'll be her day nurse all week."

"I'm Rusty—I mean, Kenny."

"A friend?"

"Yes, you can say that."

"Did you say Rusty?"

"Yeah."

"You must be the Rusty that she was calling out for in the emergency room."

"Excuse me?"

"Yeah, when they bought her in, she was yelling stuff like 'Where's my phone? Get my phone! I'm dying, and I need to call my Rusty.' 'Rusty...what was it? Blade!' Yeah, stuff like that. We couldn't figure out who she was talking about, and you are him," he says, like that.

"I portrayed this killer trucker named 'Rusty Blade' in a movie, and it's her favorite movie. She calls me Rusty Blade."

"That's sweet. I am just checking her signs and giving her medications."

"Is she okay?"

"Oh yeah, she's doing good right now and holding up well. I am hopeful that she will make a full recovery. The main thing right now is getting all of the blood and fluid out of her lung so it can heal and keeping her as calm as possible. Can I ask you a question, and I'm really not supposed to in uniform, but did you play in that one slasher movie? You look like the guy who wore the mask."

"Behind the hockey mask? Yes, that was me, and don't worry—you take care of my Kiddo, and you can ask me whatever you want."

"Deal, and feel free to ask me any questions too. I may not be able to answer them all, but I will what I can, and we can write down the ones I can't for her doctor. He comes by every morning around seven."

"Thanks."

He stares down at her as her nurse gives her medication and makes a record of everything. "Can she actually hear and feel me?"

"Oh, absolutely, and as long as she isn't in a deep sleep. Even in a coma, your brain has periods of being active, which is why you may try to wake up and you may hear and feel everything. That's why we encouraged visitors to talk to them and touch them so that they feel safe because it's scary for them. We also stress not talking about what has happened to them around them or show any extreme emotions because that can also scare them and stress them out. Soft talking, encouraging words, and touching."

"That's amazing how the brain works and understandable. No one best not come in here and show their tails around her either. I want her as comfortable as possible."

"They say that while you are talking to them and touching them, sometimes, they dream about it, and they actually know just by the voice and touch who that person is."

"Well, I think she is asleep because she hasn't responded to me yet."

"Yeah, she is in a deep sleep right now. She was trying to wake up, and we had to put her out more, but she did squeeze her mom's hand this morning and moved her eyes under her eyelids when her brother was talking to her. So I am sure she will react to you eventually."

"As long as she knows I am here."

"She will! Take care."

Kenny steps out and tells them about the nurse and what they talked about. Thinking back to her sleeping on his couch and being by his side when he was so sick, he asks her mom if he can stay in her room with her. Later that night, he arrives back at the hospital with his Canadian flag blanket she crocheted for him. He makes himself as comfortable as possible on the guest chair that converts into a bed.

He calls his brother and updates him. It's only her second night of what is sure to be a long week, and he plans to ride it out with her till she wakes up. The night is a long sleepless night for him as he finds himself up by her bed every time she tries to wake, and he always seems to calm her just by talking softly to her. Her machines beeping, her night nurse coming in her room every two hours and four hours to check on her and give her medications doesn't help either. But he doesn't once regret his decision to stay with her, for he just wants to be close to her. Her doctor comes in around 7:20 a.m. to check on her. He tells Kenny that she is still continuing to improve and in two days, they will get an x-ray on her lung to see its progress. Kenny is pleased with the news and updates everyone once they arrived. They are very thankful for him staying with her daughter, and seeing how tired he is, they talk him into going to his hotel for a nap and assure him they will call if anything happens.

Shannon continues to improve over the next two days. She still has episodes of fighting the nurses while trying to wake up but calms right down as soon as Kenny speaks softly to her. This morning, she will be getting an X-ray on her lung. Carlos, Kenny, her mom, and her brother are in her room when her doctor and two nurses come in around nine and start unplugging her machines from the wall and turning on the backup batteries. Once they take her away and with an hour or so to kill, they step out of her room. Carlos and her mom go down to the vending machines, and Kenny and her brother sit in the ICU hall waiting area.

"Thanks for being here for my sister. I imagine you have a million things you need to be doing, but you put her first."

"She didn't hesitate to drop everything for me when I was so sick that at times I couldn't even sit up. A movie is a movie, and a convention can wait, but your sister's life is only one. One thing she has taught me is you never pass up a chance to make memories or to be there for someone who loves you no matter what you are doing because that person will always be there when everything else isn't."

"Yeah, she has always been good with putting words together. I told her one time that she should write a book full of her quotes and sayings, ha."

"She totally should. I care a lot about her. And I'm just ready for her to wake up, hear her talk, and laugh again. It's hard seeing her just lying there so still and silent to the world. I mean, this is a girl who is always so bubbly, full of laughs, always talking, and cracking jokes. I am surprised but happy Jason hasn't showed up. I'm don't judge but not crazy about him because of how uncomfortable he makes her, and I don't think she would want him here, anyway."

"I made sure he wouldn't be able to be here. I'm good friends with his dispatcher. Let's just say that he will be hauling all week and far away. My sister doesn't need him here all over her, and I don't want him here. I like you because you are good to my sister, and you make her so happy. You remind me of how Craig was to her and the closeness they had. Them two were always laughing and having a great time like you two, and he was very protective over her like you are. Makes me happy to know that. If I didn't know any better, I would swear you two were a couple. I know she wants that with you. As long as you are good to my sister and don't ever hurt her, we won't have any problems. She loves you, man."

"Too kind, and Shannon is such a gentle person. She will definitely make someone a wonderful wife again, someday. I know she loves me and would probably love to date me, but I don't know if I am ready to have another relationship again. We are such close friends. I wish she would react to me so that I know she knows I am here. I guess, though, I keep getting her when she's in a deep sleep."

"Probably, but don't worry. She will."

After they roll Shannon back in her room and plug everything back in, her doctor steps out with the wonderful news that her lung is healing well and good enough that they pulled the drainage tube out. He also tells them that in two or three days, they plan to wake her up and take off the ventilator. It is a very happy and exciting day and a true blessing for Shannon. They all go in her room to see her with a more positive outlook. Kenny walks over to her bed first and gently cups her left hand with his and tells her that she's doing so good, and they took that tube out of her lung. All smiles and happy emotions, he tells her that she will get to wake up in a few days and get that other tube out of her throat. Carlos, her mom, and her brother are staring and listening from behind when she moves her eyes under her eyelids. Thrilled, Kenny asks her if she can hear him, and she squeezes his hand. Finally getting a reaction, he excitedly lifts her hand up to his lips, softly kissing it, and she twitches her arm.

"Hey, guys—look! Looks like she is trying to smile with her tube, ha ha." Kenny looks back, pointing.

"She knows it's you, Kenny." That's what her day nurse replies as she's walking in the room. "Remember me telling you that? Imagine being trapped in this endless dark place, like a big dream, and you keep trying to find a way out of it and wake up. All you can hear are voices, and you see lights and shadows and feel presence and touching. You are going to have one person that finally catches you and makes you feel safe and take all of that scariness away. That's what you do for her."

"I do?"

"After talking to families and even the patients, too, I've learned that while in their coma, there is always that one visitor that the patient finds the most comfort in and feels the most joy with, and for her, that's you. One visitor can make a huge difference in a patient's recovery."

"So you are saying that she wouldn't have improved much without me? It couldn't have been all me."

"If she didn't know you were here or if you would have left, then, yes, it could have caused her to not fight as hard as she has. She seems to have a stronger connection with you more than with anyone else in this room. Not to make any of you guys feel bad, but when you are in here talking to her, she improves tremendously. Something about you she fights for."

Over there past four days, Kenny has grown more close to Shannon. He thought about their talks on how she never thought she would lose her husband so soon, and never regretting what you wish you could have said or did. He knows that he doesn't want any regrets with her and plans to have a heart-to-heart talk with her once she is better. He and Carlos step out to give her mom and brother alone time with her.

"You okay, Kenny?"

"Oh yeah, much better. All smiles now because I know she's waking up in a few days. Such an incredible relief, Carlos."

"Yeah! Have you heard from Jaylen?"

"I don't even want to talk about her right now. She is being self-centered."

"How?"

"She hasn't called me not once to ask me how I am doing or holding up or even how Kiddo is doing. I know they aren't friends, but it's just common courtesy that when you have a friend who is going through something like I am with a friend, you show a little bit of compassion, and you check on them. The only thing she is concern about is when I'll be home and if we can reschedule our luncheon."

"That's kinda rude of her. I hate to say it, but she's acting like Kim. I'm sorry."

"Yeah. Not talking to her right now."

The day finally arrives for Shannon to be awakened from her medically induced coma that has kept her in a deep sleep and allowed her body to heal. Her cuts are almost invisible, her bruises have faded, and the swelling is gone. It's been a long seven days for everyone, and the wait is over as they are all anxiously waiting outside her door. Her doctor steps out and tells them that they turned her sedation off a while ago and it's been long enough now that she is starting to come around. He explains to them that after waking her up, if she shows any signs of distress or trouble breathing, then he might have to put her back under again and it would be a good idea if one of them was in the room with her while they remove the ventilator tube so that she won't be so scared and more comfortable, and without hesitation, they know Kenny needs to be the one and sends him in. He's standing in the corner of her room, not wanting to get in the way while a doctor is on the other side of her bed and a nurse on the other working together to remove tape and unhook pipes. Before pulling the tube out, he pulls the tube from her nose and puts her on regular oxygen. They lift the head of her bed up into a half-sitting upright position, and while her nurse holds a towel under her chin to catch anything, the doctor quickly and safely pulls the ventilator tube out. She slightly opens her blurry brown eyes and feels confused. She grabs the bed rails as she grasps for air, taking her first huge solo breath in seven days. The doctor and nurses are all talking to each other and mumbling to her as she stares out straight ahead, dazed and steadily taking in deep breaths. Kenny slowly walks over to her bed and places his hand on top of hers. "Kiddo? Hi... welcome back."

13

Shannon looks to her left and up at Kenny, smiles, and tries to speak back but just sounds too raspy and unintelligible to him; but he reads hi from her lips. She's unable to speak due to her raw throat, and her voice is hoarse from the breathing tube.

"You want a hug?" Kenny asks after she reaches her arms out to him. She nods her head in a yes motion, and he leans down, hugging her tight. She begins to cry and tremble and not wanting to let him go just yet, so he asks her doctor if he can sit down on her bed, and they give him the go ahead.

"Look at me, Shannon." He only uses her name when he's being superserious. "I am so happy to see you are awake. You just don't know how much I've missed seeing those brown eyes of yours and your sweet smile." He whispers to her, "Please don't ever leave me again."

"Sorry," she silently says to him.

"Aw, Kiddo." He places a hand on the back of her head pulling her forehead to his lips and gently kisses her forehead, and she lays her head on his shoulder. "You don't have anything to be sorry about."

Carlos, her mom, and her brother are let in by a nurse; and they see Kenny and Shannon still sitting on the bed. They go over and give her hugs, and happy tears are cried, and praises are praised. The doctor explains to them that she may be unable to speak for most of the day and gives her a pad and pen to write down her questions, answers, and conversations. They learn that she will be moved to a regular room in the morning and may be able to return home in a few days to finish out her recovery and physical therapy. Due to being in a coma and inactive for a week, she has lost muscle strength in her legs, leaving them like Jell-O, and will need therapy to help her build it back up so she can fully walk again. After the doctor and nurses leave the room, she writes on her pad of paper, "I love you, guys, and thank you for being here for me." They tell her she's welcome, and her mom and brother tell her they love her too. She didn't feel sad when Kenny or Carlos didn't say it back, for she wasn't expecting it from them even though she thinks she heard Kenny say it to her a few nights ago. She flips the page and writes, "Can I have my phone?" and her mom hands her, her phone fully charged. All throughout the rest of her day, she learns pieces about the accident that almost took her life and some of being in her coma. Not wanting to overwhelm her by telling her too much too soon, they keep it very little details for now. A therapist comes in to see her, and they start by making her stand and take a few steps around her room. Being concerned, her brother and Kenny are both right behind her with a wheelchair ready to catch her if she falls. She is put on a soft-foods diet and gets to eat dinner for the first time in seven days. Them not wanting her to eat alone, her brother goes out and brings dinner back up to her room for everyone, and they all join her. By nightfall, she is able to speak but still with a shakiness in her voice. "Good night" and hugs are exchanged, and after everyone leaves, Kenny stays behind with her. He goes over and sits down on the side of her bed facing her.

"What's on your mind, my Rusty Blade?"

"Carlos and I are flying back home tomorrow. I feel bad leaving you so soon after you just waking up, but we have to get back to working on his movie, and I have a two conventions coming up."

"It's okay, and I understand. Just the fact that you guys dropped everything to come out here and be here with me all this time means so much to me. I'll be okay now."

"Just promise me, Kiddo, that you won't let this make you depressed after I leave and that you will keep fighting to get better and that you will do whatever therapy is required."

"I promise! I'm not letting this stop me. I am ready to get back out there."

"Really? Already, after this wreck nearly killed you?"

"Of course! You can't live in fear of what happened or what could happen. You just go out and do it. That accident is one of the scariest things to ever happen to me, but I can't let it hold me back or make me too scared to face the world again. These wrecks are always a risk with my career, and I love my job. I love trucking, and I'll be back out there in no time."

"I just admire your determination and strength."

"Thank you, and, hey, you encouraged a lot of it by me seeing your determination. I'll look forward to visiting you again."

"Me too, Kiddo, and anytime after my conventions and once you are better. Don't rush it!"

"Deal."

Once returning home, Shannon worked steady and stayed on top of her doctor's appointments. She has made a full recovery over the past three weeks. Her lung has healed completely, and physical therapy has her back moving faster than what she did before her accident. Kenny had kept a very busy tight schedule with between working on Carlos's movie and traveling for conventions till he and Shannon barely had time for phone calls, but he made time to text and check on her. He misses her more now than he ever has and can't wait to see her in a few weeks. He knows that he's ready to have a heart-to-heart with her and Jaylen both. Since returning home himself, he hasn't seen or spoken to Jaylen. He has grown to love one of them and can't keep seeing both of them one-on-one anymore. It's time that they know one has his heart and one will just remain a friend. The end of May is approaching and almost time for Shannon to make her way up to see him. She had been back on the road for two weeks, and she couldn't be happier. She's taking it slow, and her dispatcher is giving her light easy hauls. She is parked at a truck stop in Washington State after dropping off her last load. She decides to go in and shower, and after returning to her semi, she sees Jason is parked beside her. Feeling annoyed, she tries to get in her semi as quick as possible, but she isn't fast enough, and what he does to her makes her so uncomfortable and frightened for her safety that she leaves. Kenny wasn't expecting her until the next day and is stunned when she backs up in his drive and pulls a trailer, which is a first.

But he doesn't mind, for he is so excited to see her and have her back at his house. She climbs down from her semi and quickly runs over to his porch where he is standing at the door. She looks at him and begins to cry before running up to him and then wrapping her arms tightly around him and burying her face in his chest.

"Sorry, I am here early, Kenny, but I had to get away. I just had to get away."

"What's wrong, Kiddo?"

"It's Jason! He won't leave me alone! You were so right about him, and I should have listened to you!"

With anger building inside, he lifts her face up and wipes her tears. "Let's sit on the couch, and tell me what he's doing! I want to know everything, and I mean everything!"

"He has been texting me and calling me nonstop, wanting to know how I am, where I am at, if I was seeing anyone yet. And he is popping up at the same truck stops and diners as me. I think he is now following me, and he just won't leave me alone. I am going to change my number—I swear!"

"Ugh, that guy! I am fed up with him and what he is doing to you. What else?"

"We both happened to be at the same truck stop. I was coming back out from a shower, and he was parked beside me, walking around his semi. I was trying to get inside of mine before he noticed me, but I wasn't quick enough, and he approached me. We started out having a nice conversation about my recovery and being back out, and I told him I was coming to visit you when he asked me where I was headed… Ugh…why did I tell him that! I could tell he was a little jealous when he asked me if you and I are dating."

"And what did you tell him when he asked you that?"

"Oh, Kenny, don't make me blush, ha. I told him I wished! Anyway, as I turned to open my door, he grabbed me, shoved me up against my driver door, and just kissed me. He kissed me, Kenny."

"You're kidding me, right? Kissed you?"

"Yeah, it was awful, Kenny." She buries her face in her hands as she cries.

"You're telling me that man forced himself onto you and kissed you?"

"I got so scared till I left and drove straight here to you." She breaks down. "I can't tell my brother. He will go after him, and I reported him to my dispatcher."

"Kiddo, don't you worry. You know you will be safe here with me. He has one time to track you down here and think he's going to come up in my yard and bother you. He will have one heck of a bad day."

"I'm glad I have you to keep me safe. I love you, my Rusty Blade. You know, even though you always portray this tough, rough bad killer in all of your roles, it's still so hard to actually picture you being that mean and tough in real life because you're so sweet and gentle."

"I am sweet and kind to everyone, but if you mess with someone I care about, then well, that's a different story. How are you feeling, Kiddo?"

"I am great! I have fully recovered and happier than I've been in a while. Facing death like that really changes you and makes you see life in a different way."

"Well, right now, I just want you to rest and relax, and later, I want to talk to you about some things."

"Okay," he says, smiling at him softly.

"Oh, how I've missed your smile, Kiddo."

"Thank you, and I've missed...you. Think I am going to lie down for a bit. Is that okay?"

"Absolutely, Kiddo."

Once she is lying down in the guest room, he steps outside and calls Carlos in a fit of rage at this Jason.

"Hi, Kenny, what's up?"

"Carlos! I am so mad right now."

"That's not like you to be angry. What happened?"

"This Jason guy keeps bothering Shannon, and I just want to do something about it!"

"What do you mean? What is he doing to her?"

"He keeps hitting on her, following her, and trying to get a hold of her nonstop. He is touching her, grabbing her, making sexual remarks, and today he shoved her up against her driver's door and kissed her—*kissed her, Carlos*!"

"No! For real? Did she report him to her dispatcher?"

"Report! She said she did, but I am all the report she needs for this jerk, and he's about to find out."

"Wait a minute, Kenny! Don't be going and getting yourself in trouble over him. He's not worth it."

"No, he isn't, but my Kiddo is!" Kenny exhales deep. "She means the world to me, and I have to protect her, Carlos. I can't just sit back and not do anything while she's scared to even get outta her semi because of him. She drives extra miles outta her way just to the next town if she sees his truck at a truck stop. Do you know how that makes me feel to know he has her that scared? Carlos, I-I love her. Whoa, can't believe I just said that, but I do."

"You have got to be kidding me? I didn't realize it was this bad—wait! Did you just say what I think you said? Kenny! You love her—like really love her?"

"Yes! Ever since she told me that she's in love with me and almost losing her in that accident, seeing her in that coma not knowing if she was coming back to me has definitely made me seen her in a different light. I never thought after Kim that I could trust and love again, especially a fan, but I do. I'm telling you, if he hurts her, I'll put my Rusty Blade hatchet through his forehead."

"I hear you, but don't get yourself in trouble. So sweet that you love her, and you actually said it. Ha ha, this is exciting, man. Have you told anyone else?"

"No."

"When are you going to tell her?"

"Soon."

"Sweet! Let me know what happens, and Camilla and I want to get together with you two and do something. Camilla really wants to see her."

"Okay, sounds great. Talk at you later."

"Bye."

It's late in the evening, and Shannon is sitting out on the porch swing when Kenny comes out and asks her if she wants to watch the sunset. She excitedly stands up and says, "Absolutely," and with a sheet in his hand, they walk through his sliding doors and out into the backyard where he spreads the sheet, and they lie down. The sky has just begun to change from pinks and orange to a soft darkness as the sun is barely visible. While lying on their backs looking up at the stars starting to peek out, she rolls onto her side right up against him, laying the side of her head on his shoulder, still stargazing. "I love these moments with you because they are so personal, private, and intimate. Craig never cared to do this with me, and so I am so happy you do. It's memories with you that I will always have when I don't have anything else. Thank you for asking me and for wanting to do this with me." She whispers in his ear, "I love you, my Rusty Blade."

"I am happy to do this with you. To be honest, it's something that I never thought about doing. You don't really think about the sun setting—it's just expected. I love seeing your love for it. Just the simplest things in life that make you so happy."

"You make me happy, Kenny."

"You make me happy, too, Kiddo."

"He he...good."

"I just love how affectionate you are toward me, Kiddo...the passion."

He is now on his side facing her. "You want to know why I asked you about watching the sunset, Kiddo?"

"Tell me!"

"It's because when I walked in that hospital room and saw you lying there with all those tubes coming out of you"—his voice breaks—"I was so scared, and the only thing that I thought about was my last memory with you was lying right here where we are lying now, staring at the sunset. A memory that I was ready to hold on to the rest of my life. Dang it! Why am I crying?"

"Aw, Kenny, you can cry—it's okay. I think it's sweet when a man cries, and I am now crying, too, with you."

"One thing that you have taught me is there is so much more out there in this world once you get out there and you find it. There is so much beauty in just the smallest things in life that we never think about, that we take for granted like a sunrise or a sunset or driving over a long bridge with water as far as your eyes can see. I admire that you don't need fancy things in life to make you happy because you get happiness just out of everything that's around you, and you have shown me how to have that happiness as well. I'm just a simple guy who likes simple things, and you taught me how to appreciate and find happiness in the simple things that are already around me. You know that saying 'you never realize what you have till it gone' is true because I realized just how much you mean to me when you were in the hospital."

"So freaking sweet, Kenny."

"Kiddo, I never fully understood how for twelve years before you met me, I could give you so much happiness and encouraged you or how I saved your life when I didn't know about you until I sat in your room every day for seven days because even though you didn't even know you were in the world, you still gave me happiness, and you gave me hope just being there with you. All I wanted was just for you to know I was there like you wanted me to know about you for those twelve years."

"I did know, Kenny. I knew you were there from the moment you stepped into my room. I felt your presence, and I could smell you. It's like when you're in that coma and you can't see, your senses just multiply by a trillion. I could hear your heartbeat. I could hear your footsteps. Every time you sat by my bed and you talk to me, I heard every word, felt every caress and every touch. I felt when you kissed me on my forehead, when your tears fell on my arm—everything, and at times, I was trying so hard to find you. I was trying so hard to say something to you, but it's like I couldn't. I couldn't find you, but I can hear you." She pauses for a second. "And at one point, I thought I heard you tell me you love me."

"Kiddo?" He just stares at her, shocked. "I did say that to you."

"You…told me…you love me?"

"Yes."

Shannon smiles at him in amazement before telling him she loves him and gently kissing his lips. They giggle and lie there for a few more minutes. She still wonders what all he wants to talk about, and he thinks of how to be more open with her so he can tell her what he wants to say. He wonders if he's really ready to take the next step with her and risk it all or just continue on with their friendship.

14

Kenny wakes the next morning to the smell of breakfast she is cooking. He walks out into his kitchen. She sets him at the table with a cup of coffee, eggs, pancakes, bacon, and syrup; and she joins.

"Hey, Kiddo."

"Yeah."

"Just out of curiosity, what did you dream about while you were in that coma?" he asks during breakfast.

"I don't really remember much of going through the actual accident itself. I don't remember the paramedics. I don't remember the helicopter. I don't even remember freaking out in the emergency room wanting to call you like the nurse said that I did. I really don't know when my dreaming actually began, because when you're out like that, you don't know what day it is, and you don't know if it's day or night. I just remembered for what felt like maybe a whole day, it was darkness. I couldn't hear anything or see anything, and I honestly didn't even know if I was alive. I think because they had me so sedated, but I started dreaming right around the time that I started hearing my mom and my brother. My first dream was seeing my mom and my brother and hugging them, wiping their tears and telling them that I was going to be okay and that I would be back. I had a dream that I was walking through a field of dandelions—I love them. Can't ever walk past one without picking it, making a wish, and blowing it up to the heavens. And I, in my dream, I picked one and made a wish, and then when I looked up, Craig appeared on a cloud, looking down at me."

"Wow! Goose bumps, Kiddo."

"Ha, it's actually funny because I used to tell him all the time that I wished I could just lie on a cloud and read a book while watching the planes fly over me. Anyway, I felt myself trying to cry, but I just couldn't get the tears out. I reached out to him, and I said, 'Come get me so I can come up there and sit with you.' He said, 'No, you can't come to me. You're not meant to, because it's not your time. You have to go back. You have to stay,' and I said, 'But why do I have to stay?' He said, 'Because of him,' and I felt somebody touch my hand, and I looked over, and I couldn't really make you out, but I could see your shadow, and I could just smell you. I knew it was you, and then I felt myself trying to get out of the dream, but I just couldn't move, and that's all I remember from that dream. Most of my dreams were you guys talking to me. I could feel you guys touching me in my dreams. I could see your shadows, but I couldn't really make you out that much, and I just kept trying to wake up. I just wanted to wake up."

"What were you dreaming about when you heard me say those words?"

"Ha, you can say them now if you want." She blushes.

"Ha!" He clears his throat.

"What, Mr. Rusty Blade? Cat got your tongue?"

"You are such a flirt."

"Only with you." She winks her eye at him. "Now look who's blushing. Okay, back to my dream. We were at the gazebo actually, and we were just sitting there talking. It was a beautiful night, and I can feel the cool breeze. You reached over, grabbed my hand, and I looked over at you. You just looked at me with those beautiful brown eyes, smiling the sweetest smile I ever seen you smile, and you said, 'I love you, Kiddo,' and it's like I woke up from the dream. Everything went dark, and I couldn't find you."

"Beautiful dreams, and I am happy you didn't have nightmares."

"Yeah, that would have been terrible."

"Were you scared?"

"No, because I knew you all were there, and that helped me to feel safe. What are we doing today?"

"Carlos and Camilla might come by today or tomorrow."

"Fantastic! I'd love to see them."

"Yeah, they want to see you, and then later tonight, I might have Jaylen to come over because I want to talk to you and her about some stuff." Shannon feels knots in her stomach from this news. This is supposed to be her time with him, and she's a little disappointed that he might have that woman over.

"What do you want to do, Kiddo?"

"You know what I think, Kenny?"

"What's that, Kiddo?"

"It's the end of May, and you don't have any pretty colorful flowers anywhere out in your yard, like around your porch or your firepit area."

"I don't exactly have a green thumb, ha. Not so good at growing flowers and keeping them alive."

"I am," he says, nodding her head and trying to drop hints.

"Do you want to plant flowers, Kiddo?"

"I would love to."

"Then let's do it."

"Seriously? You don't mind?"

"No—not at all. It may be nice to see some color out there."

Kenny gets a knock at his door and opens it, inviting Carlos in; and Shannon quickly runs over to him, wrapping her arms tight around him. He asks her has she is feeling and apologizes for Jason. He also tells them that Camilla had something to come up today, and they made plans to hang out tomorrow.

"Shorty, how did you back that trailer up in the dive without hitting the ditch?"

"Piece of cake, Carlos. I learned in trucking school how to turn that semi on a dime. It was supereasy. You just have to watch your mirrors, watch out for oncoming traffic and both shoulders of the highway. Yes, it is a little more difficult on a two-lane like that out there, but nothing really."

"Shoot! I would have taken out both sides of the road, Kenny's mailbox, maybe a few trees, the light pole, and still would have missed the drive." They all are laughing.

"OMG, Carlos, that's funny."

"What are you hauling?"

"It's empty right now. I am dropping it off at Medical Supply Warehouse when I leave here, and I'll pick up a full one to take to a hospital."

"Any plans for today?"

"Kiddo wants to plant flowers around the deck, and I am going to help."

"Oh, nice! That will be something new for you, Kenny."

"Yes, and we are probably leaving here soon to go get some."

"Mind if I tag along?"

Shannon and Kenny both agree in unison. Carlos offers to follow them in his car after Kenny said that there might not be enough room for all of the flowers, plants, soil, and gardening tools in his car. She reminds them that she has an empty sixty-three-foot-long trailer out there that will hold plenty and that they are all going together in her semi. She excitedly runs to the guest room retrieving her purse and keys and says, 'Let's go, guys,' on the way out the door past them, never missing a beat and before they can even get a word in. They walk out to her semi that's now idling and climb up in through the passenger side. This being Carlos's first time inside is curious and amazed by all of the space and storage she has, and Kenny wastes no time with showing him her Rusty Blade painting. She's ready to pull out after finding addresses for several retailers that sell flowers. Kenny offers Carlos to sit upfront, with this being his first time riding in her semi; but he declined, saying that he would rather ride upfront coming back so he can watch her back her trailer and make himself comfortable on her bunk. During the ride, Carlos asks Shannon about all of the buttons and switches on her control panel and what they all do, and Kenny is even able to answer a few for him, remembering most of them from when he asked her while out on the road with her. They make their first stop at retail shop that has all things for your home from indoor to outdoor. They walk through the inside portion of the lawn and garden area; and Shannon loads up the chart with bags of soil, fertilizer, digging tools, and gardening gloves for her and Kenny. They make their way outside to the flowers, and Kenny is amazed at all of the different types and colors. She tells him to pick out ones that he likes providing it requires sunlight, wanting him to feel as much a part of it as her. Carlos stays at a distance, not wanting to interfere in their time. They take their time walking up and down each section of flowers, picking out various types and colors that are sure to brighten up Kenny's yard. After she makes her purchases, not letting Kenny pay for anything, they head to her semi where Carlos and Kenny begin to load everything into her trailer while she starts her trailer. She climbs back down and decides to have a little fun.

"Hey, Kenny, remember the day we met outside of that restaurant, and I told you that I could bend down and walk under my trailer?"

"Oh yeah, ha, and I told you that you would have to show me sometime."

"Well, check this out." She bend downs, walking under her trailer to one side and back to the other. Carlos and Kenny both fall out in the parking lot in laughter.

"You've officially earned your nickname, Kiddo. That is the funniest thing I have ever seen."

"Ha ha, told you I could."

Once back at Kenny's house, Carlos watches from the passenger seat in amazement at her taking both lanes and perfectly backing her semi and trailer down Kenny's drive. He helps Kenny unload the trailer of flowers, and after they converse for a few minutes, he leaves. Shannon and Kenny both change into clothes more suitable for being outside in the dirt before getting started digging and planting their flowers. They both work together spending the rest of the afternoon and into the evening by starting at one side of his porch and working their way to the steps and picking up on the other side of the steps and working to the other edge of his porch. They talk about his upcoming conventions, Carlos's movie, and summer plans. They even playfully throw dirt at each other. It was Kenny's first time planting a flower garden, and he enjoyed every minute of it with her. Once done, sweaty and covered in dirt and soil, they step far back to look at what they accomplished—a beautiful mixture of bright, colorful roses, sunflowers, mini carnations, gerbera daisies, snapdragons, mums, and lilies. Please and satisfied, they high-five each other for good work and do the same around his firepit area. They head inside to clean themselves up, and having such a wonderful day with Shannon, he decides to not have Jaylen over. The next day, the month of June arrives. They head over the Carlos and Camilla's after breakfast and spend most of the early day just hanging out and having lunch out on the patio. Later that night back at Kenny's, he sits her down on the couch for a talk.

"Kiddo, I have been thinking lately that I want to give this whole relationship thing another try. I don't know how you did it, but you have opened my heart, my mind, and my eyes."

"Kenny," she said, shaking inside and trying not to show her emotional fears, "I think that's great, and hey, it's not no one's fault what your ex did to you. I always say that if you let your ex and your past continue to control your present, then you won't have a future. You will just find yourself old and alone one day with an ex who won the battle over you even after the relationship was over. So who's the lucky lady that won your heart?"

Grabbing both of her hands and with a seriousness in his voice, he says, "I want you to know that what I told you before is true in that I won't ever let another woman come in between us. Nothing between us will change, okay—trust me?"

"Of course, I trust you, Kenny."

"I've thought about it a few times, and with the years of friendship we have and connection between us, I think I am going to give Jaylen a chance. I know you two aren't exactly getting along, but maybe over time, you will, and I promise I won't let her be mean to you or keep us apart. If she is mean to you, I expect you to tell me. I still hope you will come out and visit, and everything will still be the same between us."

Shannon can't believe what she has just heard. The man that she has waited for for so many years and who knows she's in love with him just told her he's fixing to go steady with another woman. Her soul is crushed, and her heart is shattered because he's more than just her favorite stuntman and actor, he's more than just her best friend, he's more than just her protector, and he's more than just her Rusty Blade… He's her Kenny Kirtzanger, and she loves him more than she has ever loved anyone. Even though she's not the jealous type, this is one time that she actually feels jealous and not good enough, but out of love for him, she fights every emotion in front of him.

"Kenny, I just want you happy no matter who it's with just as long as she's good to you. Just as long as she says everything to you that you have always wanted to hear and makes you feel the way you have always wanted to feel because I love you enough that I can let you go and step aside. I am afraid that she may try and keep me away, but I have to trust in you that you won't let that happen. I am also worried that she may be like your ex in some ways, but that isn't for me to judge. Everyone deserves a chance to prove themselves."

"Kiddo, I feel terrible doing this to you after you telling me that you're in love with me and this wreck you had. I feel terrible because of knowing about your feelings for me, and I know that you're hurt right now and doing a darn good job at not showing it. I'm sorry, and you will always be my Kiddo. You will always be my girl just like your necklace says."

"Kenny," she says with a shake in her voice, "you have no idea about my feelings for you. Don't apologize for wanting to be happy, and don't worry about my pain, because I will never make you feel guilty for wanting to be happy. She just better never hurt you—she better never make that mistake. I better never have to drive my semi out here or hop on a plane and fly here to you because that woman hurt you. I wasn't here when the other one hurt you, but I am here now, and I care more and way more protective over your feelings than I am my own. I can't make you love me the way I love you. I know that, and I wouldn't want it, anyway, if it wasn't real. Don't love me out of pity. If all I ever get to be is your fan and best friend, then I'll die happy because having you as my best friend is better than nothing at all when I didn't have you at all this time last year. I wish you two the best of luck and happiness."

"Thank you, Kiddo. I appreciate that, and we'll always be best friends."

No longer being able to fight her tears. "I think I need a breather," she says, giving him a hug. She gets to the guest bedroom door and turns to him. "I can no longer be your girl, Kenny. You made your choice. I love you." Shutting the door and locking it, she throws herself on the bed, burying her face in the covers to muffle her cries, and cries her pain away into the darkness. This is the worst loss she has felt since losing Craig. She is truly happy for him, but at the same time, she wanted nothing more than to be with him, and even though she tried so hard, it just wasn't enough to win him.

Kenny wakes the next morning around eight to find Shannon and her semi are gone. How did she manage to sneak out without waking him, and where did she go? Knowing that she wasn't leaving for another two days, concerned, he calls her but no answer, and he sends her a text. A few minutes later, she replies that her dispatcher sent her details for a load with a nicer pay than the one she had and so she accepted it and left around six. She drops her empty trailer at a truck stop for another driver to pick up. He is impressed at how quiet she was but also a little suspicious of her leaving. He asks her is she is okay after last night, and she tells him yes. He invites Jaylen out to dinner that night where he asks her about dating, and she accepts. Somehow being in a relationship again and with a longtime friend who is friends with his ex made him feel uncomfortable at first, but he just figures it's new relationship jitters. Two weeks goes by, and Shannon has barely heard from Kenny. He has only called her three times and rarely texts back and sometimes late. She tries not to let it bother her because he is in a relationship now, and sometimes things do change in friendships when someone finds a new love interest even though he promised her, but now he's just hurting her, and she's ready to feed her depression.

Shannon is back in Vancouver, British Columbia, not far from where Kenny and Carlos live. It's a little after seven, and Carlos is sitting out on his patio enjoying the cool night when his phone rings. Seeing it's her, he quickly answers but soon realizes it isn't her, hearing a man's voice on the other line.

"Hello."

"Is this Carlos DelValle?"

"Yes, it is."

"Hello, my name is Travis. I am a good friend of Shannon."

"Okay," he says in a hesitant voice.

"I just pulled into this rest stop for the night and found her parked in the back, sitting on her bottom step. She is crying and drunk."

"What? Shorty doesn't drink."

"Well, she did today, and she is hammered. I asked her what was wrong, and she keeps saying something about losing her Rusty Blade…he's gone…how could he hurt her, I don't know. I asked her if I could call someone because she can't be in her semi drunk and she said to call you. Is there any way you can come to her or I can take her to meet you somewhere?"

"I'll be right there."

"I'll send you the address."

Carlos arrives at the rest stop and parks a few spaces over from her and finds her just where Travis said she was, and not wanting to talk right in front of her, he walks Carlos away after meeting.

"Hey, thanks for calling me. I can't believe she is actually drunk."

"Not a problem. I am glad I found her and not some crazy person up to taking advantage of her. I have been trucking for twenty years, and I've seen it. I am good friends with her brother as well, and I try to look out for her. It's just terrible what all she has been through. I've never known her to drink myself, so whoever hurt her has her bad. Anyway, we are not allowed to be drunk in or around that vehicle. No open bottles of alcohol allowed either—only sealed. If another trucker had seen her like that, they could report her, and she is too good of a driver to have that happen to her. Good thing she is off for a few days. She is able to go with you?"

"Oh yeah, I'm taking her to my house for the night. I'll get her sober. What all did she drink?"

"A little of everything. I've already gone inside of her semi and clean out all of the mini bottles, and there was a lot too. I got her bags that she told me to get, and I've locked and secured her truck."

As they walk over to her, she tries to stand and stumbles, falling against her driver's tire. Carlos catches her and helps her back to her feet. "Whoa, where are you going, Shorty?"

"I don't even know where I am," she slurs.

"Shorty, why now when you've never been drunk?"

"He hurt me, Carlos," she says, crying and slurring her words. "Kenny hurt me. Why wouldn't he just say the words to me? I just wanted to hear him say he loves me like I did in my coma, and why her? She's no different than—what's her face? Oh yeah—Kim. She is no better than me. Well, I guess so if he picked her. I actually thought he was…he was starting to feel the same way about me with how close we have gotten and with how romantically affectionate he has been toward me lately. She tries to walk away from him to the front of her semi but falls on the ground, giggling. "Look at me, Carlos, ha ha."

"Come on, Shorty," he says, helping her up. "Let's go. I am taking you to my house."

He lays her down in his backseat. He puts her bags in his trunk and takes her keys. Before heading back to his house, he texts Kenny to see what he's doing. Back at his house, Camilla helps to get Shannon in their guest room on the main floor, and Carlos fills her in on what he knows so far. He makes her his specialty drink to start helping her sober up and takes it in to talk to her alone.

"Here, Shorty, down this. It will help you not feel so bad."

"Thank you for coming after me. I am sorry you have to see me like this."

"You're welcome." He uses his fingers to brush her hair from her face. "Now talk to me. Tell me what's hurting you."

"I was happy for him—really. I was because he was happy. I was happy to see him finally opening his heart again to love, and I am proud that I helped him do that, but he promised me, Carlos—he promised me that nothing would change, but it has."

"What has he done?" His phones rings, and he excuses himself to step out and talk because it's Kenny.

"Hello."

"What is going on with, Kiddo? What is this text about saying she's in trouble, but you have her and taking her to your house?"

"She is drunk, Kenny, and when I say drunk, I mean totally wasted. One of her trucker friends found her at a rest stop sitting on her step drunk and called me. I just gave her my special sober-up drink."

"Drunk? Why in the heck did she get drunk for? What happened? Why didn't she call me?"

"Well, Kenny...you happened!"

"*Me?*"

"Yes, she is hurt by you from what she told me. I was just fixing to find out all of the details when you called."

"Can I come over and talk to her? If she is saying that I am the one responsible for her being hurt and drunk, then I want to know why?"

"I don't know if you should right now."

"She is my Kiddo, Carlos, and I want to see her."

"Okay, but if she asks you to leave, *you* leave."

"I'll be right over."

He drives over, and Camilla lets him in. He quickly scans the room before looking at Carlos genially concerned and asking where Shannon is. Carlos points him in the direction of his guest room. He tells Kenny that he didn't tell her he was coming.

"Kiddo, it's me," he says, knocking on the door. He enters the room after she tells him to come in.

She is sitting up in the middle of the bed leaning up against the headboard holding the now-empty drinking glass in her hand, and even with feeling and looking like hell, she still manages to smile and glow seeing him walk through the door.

"Hi, Kenny...I'm drunk. I'm sorry!"

Kenny walks over and sits on the bed facing her. "Don't apologize, but tell me why. Why does someone who doesn't drink anymore all of a sudden decide to get wasted?"

She breaks eye contact for a second. "I've been feeling depressed. I was sitting on my bunk thinking about you and her being a couple. I started thinking about how she's going to get to kiss you...touch you, and possibly hear you say those words to her. My mind went into the deeper intimate thoughts thinking about what couples do, ha, but—"

"Whoa, Kiddo, ha! Wait a minute now. I haven't done anything with her. Maybe a peck on her cheek, and I haven't said those words to her either."

"What really pushed me was because you hurt me, Kenny. You hurt me," she says, looking back at him.

"Well, Kiddo, that's why I'm here. I want you to tell me how I hurt you so that I can understand."

"You promised me no one would ever come between us and that nothing would never change, but yet I am barely hearing from you anymore. I feel like that over the past two weeks everything has changed and I've slowly started losing you. I feel as though, I'm losing my Rusty Blade," she says, breaking down.

"Kiddo," he says, scooting closer up to her, "it's just…these two weeks was not what I expected. The day that you left unexpectedly, Jaylen and I went out to dinner and became a couple. Four days into our relationship, it still felt a little awkward for me. Not only is she a friend of my ex, but I really hadn't fallen in love with her like I had thought I was or really reconnected with her. I've always had the same password on my phone through the years even when I would upgrade to the next newer version, and Kim knew it when we were dating. I think Jaylen found out the code from her years ago because one night she was sitting at my kitchen table with me and I got up to go to the restroom and didn't think anything of it until the next day when I discovered that your number was missing out of my phone when I went to text you. I immediately called her and ask her if she deleted your number, and she told me that as long as we are a couple, no other woman who's in love with me is going to be in my phone. I got a little heated, and I told her that nobody tells me who can be in my phone and that you are my Kiddo and that you will be in my phone whether she or anybody else likes it or not. I was very mad at her for going in my phone without my consent and deleting your number, and I felt like if she would do that, then what else would she do, and that just really hit me the wrong way. I told her on the phone that night that if this is how she is going to be—like Kim, then we were not going to be a couple. The next day, I asked Carlos for your number, and after he gave it to me, he told me that Jaylen told him if I asked for it to not give it to me. This early into the relationship and she was already making me uncomfortable, so I broke up with her."

"I'm sorry, Kenny. I mean, yeah, I can be in love with you and still be sorry for you that a relationship didn't work out because I just want you happy. I'm sorry that she did that to you instead of appreciating the chance you gave her."

"I'm sorry, Kiddo, that I haven't been talking to you much, and I'm sorry that I did make you feel hurt, but it's just been a lot on my mind between that and trying to focus on work till—"

"Oh, Kenny, you don't have to say nothing else. Just let me give you a hug," she says, reaching out hugging him.

"It's getting late. You want to come to my house?"

"Yes, I would love, too, but what about Carlos and Camilla?"

"I'll go talk to them."

"Okay… Hey, Kenny?"

"Yeah," he says, looking back from the doorway.

"Thank you for coming here and clearing things up with me. I love you, my Rusty Blade."

"I'll always come to you, Kiddo."

15

The next morning, it's early dawn as a sober Shannon is standing in Kenny's kitchen looking out of the window at the bloomed array colors of flowers that they both planted just two weeks ago. In one of her daydreams, she doesn't even notice him sneaking up behind her until she feels him warp his arms around her. He leans in close and whispers in her ear, "I love you, my Kiddo," and she gets goose bumps as chills run through her body. She reaches for one of his hands, bringing it up to her lips and ever so softly kissing it. "I love you too, my Rusty Blade." She turns around while still in his arms and wraps hers around him.

"You actually said it, Kenny. You said those words to me."

"Yes, I did, and it felt great to finally say them to you."

"Do you want to know one thing that I do love about being so short and you being so tall?" She looks up at him.

"What's that?"

"When I lay my head against your chest, my ear lies perfectly over your beautiful heartbeat."

He just smiles at her for a second before leaning down and kissing her forehead. They both get chills, and he knows that what he has been secretly feeling for her is real. He loves her as a fan, a friend, and now he has fallen in love with her, and he knows it's time to finally be open and honest.

"Let's talk, Kiddo."

"Okay," he says, walking with him over to the couch and sitting next to each other.

"So tell me, what do you love about me? What makes you love me so much?"

"Kenny, when I took care of you while you were sick, I realized how much you really mean to me. Seeing you sick like that—it scared me. A man so tall and strong weakened down to the state of a child, and that one night when I had to go to bed early because I had to leave early the next morning and you were still up watching that movie, I lay in bed and stayed awake as long I could to listen to you laugh. I love to hear you laugh."

"That was a funny movie, Kiddo."

"I started thinking about everything, like how I waited twelve years to meet you. I never gave up hope, and I thought about how I wanted to see that beautiful smile that I looked at on the internet every day in person just one time, but I never thought I'd get to see it this much. I thought about how we met outside of that restaurant and how at that convention you trusted me enough to give me your email and we become instant friends. I told you, you wouldn't regret me."

"And I haven't."

"I thought about how everything happened the way it did from losing my husband unexpectedly and how I could email you and cry and cry, and you listened to me cry every day through our emails over his passing when you didn't have to. I thought about how you invited me out to your house knowing it would stop me from driving my semi off that bridge that morning. You saved my life, Kenny. You were there for me through the worst thing that ever happened to me, and you became the next best thing. I thought about everything we ever said and talked about and how I love spending time with you. You gave me a chance to know you. I knew I would get you to trust me one way or another. I didn't wait twelve years for a handshake, an autograph, a smile, or a hug. I waited for you. I could spend all day in this house with you, just sitting on your couch watching TV with you or watching you work on movie scripts and be happier than with any material thing you could give me because any little bit of time that you're willing to give me out of your busy schedule when you could be doing anything else with it means more to me than any piece of jewelry, flowers, or any fancy dinner. I thank you for every second of your life that you've shared with me, and I couldn't imagine my life without you now, and I lay in that bed that night and cried myself to sleep because I realized I love my best friend more than I thought I ever would. I went home and told my mom that I was in love with my Rusty Blade. She smiled and wiped a tear from my eye and said, 'Well, baby, you've got to tell him,' and I said, 'I can't, Mom, because he's not even looking, because his ex-girlfriend ruined it for the rest of us, and besides, if those beautiful women out there can't even win his heart, then why should I think I stand a chance?' She said, 'Because you love you him for all the right reasons when all those other girls don't, and you will never know if you don't tell him.' So I decided my next visit I would tell you so you would at least know and I can get it off my chest, but I didn't want to risk our friendship for my feelings, so I chose to sacrifice them. I didn't want to lose my phone calls, text messages, seeing your smile, or feeling your hug. But then after Jaylen popped up, I knew I needed to tell you, and so I did."

"Kiddo, you won't ever lose me, especially not because you love me more. I would never do that to you. You mean too much to me. You're the first woman I've trusted since Kim, and that took a lot for me to do that. Tell me more."

"It's the little things you do that means so much to me. I love the way you smile at me and the way you hug me every time I walk through your front door. I love how you raise your eyebrow at me sometimes when you call me Kiddo. I love how you let me call you my Rusty Blade, and you'll even chuckle like him sometimes." Kenny chuckles. "See—just like that. I don't know how you do it, but no matter what state I am in or how far away I am from you, you make me feel safe like your right out there in my semi with me, and then I lay in my bunk every day, and I think about you, and I wish you were. Every day, no matter what state you're in, here at home or in a different country with different time zones between us, you check on me, and for that moment, I don't feel lonely. I love that you are so easy to talk to and so understanding, and you never judge me for things I can't help. All I wanted was for you to know I existed, but I also knew there was someone behind those eyes I wanted to get to know."

"Even though I am so much older than you, when you can have your pick of any younger man out there?"

"Oh, Kenny, I don't care that you're twenty-six years older than me or that your brown hair may one day turn gray. All I care about and all I love is that beautiful man behind those beautiful brown eyes of yours and the way your treat me and how you make me feel. I can't help it we were born so many years apart. I had nothing to do with that, ha, or can I help the way I feel about you? Being in love with you is the most amazing feeling in the world. It's the happiness I get to wake up to every morning and go to sleep with every night, and no one can take that away from me—not even you. I love that you trust me to be in your life, your home, around your brother and your friends. You're my absolute everything, Kenny Kirtzanger. Yeah, I could fall in love with some thirty-year-old trucker, but I'm not going to put up with him telling me I can't come see you or talk on the phone with you. I am not trading my Rusty Blade for a boyfriend. I'll stay single! Sometimes, I travel for eight days just to see you for one, and you're worth it, Kenny—every single mile that I drive and every penny of fuel I put in that tank. Sometimes, when I am sitting in your living room with you and your brother or Carlos, I just listen to you laugh or talk, and I glance over at you, and I wonder to myself how a woman who was so lucky to have you for all those years could hurt you like she did. I'd trade everything I have, Kenny, everything I've worked for, accomplished, my future black tractor trailer's savings account, even my semi—everything sitting parked at that rest stop right now for just for one minute, Kenny…sixty seconds just to feel what she felt when she was at one point the love of your life. When she got to hold your hand on a regular basis, cuddle with you, fall asleep lying in your arms feeling safe, and she got to look in those beautiful brown eyes of yours every day and know that you were hers and she was yours, and no other woman would ever compare to her. I want to be your every and only desire."

"Aw, Kiddo, dang, I love you. You just always say the sweetest words to me. Such a kind soul."

"Don't ever stop saying those words to me. They are just beautiful. I love you, Kenny Kirtzanger. I wish you could look through my eyes and see you the way I see you. The way your fans see you. I wish you could feel the love I feel for you. I wish you could have one minute behind my smile and my happiness that you make me feel every day, but it's a fan thing. Going to bed thinking about you and waking up thinking about you is the one happiness I look forward to every day."

"I love your passion for me. Kiddo, you just don't know what your kind words mean to me. Maybe in some ways, I have forgotten what being a fan is like, and I love being reminded through you. I guess in ways I don't realize, and I don't see what I mean to my fans because I am me. I hear stuff like this all the time, and at times, it's hard to believe what's sincere and what's just talk to hit on me, but you make it sound so…dang, Kiddo."

"I make it sound so…what, Kenny?"

"So freaking incredibly real," he says, grabbing her face with his hands and French kissing her, still holding each other, nose to nose, and softly speaking to her. "Kiddo, I just couldn't do it. I just couldn't be with her. I don't love her—not like I love you. You say all of the things I want to hear." She begins to cry. "You make me feel the way I want to feel, and you are my everything. I don't know what it is about you, but deep in my mind and deep in my heart, I am so attached to you. It really is true that no one will ever love you in this business like a fan will. I can't hide the way I feel about you anymore or deny it to myself. My mother once told me that one day I would meet a fan—my special fan who will change my life forever, and here you are, and I'm never letting go. Please don't let go of me, Kiddo. Please keep loving me the way you do and wanting me the way you do."

"I promise, Kenny," she says, still teary-eyed. "I'm not going anywhere. I'll never stop craving you. I love you so much."

"I love you too, Shannon."

They both cuddle on the couch under the blanket she crocheted for him and watch a movie. Right toward the end of the movie, she lets her fingertips explore the inner side of his right thigh under the blanket from his knee up to his waistline, and he doesn't stop her. She notices him tensing his leg a little as his breathing picks up, and she knows she's aroused him a little. Before getting up to go shower, she kisses him on his cheek and whispers in his right ear. "Come and get me, big boy, and show me what you Canadian men are all about, ha—yeah." She licks his earlobe. Showered and still wrapped in her towel, she opens the bathroom door to find him standing on the other side. He cups her face in his hands, bending down and kissing her, and she rubs her hands up under his shirt and claws her nails down his back. He pushes her in and up against the sink, lifting her up and sitting her on the counter. She wraps her bare legs around him for grip and helps him take his shirt off. She hops down off the counter and pulls him into her room by his belt loops and pushes him on the bed.

"You want me, Kiddo?"

"Oh yeah, and it's not going away anytime soon."

She climbs on top of him, kissing him, and he reaches up softly rubbing her left cheek with his fingertips, and she feels sensational chills run through her body. With just that one kiss from him, she is now in the moment she's been longing for…the part of him she craves, and she goes for it, kissing him back in a full seductive kiss. She slides her left hand around the back of his head, kissing in a seductive way. He rolls them over and on top of her. Her heart begins to race, her body becomes warmer, and her sex drive is high as she feels one tingle after another. It almost becomes too much to handle having never felt intimacy this incredible before as he kisses her along her neck, forcing her eyes to roll into the back of her head. She moans as she's digging and rubbing her nails along his bare back, causing him to twitch. He sets up enough to open her towel, exposing her bare body in the glow of the lamp light that she left on from the last night.

"Like what you see, Kenny?"

"Love is more the word I am thinking, ha," he says, and with a strong grip, he rips the towel right out from under her and throws it on the floor. He kisses her breast before licking her nipples when she says. "Now it's my turn."

She moves over and makes him lie down, and she climbs on top of him. Starting at one side of his neck, she kisses him all the way to the other side and moves her way down, kissing him on his chest and tonguing around his nipples, causing him to arch his back.

"Oh, dang, Kiddo!"

"What? Ha!"

"Don't stop!"

"Oh, don't you worry. I'm just getting started."

She continues to kiss all over his chest and stomach as she rubs her fingers along his sides. She licks around his belly button and kisses down to his waistband. She unbuckles his belt and unbuttons his pants enough to kiss under the band of his underwear before pulling them off, exposing him to her.

"Oh, snap, Kenny."

"Ha! Don't blush, Kiddo."

She moves up by his face. "I might be blushing, but you're fixing to see stars, big boy." She puts her hair in quick ponytail and moves back down to his private area, giving him minutes of oral pleasures, causing him to grab the headboard as he lets out a loud moan.

"OMG! Wow! You can do amazing things with your mouth." He reaches down, grabbing her under both her armpits, pulling her up, and flipping her on the bed on her back; and he gets on top of her.

"Is this really happening? Are we really about to do this, Kenny?"

"Oh yeah, and it's going to be incredible," he says, kissing her and engaging in sexual intercourse with her, and they both feel intense pleasure. She digs her nails deeper into his lower back as she squirms and moans loudly. His first orgasm causes him to collapse onto her. "Whoa, crap, Kiddo," he says, breathing heavy.

"You okay, Kenny?"

"Yeah. Just never had pleasure this amazing before, and it's been a long time."

"That's because you've never had me before," she says, pulling him in for a seductive kiss.

She rolls him over, climbing on top of him. She moves in a steady motion, giving them both more orgasms, and lifts his hands up onto her breast, signaling him to grab them at one point. He grips the headboard tight as she kisses and tongues around his nipples more while continuing to engage in sex with him.

After finishing, she stretches out on top him, lying her head on his chest. They are both breathing heavy, trembling, and their hearts are pounding.

"You okay?"

"Oh yeah, Kiddo. I'm fantastic and you?"

"Super! No regrets?" She looks up at him.

"Oh no! I don't regret that at all." They both fall asleep.

Shannon wakes later that afternoon lying in his arms tangled up together in the bedsheets. She kisses him on his cheek, and he slowly opens his eyes.

"I love you."

"I love you too, Kiddo."

"Fun morning, huh?"

"The best! You want to know something funny?"

"What's that?"

"This is the first time I've ever slept in this room."

"No way, ha."

"Yes, and it was your last."

"Why is that?"

"Because from now on, you will be sleeping in my room with me."

"I'd love to. I wish I didn't have to leave in a few days, but I'll see you at your convention in Kansas in a few weeks."

"I know! These goodbyes are getting harder. I'll look forward to seeing you there. Maybe we can have lunch together or something if it's not too busy."

"That would be great. I have a ticket for that Saturday because I am free that whole day. I should arrive in town sometime that Friday afternoon, and then I have to leave sometime Sunday."

They get up and look around at the room before laughing. The bed comforter is lying on the floor at the foot of the bed. Kenny's pants and underwear are lying in the corner by the chair. Shannon's towel and a pillow are lying up by the bedroom door.

"Did we nap through a tornado, ha?"

"No, Kiddo, I think we were the tornado, ha."

Later that evening, they are out on his porch swing taking in the beautiful warm weather. "Kiddo?"

"Yeah."

"When you came two weeks ago and we lay out there and watched that sunset, I knew right then that I love you. I knew that I wanted to be with you, but having so many bad relationships in the past that not only cost me the relationship but also the friendship, it scared me. We have such a strong bond and such a strong friendship that we've made till I thought that, even though you are the one I want, I feared that if we dated and it didn't work out, would I lose you all together?"

"You won't ever lose me if a relationship doesn't work out, and at least we can say we tried."

"When I sit you on that couch and I told you that I was going to give Jaylen a chance, the whole time I was telling myself, 'What are you doing? You don't want to be with Jaylen. You want to be with your Kiddo. Just tell her you want to be with her.' When I woke up that morning and you were gone, I knew then I made the wrong choice. All I kept thinking about was you standing there in that doorway and telling me that you are no longer my girl. I love you, Shannon, and more than I've ever loved any woman. You have put life and happiness back in me that I've lost over the years. You never think in this business that you would ever and can love a fan, truly love a fan other than just being your fan, but you proved me wrong. You made me see you other than just being my fan."

"Kenny, my dispatcher really didn't send me a better load that morning. I'm sorry I lied, but I was just so hurt over you telling me that you wanted to be with her when I just wanted to hear you say those words to me. I just cried all night because I knew waking up that morning, I would see you knowing you were going to be her boyfriend, and I couldn't take it. I didn't want to make you feel guilty that you chose her. I didn't want to make you feel bad for wanting to be happy, and I didn't want to seem selfish, and so I left. I'm sorry."

"I had a feeling that it wasn't true with you just getting here after being away for so long due to that wreck, but no harm done.

I totally understand, and if we're going to make confessions, then I have a confession of my own."

"What's that?"

"I really wasn't going to miss my flight, Kiddo. I just didn't want to miss you."

"What? Ha!"

"Spending that weekend with you at my convention, having you at my table with me all day and playing games with you across the hall like two big kids. I wasn't ready for it to be over. I just wanted more, and I wanted to spend time with you alone to see what you are really like outside of our visits. I wanted to see how you work and what your life is really like out there. So I told you I was going to miss my flight to get you to come back. I knew you would come back for me."

"You sneaky tail. I had a feeling too. For someone who flies all the time, I wondered how you misread the flight time, and I felt a little suspicious, but I didn't care. I just knew I was going back to get you, and I was going to have you in my semi with me, and I was going to get to spend time with you. That's all I cared about. That's the kind of fun I always want to have with you."

"I feel the same way too."

"This is, too, perfect what we have going on between us."

"Shannon?" he says, grabbing both her hands.

"Yes."

"Are you sure that I'm the one that you want to be with? Are you sure I'm the one that you want to give your heart to, and am I the one you want to love for the rest of my life?"

"Yes! I gave my heart to you when I became your fan all of those years ago, and you will always have my heart, and don't you mean for the rest of my life? You are the only man that I want to give my all to. Even after you're gone, Kenny, my heart will forever belong to you because now that you love me, no other love will ever compare."

"I want to be with you, too, Kiddo. I want to give us a try and see where it goes. I know there's a lot of years between us, but you are so mature for your age. I know you truly love me even if I had nothing."

"Absolutely, Kenny. I'd rather be poor with you than to be rich without you. Not that your financial income is any of my business, but I would take care of you."

"For however many years I have left on the earth, you're the one I want to spend them with. I want you in my life for the rest of my life."

"You're going to make me cry."

"So, Shannon?"

"Yes."

"Will you be my girlfriend and forever my Kiddo?"

"Yes! Absolutely, if you'll be my boyfriend and forever my Rusty Blade."

"Perfect! Ha, yes, Kiddo, I will."

"Whoa, you're my boyfriend. Now *what*! I am yours, and you're really mine."

"Yes!"

"Will your other siblings like me?"

"Oh yeah! Most already do just from me telling them about you and how you came out and took care of me. Daniel already adores you. He didn't seem too happy when I told him that I was dating Jaylen because he knew I love you beforehand."

"That makes me happy, and my whole family already knows about my feelings and pretty much accepts you already."

"Great! I look forward to meeting them all."

Daniel pulls up and walks over to find them still on the swing cuddling, giggling about something, and just glowing in that new love glow. "What are you two up to besides glowing brighter than the evening sun? Wait a minute... Are you two...?"

"Yes," Kenny answers.

"Aw, I think that's just beautiful. It's about time you find a great girl."

"And she is! I'll be back," he says, excusing himself and walking in his house. Daniel sits on the swing beside Shannon after she invites him.

"I know you truly love my brother. I also know you'll be good to him. You have shown that to us. I thank you for loving him so much and for being here for him in every way possible."

"I will always love your brother and take care of him."

"All we have ever wanted was for him to find the one whom he can just be happy with for the rest of his life. He deserves that!"

"Our age difference and only knowing each other for ten months won't bother any of you guys, will it?"

"Oh no, honey. Age or time doesn't define love as long as it's real love and real happiness. You have made him a heck of a lot happier than the ones he has known since you were little, ha."

"Oh no, ha ha."

"Paula told me what you said to her the night of the cook out back in April."

"Oh." She scans her memory and quickly remembers. "Oh, that...ha...yeah, well it's true."

Standing in his kitchen, Kenny overhears everything for his window is opened. He steps back out, and she excuses herself to use the restroom, and Kenny's curiosity of what his girlfriend said to his sister-in-law kicks in. "Hey, what did she say to Paula?"

"You heard us talking?"

"Kitchen window is open."

"Paula just clicked with her that day and just thinks she is so sweet. She told me that after you and I walked away, and after hugging each other good night, Shannon said, 'Awe, you get to go home a Mrs. Kirtzanger. I wish that I was Kenny's little Mrs. Kirtzanger.'"

"Hmm...ha, well, she just might be one day. This is the first time in my life where I can honestly say I am truly in love, and it feels a little scary, and it also feels truly incredible."

"Nothing to be scared about when you have a great woman by your side who never lets you feel any fears, except maybe losing her, and you shouldn't even fear that because you know she isn't going anywhere. Well, brother, I just wanted to stop by and check on you on my way into town." He stands up to leave. "And I am glad I did. I am happy for you two, and I wish you both the best."

"Thanks."

Kenny joined Shannon back inside where they decided to spend the rest of their time together as a couple and indulge in each other. He eventually drives her back to her semi, and it's a harder goodbye for them both now that they are a couple. Through their goodbye hugs and kisses, they hang on to each other as long as possible, and he promises her that they will definitely have fun at his convention in a few weeks. She climbs up in her semi, and he watches as she drives off. He makes the drive back to his now-quiet home. Two weeks is all that stands in between them, and counting the days is now on.

16

Over the next few days while out on the road, Shannon chooses to only let close family and friends know about their relationship and keeps it off social media to respect the private side of Kenny's personal life. With everyone's full support, she is the happiest she has been in a long time and truly free to continue giving love and support to her Rusty Blade as his fan, best friend, and now his girlfriend. Oh, how that word makes her weak in her knees. Just knowing that he is her boyfriend now and he loves her back the way she has always hoped he would. He receiving the same loving support from his family and friends makes their relationship stronger. She has been gone for about five days when Carlos stops by to check on him finding him out by his firepit.

"How's things going?"

"Great, Carlos, just great."

"You miss her, don't you?"

"Oh yes, very much. We talk almost every day, but I still worry about her since having that accident and Jason inappropriately touching and kissing her a while back."

"Are you worried about when he finds out that she's dating someone?"

"Nope." He looks up at Carlos with a serious look and his brown eyes sparkling in the bright noon sunlight. "Because I'll hurt him if he does or say anything wrong to my Kiddo. He doesn't want to play with me."

"I believe it too. When she comes back for a visit, Camilla and I want to double date and toast you two on finding love and happiness in each other. It's just wonderful, and we're so happy for you two."

"Well, thanks! That's sweet. I don't know yet when she will be back, but she is coming to my convention a week from this Saturday, and we plan to spend as much time together as we can in between me meeting fans, interviews, and Q and As. Has she ever mentioned to you in the past about how it bothers her that I don't have a son?"

"Yes, but she never went into details. Just got emotional and shut down about it. Has she to you?"

"Just the same with you—a few times actually. I don't know why, but I want to know why it bothers her so bad."

"Well, if you find out, let me know."

"I am going to try to at the convention."

The weekend before his convention, she called Kenny from a rest stop right outside of Seattle, Washington, with an idea in mind. She asked him if he can get away now because she wants to take him on the road with her and to his convention, assuring him that she can get him there in time for Friday afternoon. Flattered by this kind gesture, he calls Carlos to see if he can drive him a few hours out to meet her. He quickly packs everything he needs and locks his house up. He lets his brother know as he always does and waits for Carlos. She offers to drive across the Canadian border and meet them halfway. There's nothing she wouldn't do or anywhere she wouldn't drive her semi to see him. She arrives at their meeting location and waits out by her semi that she has left running to keep the cab cool for them to arrive a few minutes later. Once they arrive, she and Kenny, excited to be together again, hug each other tight and share a kiss. Then she runs over to Carlos, giving him a hug and thanking him for bringing Kenny out to her. They say their goodbyes to Carlos, and he tells them to be safe and have fun but not too much fun, and they laugh. Kenny climbs up in her semi and gets settled. She is thrilled to see he bought his blanket with him that she crocheted for him, and he tells her that he wouldn't leave without it. She takes her time driving through Canada and crosses back over in the United States, and after they stop for dinner, she returns to the same rest stop that she called him from for the night. Around nine, it begins a steady rain pours, and the sound of the rain hitting Shannon's semi makes her sleepy, and she lies down in her bunk. She's a daydreamer who loves clouds and a calming rainstorm. He lies down in her bunk beside her and cuddles her deep in his strong arms.

"Hey, Kiddo, the last time we did this, we weren't even a couple."

"I know right, and now we are, and it feels even more amazing to cuddle with you in my bunk. I love you."

"I love you, Kiddo. Where are we going in the morning?"

"Twin Falls, Idaho, for a dry grocery pickup that I will drop off in Salt Lake City, Utah, and I don't know yet from there, but we are making our way to Kansas. So glad that you are here and wanted to come."

"Absolutely, Kiddo. I thought it was so sweet of you to offer. I didn't have anything planned for this week. I just would have been working around the house, but I much rather be here in your semi with you."

"You know, I used to lie here after Craig died and ask why? What was the reasoning I lost him? How would I ever move on? And now I know. It is you, Kenny. You are my present and my future."

"I'm happy to be too, Kiddo."

"We only get one life, one chance, and one opportunity to know someone. I've told you that before, and this is my chance to know you, to love you, and to have you. I believe that people are put in our lives at the right moment when we need them the most, and you were put in mine when I needed you the most as I was put in yours. To look past me just being your fan and me look past you just being my favorite actor, to see each other for who we are with all we've been through, and to grow to love each other through our eyes."

"Did you ever doubt that you would ever meet me?"

"Sometimes—yes! I mean, as a fan, you always hope and believe that you'll meet your favorite celebrity, but when year after year comes and goes and you find yourself being a fan for nearly half of your life, then you begin to wonder, but I never gave up hope, Kenny."

"Well, I am glad you never gave up on me, Kiddo." He holds her tighter and kisses her forehead. "You only have a ticket for Saturday, right?"

"Yes, because I wasn't sure when I purchased it last month if I would be able to attend Friday. I know I can't Sunday."

"Well," he whispers in her ear, "how about getting a ticket for Friday, and you can stay in my room with me?"

"Definitely."

It's the first weekend of July and time for Kenny's three-day convention. Shannon, with a full trailer to drop off in town a few hours away, drops him off at the hotel of the event Friday morning around ten so he can check in and get set up. She returns around six that evening, parking in the loading dock with the other semis, and heads inside to buy a ticket for tonight. With the convention just starting, the lines are long but move at a steady pace. After purchasing her ticket and getting her wristband, she decides to walk around some first instead of going straight to Kenny. She doesn't want to take time from his other fans knowing she will have time with him later but texts him to let him know she's in the building. She finds a table in the far corner of the room selling horror merchandise and buys the same hockey mask shirt as the one that Kenny was wearing back at her convention last August and changes into it. She makes her way through the large crowd trying not to bump into people. She takes pictures of displays, fans in crazy costumes, and even zooms her camera in and sneaks one of him from across the room and giggles to herself. A part of her still can't believe he's her boyfriend. Even though she doesn't see him as a famous person and only as Kenny Kirtzanger with a wicked cool career, she never thought she would be good enough to win his heart when he's surrounded by all of these beautiful women. Around eight and with only two hours left in the event, she goes into room that has TV screens hanging everywhere and a small bar. They are all playing different upcoming movie trailers, clips, and interviews. She's sitting in a chair watching a few of them when she feels someone approach her from behind, and when she turns around, she is shocked and surprised all at the same time as to who is there. After they exchanged words, Shannon, not wanting to slap this person, storms off in tears and leaves the building. Kenny just finished up meeting his last fan in line and has thirty minutes till photo opts with fans in his slasher costume when he hears a familiar voice call to him. He looks up displeased at the woman standing in front of him.

"What are you doing here, Jaylen?"

"I came to see you."

"Why? You've never came to a convention before to see me, and now is not a good time. I have an hour to rest and mingle around before I have to get in costume."

"Anytime is a good time to see an old"—she clears her throat—"friend, Kenny, and rekindle things."

"There is nothing to rekindle between us, and I can't tell you, you can't be here. Just leave me and my fans alone, for this is not the place or the time. Now if you'll excuse me, I want to check on, Kiddo," he says, turning to walk away with his phone in his hands.

"She's gone!"

"She's what?" He turns to look back at her, confused.

"She left!"

"And why did she leave, and how do you know that?" he says, walking over to her, trying not to talk loud.

"I found her by the bar, and we exchanged some words after she told me you two are dating, mostly me telling her she can get in her semi and carry her worthless self somewhere else because I am here to get you back."

"You told her what!" he says, trying to keep his voice down.

"She isn't good enough for you, Kenny—not like me. I deserve you more than she does. I've known you longer, and I'm better than her, prettier, and I can give you everything you need."

He grabs her by her arm and pulls her into an empty room, slamming the door shut. "You listen to me, Jaylen, and you listen to me good! Shannon is my girlfriend! She is my best friend... She is my everything. I love her more than I've ever loved you, Kim, or anyone else. She has been there for me physically, emotionally, and mentally more than any of you have. It doesn't matter how attractively beautiful you are on the outside. It's about how beautiful you are inside out. You have nothing to offer me, nothing to give me, and you'll never be to me what she is, and if you can't respect that, then we can't be friends anymore either. Now it takes a lot to make me angry, but it doesn't take much to hurt me, and you just hurt me bad, Jaylen. You stay away from my Kiddo—you understand? You don't say nothing more to her, and you better hope she comes back. Don't call me or text me anymore until you hear from me first. This is just what I need on my mind right now while I have to go get ready for my photo opt soon. I can't believe you did this to me. Stay away from me and her this weekend, or I'll have you thrown out of here. Don't even try me!" He walks out of the room and slams the door behind him. As he heads to get ready, he calls Shannon, who's outside in her semi, but she sends it to straight to her voice mail, and he leaves her a message: "Kiddo, I found out what happened. I am so sorry! Come back inside and wait for me. She won't bother you anymore—I promise. I love you." She listens to the message and heads back inside. She texts him back, and he asks her to come to the dressing room. With a few minutes to spare, she walks in to see him fully dressed in costume except for the hockey mask. She giggles a little through her tears, causing him to laugh.

"What, Kiddo?"

"I feel like I am in the middle of a movie set or something. Look at you!"

"Come here, and give me a hug."

"Sorry, I didn't answer your call. I was scared. I know that sounds silly. I almost left altogether. She hurt me, Kenny! Just said the ugliest things to me and—"

"Shh…it's okay, Kiddo. You don't owe me an apology. I'm sorry about her. I had no idea she was here. Don't worry about anything she said to you, because you know I love you for everything that makes you—you. Her opinion doesn't matter. You trust me, right?"

"Of course I trust you. I just don't trust her. I love you," she says, looking up smiling at him.

"I want you to go up to my room and wait for me," he whispers to her and slips his room key in her back pocket. "Second floor, room 223." He kisses her.

"Yes, sir."

"I'll give you a 'yes, sir.'"

"Don't tease me if you aren't going to please me…Mr. Rusty Blade. What, Kenny? Are you going to 'eye for an eye' me? Or slash me with that machete?" she says in a flirtatious tone.

"Ha ha."

"I love it when you blush. See you upstairs."

Around ten twenty, she gets a knock at the hotel room door and opens it to see him on the other side back in his regular clothes and his face clean of the dark makeup that was around his eyes. The hall is filling with fans and other guests as everyone is making their ways to their rooms. She grabs his shirt sleeve, pulling him in, and closes the door. She may be over a foot shorter than him, but she's tough and pushes him right down on the king-size bed, climbing on top of him. Having already showered, she is wearing a button-up short-sleeve pajama top with matching shorts. He grabs her shirt right at the buttons and rips it open, sending buttons flying across the room. He snickers with an oops; and she giggles, quickly taking her shirt off, exposing her bra and throwing her shirt on the floor. She slides her hands under his shirt, clawing her nails gently down his chest. She asks him if he wants a rub down and helps him take his shirt off. She spends the next twenty minutes rubbing down his chest, both sides, stomach, and arms.

"Great massage, Kiddo. Feels so nice—thank you."

"This is what you deserve and need after standing out there for all of those hours meeting your fans, signing autographs, and taking endless photos. Just a good rub down to help you relax. Now roll over, and I'll rub your back."

Before he rolls over, she pulls his shoes, socks, and pants off. She massages his back, shoulders, and the back of his arms before moving down to his legs, rubbing them. He is so relaxed by this point and jokes that she's about to put him to sleep, in which she tells him to go ahead if he wants because they will still have tomorrow together. She moves back up to his head and rubs her fingers through his hair, giving him a deep head and scalp massage. She leans down, kisses his ear, and whispers to him that she loves him with her entire heart before moving down and giving him a foot massage, which finally relaxes him into a sleep. Once he's asleep, she covers him up, turns out the room light, and snuggles up beside him in bed. He wakes the next morning to his alarm in a very good mood. He tries to get ready without waking her, but with her being a light sleeper, she wakes up.

Once dressed and ready, he lies back on the bed next to her for a few minutes.

"Don't you worry if she shows up today. Don't pay her no mind at all. You just walk away, and come to me. I'll take care of her. I have a super long day today with meeting fans, photos, and a Q and A, and I'm not having her crap today. I'll have her thrown out."

"I'm not worried about her. She means nothing to me. I'm sorry to say that with her being your friend, and I've tried to be nice to her. She don't want to mess with me, or I'll make a *Unjoyful Ride 4* out there in that parking lot with her, ha."

"Oh no, Kiddo, ha ha."

"What! I won't kill her. I'll just have some fun with her."

"Ha ha ha ha, don't make me laugh at that, Kiddo."

"He he, but you are."

"You're a mess—I swear. I've got to head down, Kiddo. You come down whenever you're ready."

"I wish you a fun-filled, superamazing time."

"Gosh, you're so sweet."

Day two of the convention starts around ten that morning, but with her having a bad headache, she doesn't make her way down until around noon. Rumors are slowly starting to spread about her and Kenny being a couple after them being seen together a lot, but to keep respecting his privacy, she calmly declines to talk about it or admit to them dating. She feels that it's something they should announce together and when he's ready to be open to the public about them. The event is packed but not overly packed, and the lines aren't that long. She makes her way through Kenny's line like a normal fan just for fun, meeting him, giving him a hug, and even paying like the rest of his fans to have her photo taken with him at his table. She doesn't spend too much time walking around because she has to hit the road early and doesn't want to tire herself out. Her autoimmune diseases have been bothering her a lot lately making her have bad headaches, exhaustion, and causing her much joint pain in her hips and lower back. With Kenny's concern, she made a doctor's appointment that she has coming up soon. She goes back up to his room around five to lie down until it's time for his hour-long Q and A at eight o'clock, which she plans to attend. She may be his girlfriend, but she is still his fan and still loves being a part of the crowd, giving him support even if she doesn't feel good. That's just who she is, and that is what he loves about her and finds beautiful—that she can still manage to make someone happy or laugh even when she is hurting or sick. After his photo opt and Q and A, they make their way to the VIP room; but after an hour of mingling with others, they return to his room to spend the rest of the night together. Tomorrow is the last day of the convention, and Shannon has to leave around eight o'clock in the morning. She slips into her pajamas, and he changes into something more comfortable, and they lay in bed together.

"Can I ask you something, Kiddo?"

"Of course!"

"I don't know why I keep thinking about it, and I am curious."

"About what?"

"Why does it bother you that I don't have a son? Tell me, Kiddo."

"Um…okay…I'll tell you. What happens when you have a son, Kenny? He takes after the father, right?"

"Ha, sometimes."

"*Sometimes* is exactly right. He looks and sounds like his father… same eyes…same smile…sometimes the same height and personality and maybe even the same career choice. A son is a piece of his father left behind for us after he's gone"—her voice breaks—"a piece of the father that we will still get to have, but when your time comes Kenny, we won't have that."

"Awe, Kiddo."

"That's not to make you feel guilty because you don't have a son. It's just the realization that once you're gone, all we will have are your photos, movies, interviews, autographs, and memories… priceless precious memories, Kenny."

"Oh, wow, Kiddo! You are going to make me cry. That's the sweetest thing anyone has ever said to me. That's deep! That's real!"

"Just think if you did have a son, he would be close to my age, and what if we had fallen in love and got married? Then I would be your fan, your best friend, and your daughter-in-law."

"Well, I guess it's not a good thing then, because you wouldn't be my Kiddo or my girlfriend, and I much rather have you for myself."

"Yes, and I so rather have you, and now," she says, pulling him in and seducing him with a kiss, and they spend the rest of the night sharing their love with each other.

Early morning wakes them, and they cuddle in bed together. "I hate that I have to leave, Kenny. Between my scheduled loads and my doctor's appointment, I don't know yet when I'll be out to see you. I wish I could spend Canada Day with you. That would be such an amazing experience, but there's always next year."

"Me, too, Kiddo, and it's always fun. A lot of festivities, parades, good food, and fireworks."

"I want some of those tulips that look like the Canadian flag too. We need those around your porch."

"They are pretty neat. We'll get some, then."

"Kenny, I've been thinking about it a lot, and I want to know how would you feel if I moved to Canada and haul freight over there? I'm not trying to move in on top of you. I just hate living so far away from you, and living in Canada has always been a dream of mine. I have no problem renting an apartment or just living in my semi in between our visits. I just want to be closer to you."

"Seriously? You would move to Canada? What about your family and friends, though?"

"Yes and yes, and my family has had me for thirty-one years, and they will always have me, but I am ready to have you, see you more, and spend more time with you. I love you so much, Kenny, till I am ready and willing to move to another country and move my career, too, to be with you. I have already been looking into trucking companies and even talked to a few dispatchers over there."

"I think that's amazing, Kiddo. I'd love to have you closer and be able to see you more too. To know I mean that much to you."

"You do, and I can always travel the USA anytime, but I'll mostly haul in Canada instead like I am doing here. I know we have different lives and different careers, but we can work around them for us, and sometimes you have to make sacrifices for love. Just the love of a fan."

"Let's definitely look into it, Kiddo."

They say their goodbyes, and she leaves with a long three weeks standing in between their next visit, and he watches her pull out onto the road from his hotel window.

17

A few weeks has passed since Shannon told Kenny about moving to Canada. As she's driving her semi to Jackson, Mississippi, for a pick, she gets a call from him with an idea. He wants to talk about her wanting to move to Canada. He doesn't know how he feels about her living alone, and he doesn't like the idea of her continuing to live in her semi 24-7 in between their visits. He tells her that she needs to be able to get out of her semi and relax. An apartment or condo would almost be a waste of money for her as well. She assures him that she won't mind, because it will be worth it to be closer to him and living in Canada has always been her dream. Then he asks her something that she never saw coming and shocked her to the point that she almost had to pull off the road.

"How do you feel about moving in with me, Kiddo?"

"With you? You mean living in your house with you?"

"Yes! I'd love to have you here and know that you're safe."

"Are you sure it'll be a good idea so soon into our relationship? I'm sorry, I've just never done this before. I waited till marriage to live with Craig."

"Absolutely, Kiddo. It won't be any different than when you are for visits except we'll just have more visits. It will be fine."

"Okay, but only if you let me help out by paying my fair share of everything. I don't want to feel like I am freeloading and taking advantage of you. I'm not that kind of girlfriend, and I won't hang picture frames up everywhere, ha."

"Maybe!"

Throughout the rest of June and the first half of July, in between hauls, doctor's appointments, and the summer heat, Shannon makes numerous trips into Canada, moving everything she owns from her parents' house in South Carolina to Kenny's house in Vancouver, British Columbia, Canada. It was a hard and painful goodbye for her close family and friends but a much-needed new beginning in her life. She wants and needs this to help her continue to move on from the life she once had. It's been a few days since she delivered her last load for her company who doesn't haul international, and it was even a hard goodbye for her dispatcher who has enjoyed having her as an employee. He even helped her to get hired on with one of the best trucking companies in Canada who do haul international, and she will start hauling for them in a week. She just needs some time to fully settle into her new life with Kenny. He is sitting on the couch looking through a manuscript when she joins him with her new logbook figuring that they can do their studies together.

"Is that your new one?"

"Yes, and every company is different. So new rules and ways of how they want theirs filled out. I just never would have thought any of this. It's just amazing! You're amazing, Mr. Kenny Kirtzanger."

"You're amazing, too, Ms. Shannon Keeler."

"Just hearing you say my name gives me goose bumps every time. You know, it's almost August, which means it will be a year since we first met, a year of friendship and fourteen years of me being your fan all in one month."

"Fourteen years, Kiddo. That's a long time when you think about."

"Yes, and being your fan has been worth every day of it too. It's an honor being your fan, Kenny."

"Well, thank you, and I am proud to have you as my fan."

"I can't make anyone your fan, but that doesn't mean that I still can't tell people about you, talk about your roles, brag about how sweet and gentle you are and how you love your fans so much. If I can get them to watch just one interview or just a few minutes of a movie clip, then my job is done whether they choose to be your fan or not. At least just get them curious. I have even started telling people about Carlos DelValle too."

"I appreciate that, Kiddo, and he will too."

"Whatever it takes to get you both the recognition you two deserve. You may have been a stuntman for all these years, but you are also one heck of an amazing actor, too, and people need to see that. You are so underrated as an actor—not right! Maybe you should try new roles, Kenny."

"What do you want to see me in?"

"Well, not everyone is a horror fan. Maybe if you branched out and play in a romance movie, more comedy, or something, that would reach other fans."

"Never thought about that, but it's an idea to think about."

"You're a big guy who plays a tough character well, but you are also a sweet, gentle, man who could easily be such a romantic actor. Don't be afraid to try it, Kenny, and that's coming from a fan who would never tell you to do anything that I wasn't sure about."

"Maybe it's a good thing having a true honest fan around that I can learn and grow from. New discoveries every day. It's almost dinnertime. You want to go out, Kiddo?"

"I'd love to," she says, smiling at him. "I never want to know my life without you anymore, Kenny. You are everything that makes me who I am now. All I ever wanted was just a little bit of your heart, but I never thought that I would get all of it."

"You will always have my heart. What would you like to do, Kiddo?"

"You know what I want to do? I just want to go out for a nice walk together. I like walks. They can be relaxing, a good way to clear your mind, and they can make for a private, personal, intimate connection. Just you…me and our conversations."

"That sounds nice. Let's go get ready."

Shannon goes to the guest room that she has all of her stuff in. She wants to look more like a lady tonight and less like a trucker. She digs through her clothes and finds one of her favorite summer dresses and changes into it. It's a midnight-blue tank dress that stops right at her knees with small white moons and big stars all over it. It has layers of white-and-blue tulle to give it some fullness and zips in the back. She slips into her dark blue fabric flats with silver stones. She brushes her shoulder-blade-length hair over to one side and does a quick loose side French braid. She applies foundation, black eyeliner, and mascara, black-and-blue eye shadows, a soft pink blush, and lipstick. She puts on her deep-blue heart-shaped necklace with a small diamond for a bit of sparkle. She walks out into the living room, and Kenny walks out at the same time wearing dark-blue pants, a white button-down shirt, and black shoes. They point and make jokes about how they choose the same colors without knowing. He tells her that she looks very lovely and that he loves her dress. She tells him that he looks very handsome and that she loves everything. She jokes about how dressing like a lady versus a trucker makes a world of difference in how beautiful you can look, and he takes her hands and tells her that she looks beautiful regardless. She almost feels her knees buckle at hearing him say those words to her, for she never really thought of herself as beautiful before. They drive downtown to Gastown, which is one of her favorite places to go in Vancouver. Everything about it is beautiful from its whistling steam clock and mix of souvenir shops, indie art galleries to its decor stores in Victorian-style buildings, which are what she loves about it the most. The trendy food and drink scene includes chic cocktail lounges and restaurants where you can get everything from gourmet sandwiches to local seafood. They casually walk hand in hand, gazing and stopping to look in the windows of shops and conversing about certain things they see. She darts in and out of souvenir shops adoring all of the Canadian souvenirs.

"You know, Kiddo, I never really came here much before you."

"No?"

"It never seems like somewhere to go alone. I've been to some of the restaurants with Carlos and with my family, but coming with you is different. It's great and more enjoyable. It is nice to just get away from everything and do something like this. I am glad you wanted to."

"Walks are adventurous little ways to still have alone time together and discover things together in our own little bubble. There may other people around, but we can still make it our own intimate time."

After walking around for a few hours, they head over to a deli shop where they both enjoy freshly made sandwiches, homemade chips, and drinks. They head over to one of Kenny's favorite sweet shops where they indulge in triple chocolate ice cream. It is a simple kind of date, but to Shannon, it couldn't have been more perfect.

"How's Carlos's movie going?"

"Great! We are working on it some next week."

"Being an outsider to this business such as myself, you don't really realize the money, countless hours and months, amount of people, stunts, retakes, and flip-lop schedules that go into making a movie. But it's a lot and a lot of hard tiring work that you guys put into these movies, and for it to only be a few hours long, ha."

"Yeah, it's a lot! Sometimes, you are on set all day, from sun up to sun down, and only have enough time to go home, shower, eat, and sleep for about four hours. You never know how well they will do, ideas get lost, and then the funding. At times, you feel like it was all for nothing."

"It's never all for nothing, Kenny. It's still an amazing thing to be able to get out there and do what you do. You should always feel proud because as fans, we are."

"Thanks, Kiddo, and I am always proud of myself."

"I've always been into stunts. I don't know why. I just love how stuntmen and stuntwomen aren't afraid to get in there and take the blows to make each scene amazing. You guys have the guts that the other actors and actresses don't have. You guys just give them an extra coffee break."

Kenny chuckles.

"I am actually glad you aren't so much of a stuntman anymore."

"No?"

"Yes, because I would be devastated if something happened to you on set. I mean, I know anything can happen even with you just acting now, but I know that stunt work is a lot more dangerous and harder."

"It is but very rewarding too. I have suffered from being a stunt-man such as broken bones, burns, muscle strains, and so on. But I wouldn't go back and change nothing about it."

"Do you miss it?"

"Sometimes, like in the slasher movie, I couldn't do certain scenes that I really wanted to, but I am much happier being an actor now. Especially at my age."

"Oh, Kenny, age isn't nothing but a number, but I am happy that you have decided to slow down some and take better care of yourself. I'll always be in your corner to help you in any way. If there's ever a day that you can't take care of yourself, I will, my Rusty Blade, because I love you."

"I love you, Kiddo," he says, winking his eye at her.

"Do you ever go back to your hometown of Saskatchewan, Canada?"

"Yes! Still have most of my family there."

"I would love to go sometime. Maybe I can get a load to haul there or something."

"Or we can go, Kiddo."

"He he!"

They return home, and after changing back into comfortable night clothes, they cuddle on the couch. Her phone chimes, and after looking at it, she uncomfortably tosses it away from her. He notices and asks her what's wrong. She tries to play it off, but he doesn't let it slide. She finally tells him that it was a text from Jason.

"What did he say?"

"He's whining because I didn't tell him how soon I was moving out of the country or that I switched companies. He wanted to hang out before I moved, but I didn't want to. He has also been a little harsh since finding out about me being in a relationship with you. I think it's time to end my friendship with him, but how? How do you tell someone that you no longer want to be friends? That isn't me! I don't hurt people."

"You just have to, Kiddo. There isn't ever an easy way, but sometimes you have to move on from the ones who hold you back. Look at how uncomfortable he makes you. No friend should make you feel scared or afraid to read their text. You have given him chances, and he still acts this way, and that isn't fair to you because you are too good of a person. It's not hurting people. It's freeing yourself. After her behavior at my convention, Jaylen is making me second-guess our friendship too. So you aren't alone in this."

"Well, guess I should call him and just get it over with," she says, dialing his number and ending their friendship.

August fifteenth arrives and the fourteenth anniversary of Kenny's slasher movie that saved Shannon's life and made her his true fan. It's around four o'clock that evening when she backs her semi up their drive and quickly runs up behind him standing in the yard, wrapping her arms around him from behind, and wishing him a happy fourteen years of her being his fan and he being her favorite stuntman and actor. He turns and kisses her and wishes her a happy anniversary too.

"Kenny, let's go sit. I need to tell you about Edge Wood."

"Edge?"

"He's your fan," he says as they sit together on the porch swing. "Who's Edge, Kiddo?"

"He is someone that I became friends with over social media back in May. We are both fans of the female pop singer who had that tragedy at her concert where a lot of fans were hurt and killed. I commented on a post, and he saw it and discovered that I am also your fan. We started talking and quickly became friends. He absolutely adores you. You are his favorite actor to play the slasher role."

"Oh yeah, that's cool."

"He's sixteen and lives in Philadelphia, Pennsylvania. He suffers bad anxiety from years of being bullied, and he's very shy. I haven't even seen his face yet, but that doesn't matter. I can wait till he's ready to show himself, and because of my depression, I can easily relate to him and understand him. We talk about you, singers we like, books and stuff, but mostly you all the time."

"That's you, Kiddo! Always trying to help people. I swear you can make friends with anybody. That's really great."

"He's been your fan for like a year now. He hasn't met you, but he called into a radio station once and asked you a question. I waited till last month to tell him that I personally know you because I didn't want that to be the main reason he talks to me, and OMG! He freaked, ha ha. He asked me if he could write you something, send it to me, and show it to you. I told him sure because he's a great friend, and I remember wishing I had a way to talk to you. He sent it to me this morning, and I wanted to let you read it," she says, handing her phone to Kenny and letting him read the email from Edge.

"That's sweet. I will type him up a little reply."

"I actually told him that if you wanted to reply, I would send it to him. Kinda like a middle messenger. He understands that you don't know him and can't have your email address. I told him that you're private and has to build trust first. He was so excited to send that, Kenny. He just loves that we are dating and that I live with you."

"We live together, Kiddo, not just you living here with me. I think that's pretty sweet of you for wanting to help another fan, and I won't mind communicating with him through you as long as he doesn't hound you too much or send anything awkward. I'll go ahead and reply back a little message, letting him know it's me."

"Hey, his birthday is October fourth, and I thought if you didn't mind, maybe you can send him an autograph photo as a surprise. I have his address. I'll pay you for the autograph and to mail it to him. He wants your autograph so bad."

"I would be happy to send him an autograph photo. Maybe I'll send a couple and really put him in shock. Let me knows if he replies back to my reply," he says, handing her, her phone back.

"I think I finally want to make use of your garden tub," she says, running her fingers along his chest. "Care to join me for a nice bubble bath," she whispers in his ear, "Rusty Blade?"

"Ha…yes."

Shannon goes into the bathroom and starts filling up the garden tub and pulling her bubble bath gel under the running water. After about forty minutes, the tub is filled at a safe level. She undresses and sits down, feeling the hot water caress her body. She calls Kenny to come join her, and he does. She checks with him to make sure the water isn't too hot for him, and he tells her it's very relaxing and he is surprised at how well he still fits because of his height.

"I've been wanting this since I saw this tub. While I was washing your hair that day, I just wanted to stumble and push us both in. You know, like an oops kind of thing."

"You are such a silly goofball. I am so enjoying this, Kiddo," he says, chuckling.

"Well, how about you enjoy this too?" she says, leaning in, French kissing him as he pulls her over onto his lap while intertwining his fingers in her hair.

"You're so hard to resist, Kiddo. I am so addicted to you and what you do to me. You can have me as much as you want me."

"Don't mind if I do," she says, going in and seducing him with a seductive kiss. It's a hair-pulling, butt-grabbing, neck-kissing, ear-lobe-nibbling kind of sex and a night of passion that is sure to change their lives forever and put them on a path they never expected.

18

For three weeks, Shannon has been nauseous in the morning and not feeling well. She's experiencing headaches and exhaustion more than usual, and her menstrual cycle is late, which is normal for her having polycystic ovarian syndrome, known as PCOS. But with a hutch and a little hope, she takes a pregnancy test at a local truck stop before heading home and nervously waits for the results. When she finally looks, she almost faints. She takes the other one in the box just to double-check and gets the same results. She runs back out to her semi and sets in her bunk crying and shaking uncontrollably, excited and scared because she's having a baby, Kenny's baby. But what if he won't be happy? What if he doesn't want to be a father? It could destroy their relationship, but she has to tell him. As she backs into their drive, her heart is pounding. It's one of the happiest moments of her life but also terrifying. She has always dreamed of being a mother, and now she's pregnant. She walks in and finds him in their bedroom, unpacking from an overseas convention.

"Kenny, I need to talk to you," she says with a nervousness in her voice.

"Hey you, come here. Everything okay?" They sit on the bed together.

"Sorry, I am just nervous."

"Don't be! Just tell me."

"You know how I haven't been feeling good lately."

"Yeah."

"I had this crazy feeling to take a pregnancy test today. I took two actually, and they both came back the same result."

"Which is?"

"Positive," she says, looking up at him with tears in her eyes. "I'm sorry, Kenny."

"Sorry for what?" he says with his heart now pounding and flutters in his stomach.

"I wasn't sure if you would be happy or even wanted to be a father. I was scared that I may have ruined everything, our friendship, our relationship, and with my health and taking all of these medications, it's a miracle. A miracle baby and our baby, Kenny."

"I never not wanted kids, but I never tried. I've often wondered what this moment would feel like, learning that you're going to be a father. I must say it actually feels pretty amazing, and I feel nervous all at the same time. It's a life coming into the world and our lives. It's pretty crazy to think at my age, too, that I'm having a child, but knowing that you'll be my child's mother makes me happy. You didn't ruin anything, Kiddo. We are having this child for a reason, and I love you. A baby! I am going to be a father."

"Yes, and I know that you will be a great father to our baby Kirtzanger, ha," she says, holding her stomach. "Can you believe it? We have a baby in here."

"Yeah, and maybe a boy, Kiddo."

"Whoa, how freaking cool would that be? Your son...our son... my other little Rusty Blade."

"We have so much to do and learn now to get ready for our son or daughter, and now that you're pregnant, I want you to take it easy, Kiddo. I not only have to protect you, but have our child now, too, and that you will have to help me protect. No heavy loads and no long hauling hours. I don't care what your dispatcher wants."

"I agree because I am already scared I won't carry it full-term, with my health. I know I will have to stop some, if not all, of my medications until after the birth."

Over the next few weeks, as they let family and friends know about Shannon's pregnancy, they are met with outpouring love, excitement, and support. They attend their first doctor's appointment where they get their first glimpse at their baby and learn that she is a little over a month, and they get to ask any questions they may have. She is pulled off most of her medications for autoimmune diseases as they are too dangerous for the baby. She also needs to put on light-work duty and start to take supplements for her pregnancy. Two months into her pregnancy, Shannon's body is making changes to adapt to the tiny little human growing inside. Her breasts are sore, growing, and feeling heavier. She has increasing fatigue, morning sickness, pregnancy cramps, and even weird dreams. Due to feeling more tired and weak from being off her medications, she's even had to cut back on hauling across Canada and staying closer to Vancouver. Sometimes, if she's really having a hard time, Kenny comes out with her providing his schedule allows it. Still nervous and not knowing what to really expect, he's anxious about becoming a father but excited to meet his child. During her third month, shortly after his fifty-eighth birthday, they get to hear their baby's heartbeat for the first time, and it's a very emotional moment for both Shannon and Kenny. One night, while Shannon is lying in bed, he lays his hand on her belly and tells her that he can't wait to feel their baby move and kick. He tears up a little wishing his parents were still alive and could share this with them and see their grandchild, which causes Shannon to cry. He's excited at the thoughts of doing everything that comes with being a parent and promises her that he will always be there for her and their child and that he'll always do his best in raising their child together. He hints around that he would love to have a son but will be happy regardless. She's approaching her fourth month, showing and definitely feeling more pregnant. Sometimes, the pressure in her hips and back gets to be too much and puts in down for the day. Kenny does his best to make her comfortable and limits her so she doesn't overwork herself. The guest room that was once her room is slowly becoming a nursery, as it's already filling up with baby items, and they couldn't be happier or more in love. They will soon discover, though, that not everyone is happy for them, as betrayal from two unlikely suspects will shake their lives and turn their world upside down, and Kenny will face the possibility of losing not only Shannon again but also his unborn child.

19

I t's the first week into December, and Shannon is fixing to pull out and head over to the United States for her first delivery since moving to Canada. She's feeling pretty excited, too, as she also plans to drive to South Carolina to visit family since her move as well before making a loop and heading back home to spend her first Christmas with Kenny. With a full trailer of various toys for a toy store in Colorado, she hits the road early morning solo as Kenny is busy with Carlos's movie as well as studying a book on scriptwriting. He was a little concerned about her going on this long journey and without him, but he also has confidence in her. She promises him that she'll text him every couple of hours and let him know that she's okay and once she settles for the night, she'll call him. About three hours into her trip, she reaches Seattle, Washington, and texts him to let her know that she crossed the border and she's fine. Being four months pregnant, she finds herself having to stop more frequently as the baby is resting against her bladder and to satisfy her cravings. She drives another nine hours and reaches Missoula, Montana, stopping for lunch and dinner. She parks at a truck rest stop for the night and calls Kenny. As they talk about each other's day, it brings back memories from their first conversations. She tells him that Jason has been bothering her through social media, and she warned him to leave her alone and even blocked him. He isn't happy hearing that this guy is still bothering her. Deep down, she is a little scared about possibly running into him but doesn't repress it, and Kenny never once thought about that until she mentioned him. Now with growing concerned on both ends, he makes it very clear to her that if she sees him to leave immediately, but like with a villain in a horror movie, you can't always escape what won't go away if you can't always see it.

Morning comes, and she hits the road, planning to travel as long as possible. She reaches Casper, Wyoming, by nightfall, and tomorrow she's scheduled to deliver her trailer in Colorado Springs, Colorado. After talking to Kenny, she settles down for the night at a truck stop and pays no mind to the semi she hears backing into the spot next to her, and it's a decision that she'll regret in the morning. Kenny begins to grow concerned throughout the day as he has not heard from Shannon and she isn't answering her phone. He hits panic mode by the afternoon and calls her mom, who hasn't heard from her either. He dials the number that she left him for her dispatcher and learns that she hasn't delivered her trailer yet and is now an hour late, which is totally unheard of for her. The dispatcher tells him that they have been trying to reach her through CB, but she isn't responding. Kenny tells him the last time he talked to her and where she was staying last night and her dispatcher tracks her semi still at that same location through the tracking device in her semi and decides to call about seeing if an officer can go out and check on her. He tells Kenny he'll call him back as soon as he hears something. A little later on, Kenny gets a phone call not from the dispatcher but the Wyoming police officer who was sent out to check on her well-being. He tells Kenny that her semi is unlocked and her purse, keys, and phone are lying on the passenger seat and she isn't anywhere inside the store or outside. His heart starts pounding. He feels flushed and almost faints. Shaking, worried with fear, and concerned, he tells the officer that something is wrong. She wouldn't have left with anyone without telling him, and she wouldn't leave her phone or purse behind. She never leaves her semi unlocked or unattended. He tells the officer about their phone conversations, her brother who is a trucker as well, and Jason, going into all of the details he can remember about him. He begs the officer to do everything he can and that she is the love of his life and he can't lose her. He also tells him that she's pregnant. Kenny tells him that he can get the next flight out, but the officer suggests him staying put in case she pops up there and tells him someone will be in contact with him shortly. Kenny calls her mom and fills her in on everything. Scared, crying, and freaking out, he texts his brother and Carlos to come over right away, that it's urgent.

Living closer, Carlos arrives first and finds Kenny an emotional wreck and pacing his porch. A few minutes later, Daniel arrives.

"What's going on, Kenny?" Daniel asks.

"Kiddo…my Kiddo," he says, barely able to speak.

"What's wrong with Shannon? Is it the baby?" Daniel asks again.

"No! She's missing," he says, finally breaking down.

"What do you mean Shorty's missing?" Carlos asks in a frantic voice.

"She never made her delivery, and I haven't heard from her since last night. Her semi is still at the truck stop. Her phone, purse, and keys are still inside; and she isn't anywhere. My Kiddo…our baby…I can't… Where is she? What happened? I am so scared, guys. I talked to her mom, and she hasn't heard from her either, and she isn't with her brother. No one has seen or heard from her."

"I am at a loss for words. I can't believe this! Let's go in and sit," Daniel says and walks Kenny inside to his couch after he almost collapses on his porch.

"I told the officer out there that I can fly out, but he told me to stay here in case she pops up. I need to be there! I need to go look for her! How can they expect me to just stay here while my girlfriend who's carrying my unborn child is missing?"

"Kenny, you wouldn't know where to start," Daniel says.

"That's beside the point. Sitting here isn't helping either. I love her, Daniel!" His voice is breaking. "I love Shannon! Just think if you two were in my shoes right now. I almost lost her once from the accident. I had to watch her lie there in that coma every darn day—not knowing if she was going to come out of it, and now she's missing! I shouldn't have let her take this load. I should have talked her out of it or cleared my schedule and went with her."

"You had no way of knowing this would happen, Kenny," Carlos says.

"No, but at least I could have been there to stop it. What if she's hurt? Scared? What about our baby? If something happens to her or my baby, I don't know what I'll do," he says, breaking down.

"What are they doing?" Daniel asks

"The officer said he was going to call in another officer and a detective to look at the store's cameras, and depending on what they see, if they see what happened to her, they will know if it's a kidnapping or if she left willingly. Someone is supposed to be contacting me soon."

"Kidnapping? No, Kenny! This can't be happening to Shorty." Carlos's voice breaks.

"It's going to be okay. They are going to find her." Daniel tries to assure Kenny.

"But what if something happens to her or our baby, Daniel? She isn't strong enough to defend herself."

"No, now you have think positive. She is strong, Kenny. You know she'll fight to get back to you and for the baby. You know she's going to do everything in her power to protect the baby."

"I just want her back here with me where she belongs. Where's my Kiddo, Daniel? Where is she?"

"I know! I'm so sorry. She's going to be okay. They are going to find her, and then we are going to bring her back home. You aren't going to lose her or your baby," he says, pulling Kenny in for a hug and checking on Carlos, who is still upset.

An hour later, Kenny gets a hard knock at his door and finds two Vancouver detectives, a male and female, standing on the other side. They introduce themselves, and he invites them in, and they also greet Carlos and Daniel. They explain that they will be working with him and keeping him informed from here on along with the Wyoming police and detectives to help find Shannon. They tell Kenny that after watching the store's surveillance cameras, it appears that she has been taken by another truck driver, and Kenny immediately says, "Jason!"

"What can you tell us about this Jason?"

"I've only seen him once, but he's like late forties, about five feet ten inches tall, and I would say about one hundred ninety pounds. When I saw him, he was clean-shaven, bald, and has a roughness about him. I don't think she has even told me his last name."

"Has she ever had any kind of relations with him that you know of?"

"No! They have been friends for a few years after meeting through her brother, Jeremy, who's also a truck driver. After her husband died, he became obsessed with her. Just texting her all the time wanting to take her to dinners. He texted her almost every day asking where she was or where she was going. She kept telling him that she only wanted to be friends, but he couldn't seem to accept that, and a few months ago, she finally called him and cut the friendship off. He was very hurt and screamed at her over the phone and blamed our relationship. He just couldn't seem to understand no matter how much she explained that he was too clingy and made her feel uncomfortable at times. The day that she left for this delivery, we didn't even think about him."

"We will definitely look through her past text messages between them to help get more of an understanding."

"How was she taken?" Kenny asks while tearing up.

"The cameras showed her about seven this morning walking around her semi and trailer. There was another semi back in beside her with a trailer as well. She was in between the trailers checking her wheels when a man hit her in the back of her head, knocking her out. He grabbed her, put her in his trailer, and drove off. No one else was in the parking lot, and the store clerk saw or heard nothing. Seems like it was planned."

"Was it him? Did Jason kidnap my girlfriend?" he says, holding back anger.

"We do have pictures from the tape that we are going to show you. It may be hard to fully make them out, but try your best. If you can't, it's okay. Take your time looking through them, and I know it's going to be hard seeing her kidnapping in the photos, but we need your help."

The female detective pulls five photos from a folder and hands them to Kenny. He almost breaks as he slowly looks through the last known images of Shannon Keeler.

"Yeah, that's him—Jason, and that's the color of the semi he was driving when I saw him."

"One hundred percent sure?" the female detective says.

"Yes! He has her. He has my Kiddo and my baby."

"Baby?" the male detective says.

"She's four months pregnant with our child."

"We are going fax all of this to the detectives working this case in Wyoming. The police will most likely look into Jason and get a hold of his dispatcher too. Trust us, Mr. Kirtzanger, we are going to work as hard as we can to help find her and return her and your unborn child safely back to you."

"Please do! I love her so, so much. I can't lose her!"

"We'll be in touch. Here's our card. Feel free to call anytime you have concerns or questions."

"Thank you."

"Anytime!"

Once the detectives leave, Kenny loses it, and both his brother and Carlos catch him before he hits the floor.

*****

Shannon wakes to a sharp pain in her head and in a daze. Lying on her side, she tries to see but finds herself in a dark, musky long-empty trailer and can tell it's moving by the swaying and the sound of the road under her. She feels around her pockets to discover that she doesn't have her cell phone and begins to panic. She can't seem to remember much right now but knows someone has taken her. She cries and trembles in fear of not knowing who, why, or what will happen to her and her unborn child. All she can do is think about Kenny and their baby. Through her tears, she manages to pull herself over to the trailer's wall and sit up against it. She says a little prayer asking God for his protection and to help her escape to safety. She asks him to protect her miracle baby and to guide Kenny to her. At one point, she even asks Craig to be with her and protect her. She estimates about four hours have passed by time the semi finally comes to a stop. She's cold, shaking, starving, and knows she needs to eat soon for both her and her baby. She becomes more scared as she hears footsteps approaching and fears what's coming next. When the doors swing open, she can't believe who is staring back at her. Before she can scream out for help or even say a word, he's already up in the trailer duct-taping her mouth closed and blindfolding her.

"How's this for your love of those *Unjoyful Ride* movies? Now you can feel like you're in one except I ain't your Rusty Blade." He drags her to the edge of the trailer and carries her into an old abandoned warehouse. Once inside, he ties her to a chair before removing the blindfold and threatens her with her life if she screams before removing the duct tape.

"Why are you doing this to me, Jason?"

"Why? Because I always get what I want"—he leans in close to her—"and I want you just like all of the others before you."

"Others?" she says with a tremble in her voice.

"You don't think this is my first time, do you? Oh no, sweetheart, I've been doing this for years. Getting rid of dirty hookers, druggies, hitchhikers, and getting back at heartless girls like you is my pleasure. Oh yeah...I'm going to have fun with you. You're extra special."

"Please don't do this," she says, tearing up. "Please let me go."

"All I wanted you do was love me because I love you. I've been there for you through everything, and I just wanted a chance, but you couldn't give me that. Instead you just wanted to be friends, just like all of the other stupid girls I've tried to be there for, and then you go a cut off the friendship because you started dating your perfect little actor boy—"

"It wasn't because of that, and he isn't little," she says with a sneakiness in her voice and a slight smile.

"Shut up!" He balls his fist at her. "It sure seemed like it to me. As you two got closer, I got pushed to the side."

"No! You wouldn't leave me alone. You became too clingy and obsessed with me, Jason. That's why I cut off the friendship, because you made me uncomfortable."

"Uncomfortable?" he says, shaking his head. "Well, uncomfortable this," he says, slapping her across her face, and she cries out in pain and fear.

"Stop! Don't hurt me!" she says, crying uncontrollably. "You don't hurt people you love, Jason!"

"Yeah, well, you hurt me."

"What are you going to do to me?"

"What I've done to all of the other girls I've taken. Torture you, watch you bleed, enjoy hearing your cries, have my way with you, and finally make sure your body is never found like the other missing but forgotten girls."

Shaky inside and fighting back her tears, she says, "You? But how?"

"Easy, Shannon, our career. I picked up a girl from one state and dumped her in the next. I never cared about them or planned to help them run away. It was all fun and games, but I really did love you and wanted to be with you. I actually never would have hurt you, but now I just see you like the rest of them," he says, cutting across her cheek with a razor blade.

"Please! Don't!" she says, crying.

"Your pleases don't mean s—t to me anymore, and neither do you."

He cuts her arm three times, and she screams out in pain. "Why are you crying? It didn't hurt when you slit your wrist fourteen years ago. Why don't I just recut it for you?"

"No! My baby! Please, I'm pregnant. You're going to make me miscarry."

Leaning in close, he says, "I know you are, and I don't care, because by getting rid of you and that baby is one way I can hurt him, too, and just like you hurt me. If I can't have you, then nobody can have you."

"I never told you I am pregnant," she says, looking confused.

"No, but an old friend of Kenny's did."

"Who?"

"That's my little secret."

She cries out begging him to stop and let her go, and becoming frustrated, he punches her, knocking her out cold.

*****

Daniel stays with Kenny all night to try and keep him sane and to keep him from leaving. It becomes a long rough night for them both with him being an emotional wreck. He's restless, angry, scared, and fighting urges to fly out and look for his Kiddo. He's up and down all throughout the night, pacing his floors and looking out the windows hoping, by some miracle, she'll come running up to their front door. Around three in the morning, Daniel wakes to find him sitting on the side of his bed looking down at Shannon's Christmas present.

"Kenny, is that a—"

"Yeah. I was going to give it to her Christmas Eve."

"Was? You mean you still are. It's beautiful too. She will love it, and she's going to be found."

"I miss her so much, Daniel," he says, crying.

"I know you. I can't even begin to imagine the pain you feel. I miss her too!" he says, sitting down beside him.

"I love her so much, and I just need her back here with me. I want my Kiddo. I know he has her, and the thoughts of what he might be doing to her are killing me inside."

By nightfall, Jason shakes Shannon until she comes back around. He unties her after threatening her if she tries to run to allow her to use the restroom, and he even feeds her. He walks her to a corner in the building where there's a mattress on the floor and two ankle chains that have been bolted into the concrete. He forces her to lie down, and he cuffs her ankles as she cries out for mercy. He throws a blanket over her and leaves her. She places her hands on her belly to feel her baby and mumbles through her tears, "I love you, my precious baby, and Mommy's sorry that this is happening. I will fight for you—for us both. We will make it out of here and return home to Daddy, I promise." She says a little prayer, talks to Craig, and cries herself to sleep.

20

The next morning, Daniel answers a knock at Kenny's door and yells for him. He looks pretty rough from his sleepless night as he comes over and greets the male detective.

"Good morning, sir. I imagine you didn't have an easy night."

"No."

"I wanted to come and give you an update on new information that we have."

"Okay."

"A few truckers have given statements about how Jason is in love with Shannon and how zealous he is over her. Some have mentioned that he gave them weird vibes, and a few even confessed that he has often joked about kidnapping hookers, hitchhikers, and girls that have turned him down, torturing and killing them. A lot of them didn't take him seriously because he is known to joke about a lot of things, but after further investigation and putting his picture out, women have come forward claiming that he has tried to or did rape them."

"I can't believe this. She was friends with that monster. Why didn't they come forward sooner and get him off the streets?"

"He threatened that he would come back after them and kill them. His face and semi are plastered everywhere. Truckers are even helping look for her and won't stop till she's found."

"I am so grateful for that."

"We didn't think it was a good idea at first, but they can cover a lot of ground out there during their travels. She is loved by many of them. They all said nothing but amazing words about her."

"Just please find her. A killer! A damn killer has her. I just can't! This can't be true."

"We will find her, Mr. Kirtzanger. I can see you really do love her. I almost shouldn't say this, but I wish more people with missing loved ones show as much concern as you have. I can see she's special to you."

"She is!"

"Jason's dispatcher is trying to track him, but he drives an older model, and the tracker isn't like today's that will still track the semi even when it's not in use. Apparently, he hasn't driven his semi since yesterday. We do have the last location, and a SWAT Team will be en route to that location soon. I'm sorry, but I can't tell you the location right now out of safety."

"That gives me a little hope that maybe she will be rescued. I just want her to be there so they can rescue her and put that monster in prison. I'm telling you right now! If he hurts her or our baby, I'll split him with my hatchet."

"Oh no, Mr. Kirtzanger, we can't have that. Let's not get you in trouble because then she and your baby won't have you. We'll give you guys the justice you all deserve without you getting yourself put in jail. Take care, and call me with any questions or concerns, and we will keep you posted."

"Thank you!"

"You're welcome, and good day, sir."

As the detective is heading out, Carlos and Camilla are walking up the porch, and Kenny invites them in. They sit down, and Kenny updates them on everything.

Shannon awakened to Jason kicking the side of the mattress and demanding her to get up. He frees her ankles and helps her to her feet, and after threatening her, he allows her to use the restroom. She cries at her dirty reflection in the mirror. She has smeared dried blood all over her face from the cuts on her cheeks and on her arms from the cuts on her arms. She is also wearing Jason's massive handprints from his double slaps, and her head is pounding from her cries. She is weak, exhausted, and scared for her baby; but she feels him move, and it gives her hope. He lets her eat before tying her back to the chair.

"Why don't you just kill me or do whatever you plan to and get it over with instead of toying with me?" she says with a seriousness in her voice and a cold dead look in her eyes.

"Because that would be too easy. You are a special girl to me."

"Special? You don't hurt people who are special. You don't tie people you love to a chair, and you don't cut them and slap them, Jason."

"Well, maybe I don't love you anymore."

"Yes, you do, because if you didn't, you would have killed me already and threw me out like a piece of trash like the others. Look at me, Jason," she says, trying to convince him and by herself more time.

"No! No! I don't! Stop saying that." He covers his ears, moving around in circles and squinting his eyes. "Shut up!"

"You do, Jason! You still love me!"

"Shut up, b—h!"

"Could you really live with yourself if you killed me? Could you look at yourself every day knowing you killed your best friend whom you loved so much?"

"I'm sorry…I'm sorry," he says, mumbling to himself over and over.

"It's okay, Jason! Everything can be okay if you just let me go."

Jason breaks and goes into a rage, throwing stuff all around her and yelling at her. She tries to calm him, but nothing seems to work, and he just becomes more insane. He opens a drawer in an old dirty broken desk and pulls out a small handgun. She screams and begs in fear for her life knowing that this is it, he's fixing to shoot her. She mumbles, "I love you, Kenny, my Rusty Blade, and my baby," before closing her eyes to not see him shoot her; and she hears it, the sound of the gun firing off.

*****

Later in the evening, Kenny and Carlos are sitting on his porch when two male detectives that they haven't met before pull up and walk over to them.

"Mr. Kirtzanger?" They extended a hand.

"That's me!" He stands and shakes his hand.

"They found her!"

Kenny cries out in relief and falls to his knees, and Carlos leans down over him in tears as well. It's a joyfulness moment.

"Is she alive?"

"She is alive but very weak and in bad shape. She has bruises, cuts across both her cheeks and arms, and marks around her ankles and wrists. He kept her tied to a chair during the day and chained her ankles where he made her sleep on a mattress. She has been taken to a hospital for medical treatment."

"The baby! What about our baby?"

"I don't have an answer for you on that until she is examined. I'm sorry!"

"Where was she found?"

"In an old abandoned warehouse about six hours out from where he took her. She was still tied to the chair when we found her. She would have died right there if she wasn't found."

"What about, Jason?" he says, holding back anger.

"He's dead!"

"He killed himself?" Carlos asks.

"Yes, sir! Shot himself in the left temple. Shannon saved herself. She fought using words against him. She kept telling him that he can't hurt someone he loves and that he wouldn't be able to live with himself if he did and no matter how many times he denied it, she kept convincing him that he still loves her. She is her own hero. She knew how to use words in her favor. She has given a written statement about everything he confessed to, said to her, and did to her. It'll make your hairs stand up. He was a true monster in disguise that needed to be taken off the streets. So as we close this missing case of Shannon Keeler, we are opening up cold cases of missing women that he made be responsible for their disappeared."

"She is such a strong-minded person. She never gives up! I need to get to her. I've got to bring her home."

"We will get you the hospital's address, but first, we have a few questions for you, Mr. Kirtzanger."

"Me?"

"Do you know a Jaylen?"

"Yes! I have been friends with a Jaylen for over twenty years, and we briefly dated for little over a week before I started dating Shannon. Why?"

"Who ended the relationship?"

"I did because of her jealous and controlling ways."

"After going through Jason's phone and all of his social media pages, we discovered that apparently he and Jaylen were friends online and—"

"Wait a minute! Are you telling me that she—" Carlos asks.

"Yes! She was in on this and the main one behind it."

"What?" Kenny blurts in disbelief, and Carlos almost vomits.

"She expressed hatred for Shannon, and she wanted her and your baby out of the way so she could have you. She planned this with Jason. Promised him everything under the sun if he did it for her."

"So you mean Jason really didn't want to do this to Shannon?" Carlos asks.

"No! He refused at first because he cared too much for her and didn't want to hurt her, but Jaylen just kept using her charm until she got her way. Before he shot himself, he kept apologizing to Shannon over and over. She was there with his lifeless body for a few hours before the SWAT found her."

"I can't believe she would do this to me! How could she? Why? She is just as much of a monster in disguise as he was."

"She knew that losing Shannon and your unborn child would completely devastate you and then she could come to your aid. It was her plot to win you back. She is the last person anyone would ever suspect. She used Shannon's estranged friendship with Jason as her secret weapon. She knew that he would automatically be a suspect and case closed."

"She was an enemy dressed as my friend. I am truly hurt by her and so angry at her. I never want to see her again or talk to her."

"What will happen to her?" Carlos asks.

"She will be bought in for questioning. Hopefully we can get a confession, but with the amount of evidence, we are hoping to get a warrant for her arrest. Shannon is pressing charges against her as well."

"What if she tries to claim she was hacked and that wasn't her?"

"This planning has been going on for a while now, and she would have known if she was hacked, and the messages would have stopped. She has no proof and can't use that. All that matters is we got Shannon alive and she's safe. She should be able to come home to you soon."

"We just can't think you all enough for finding her," Carlos says.

"That's our job! Best wishes to you, her, and your baby. It was good to come and give you this news, and we'll be in touch once Jaylen is apprehended. We may need you to give a statement."

"I'll give you whatever you need, and she has it coming to her."

Daniel and Paula stop by shortly after the detectives leave, and Kenny fills them in. The following day, Kenny, Carlos, and Daniel fly out to be by Shannon's side. Walking in her hospital room was rough for Kenny. Seeing the cuts she now wears on her cheeks and arms and Jason's handprints across her face. She has a bruising around her wrists, ankles, and upper arms. She cries out at seeing Kenny. He runs over to her bed with tears in his eyes and holds her tight in his arms.

"I love you so much, Kiddo," he says, holding her face close to his and kissing her forehead. "I was so scared that I had lost you and our baby for good. I'm shaking, ha."

"I love you too," she says, tearing up. "I wasn't letting him win, Kenny, or her. I can't believe they did this to us."

"I am so sorry this happened to you. I should have gone with you. I should have been there to keep you safe."

"You can't blame yourself. No one knew, Kenny. I was Jason's friend for two years and never saw any of this in him and Jaylen, that horrible woman. I'm sorry she turned on you."

"She's going to pay for this, Kiddo, and she's going to pay good. I'm just happy to have you back."

"I had never been so scared in my life. I thought about you and our baby the whole time. I prayed! I begged Jason to not hurt me. I just kept begging him. I missed you so, so much, and I just wanted you so bad."

"I missed you too. I had sleepless nights and bad dreams when I did sleep. I would look out the living room window hoping I would see you running up to me. I'm taking you home, Kiddo, and you aren't leaving me for a while."

"I'm ready to go home, but first, I need to fly out and to get my semi."

"No need to! Your brother is arranging for him to drive it to our house, and a friend is following in his semi to give your brother a ride back to his. So your semi will be home and safe."

"My brother is the best!"

"Yes, he is!"

"How's our baby, Kiddo?" he says, placing his hand on her belly.

"I don't know, but he's kicking and moving. We are getting an ultrasound soon."

Kenny rubs his hand across her belly and feels his baby kick and gets a sense of enticement and chills. Just feeling his tiny foot kick at him made his whole day. An hour later, they go for an ultrasound and see their baby. It's growing at a normal pace, and its heart is still beating strong. The nurse asks them if they would like to know the sex, and they both say yes while grabbing each other's hand nervously. It's a quick moment of silence, and then they hear those three beautiful words, "It's a boy!" Shannon just can't believe it. She's having Kenny's son—a son who will take after him, a son who will be a part of him left behind. It is one of the best feelings she has ever felt. The following day, she is discharged; and Kenny, Carlos, and Daniel take her home on a plane.

21

I t's a chilly Christmas Eve in Vancouver, British Columbia. Shannon has fully healed from her abduction and has been seeing a therapist to help her get through the nightmares, tough days, and upcoming trial against Jaylen. Everyone is excited about the son that she and Kenny will welcome into the world in May. She decided she needed time off the road, and Kenny encouraged it but plans to return after the first of the year. This will be their first time spending Christmas together, and for the first time in over four years, he decorated with her help. They return home around nine after a beautiful romantic triple dinner date with Carlos, Camilla, Daniel, and Paula. He starts a big fire in their fireplace and builds a cozy lounge on the floor in front of it. She comes out of their room into the living room to find all of the lights turned off except the Christmas tree lights, decorations, Christmas music playing low, and the soft glow of the fireplace. Kenny, still dressed in his dress pants and dress shirt, is standing by the fire facing her. He asks her to join him, and she is almost swept away at how beautiful this all is.

"Well, aren't you just so romantic, Mr. Rusty Blade?" she says, smiling while walking over to him.

"Only with you, beautiful! Come over and sit, Kiddo. I want to give you your Christmas present tonight," he says, helping her down on the blankets and sitting next to her.

"Kiddo, this is the first Christmas in years that I have looked forward to. I mean, last year was great having you in my life, but this year is going to be every better because you are actually here."

"I have been so excited about it too. Didn't think it would happen when I was tied to a chair, and I can't wait to wake up in the morning next to you. Just the best Christmas ever, Kenny, because I have you and our baby. I already have everything I could ever want, and I love you more now than I could have ever imagined loving you."

"Shannon, I am so grateful to have you and our son that's coming. I didn't imagine this being my life a year ago, but I am thankful for it. You have been the most amazing fan, the greatest friend, and the most loving girlfriend. I've almost lost you twice," he says, voice breaking, "and that saying 'You never know what you have till it's gone' is certainly true and hits you hard when faced with that possibility."

"Kenny, you won't ever lose me. I'll always find my way back to you."

"I can't live without you. I wouldn't know how, and I just want us to keep moving forward and growing. I don't just want you as my girlfriend anymore, Kiddo, and I don't want our baby and me sharing the same last name without you either."

"What are you saying 'not just your girlfriend anymore'?"

"Shannon, this past year of friendship with you has been the best year of all my fifty-eight years. You came into my life when I was alone, was hurt, and had nothing left but these conventions and my fans. I didn't realize how lonely I was and how much in life I had missed out on. You told me if I gave you a chance, I wouldn't regret you, and I can say that I haven't. I don't. You went from being my fan to my best friend, and when I gave myself a chance to let you love me more, you become my girlfriend, and I couldn't love you more if I tried. I want to keep waking up beside you every morning and holding you every night. I want to keep experiencing new things with you and share our journeys together. I want to be the only guy you keep coming home to and the only drive you back your semi up in. I want to be the only guy you think about out there on them highways and smile. I love you, Shannon Keeler, and even if one day you decide to leave me, I will still think highly of you and remember the amazingly sweet, gentle kind person you are. I know in my heart, mind, and soul that there are so many more things we can be, and so, Shannon"—he pulls a ring box from his pocket and opens it—"will you marry me? Will you become my little Mrs. Kirtzanger?"

In shock, Shannon just stares at the ring as she starts to tear up before looking up at him. "Yes, Kenny Kirtzanger. A million times. Yes, I will marry you."

He removes the ring from the box and slides it onto her ring finger. They hug tight and share a kiss. She tells him it's absolutely beautiful, and he tells her it's not as beautiful as she is. She looks down at her hand to adore her engagement ring. It's a three-stone diamond ring with small diamonds going around the band set in white gold. She just can't believe that she's his fiancée now. All of the years she waited to meet him, wanted to know him, and have a friendship with him; and now she will get to spend the rest of her life as his wife and the mother of his child that's growing strong inside of her. They spend the next few hours cuddling in front of the fire talking about their future together, their son, and even about names for him.

The following morning, they have a private Christmas morning alone and talk about how next Christmas will be their son's first. Kenny opens his gift from Shannon. They spend most of the day visiting Carlos and Camilla and then Daniel and Paula. It's a day of engagement celebration. He introduces her to his other siblings through video chats as they all have already fallen in love with her. In return, she video calls her mom, and he gets to meet her older brother and her dad. She also video calls her best friend Tammy so he can meet her husband, her niece, and three nephews; and she calls her other best friend Britney. It's not as hard as she thought it would be being so far away from her family. Being with Kenny is something she has wanted since she met him in that parking lot that warm August morning, and he is worth every sacrifice she has made. She was just a simple fan who adored him, who lived in her fantasies; and with every ounce of love in her heart for him, she fought to have him, proving that a fan can be more than just a fan. The love of a fan can mean many things. It's a strong love with years of devotion and loyalty. It's a connection between the fans and their idol and a desire that never goes away. New Year's comes to pass and mid-January, Shannon hits the road again for the first time since her kidnapping but won't be hauling to the United States for a while. At five months pregnant, she is becoming more easily exhausted and stays sick all the time. Not being on medication for her autoimmune diseases to protect her baby is taking a major toll on her body. She left out for a four-day haul to Edmonton, Alberta, Canada; and Kenny accompanied her for the journey because after a year and a half of an online friendship, she made plans to meet her best friend Colleen Marie Murphy who is also a fan of his who met him a while back. He thought it would be fun to meet her again in which she knew nothing about him coming, for they wanted it to be a surprise. They met at a local restaurant, it was a superfun surprise for Colleen when she saw him climb down out of that semi. She and Shannon hugged tighter than what her baby probably liked, for he kicked hard enough; Colleen felt it too. After having lunch and talking, they took photos together, and Colleen had to head to work. It was a short meeting, but it was a wonderful, and Shannon was so happy to have finally met her best online friend, and they start their journey back home.

The following weekend after returning home, Kenny has a convention in Novi, Michigan, and Shannon flies out with him to be there and give him support. Most of his fans are already aware of them as a couple and her pregnancy due to Jaylen's arrest hitting the airwaves and all over social media. Most of his fans even congratulate him as they meet him, and some asks Shannon how she is holding up. She still loves seeing him afar at his table. Nothing compares to the smiles he wears all day and the laughs he gives as he meets every fan. It never gets old seeing how much joy he gets from meeting his fans and how much he loves them. She may be his best friend and fiancée; but she will always be his fan first at heart and still loves to wait in his line like the rest of them for a hug, for a smile, for a handshake, and to hear his laugh. She makes her way up to him, and his fans have a ball, cheering them on and taking pictures of them together. With her wearing a fitted shirt, her growing belly becomes the star of the encounter between them. It turns out to be one of the most fun conventions Kenny has had in a while.

Valentine's Day is approaching, and Shannon is a few weeks from her thirty-second birthday and her sixth month of pregnancy. It's a chilly evening, and she's standing outside on the porch, leaning down on the post watching the sun as it begins to settle when he walks out with his crocheted blanket and sits her on the swing next to him, covering them both.

"I know how I want to marry you, Kiddo."

"How?" she says, with a curious grin.

"Under a sunset just like this one. Just you and me."

"Seriously?"

"Yes! This is my first marriage, Kiddo, and I want it to be private, romantic, and intimate. I figure we can get married now, and then after you have our baby, we can have a party reception like ceremony with close family and friends. We can dress up and maybe even recite our vows. I want you to feel beautiful in your wedding dress, not pregnant, ha. What do you think?"

"I love it, and the fact that you want to under a sunset is just beautiful, Kenny. Just the fact that you thought of that shows just how much you have truly valued my little loves in life that make me happy, and it shows how romantic you truly are."

"I want to kiss you as my wife under the stars, Kiddo. If you picked, where would you marry me?"

"I will marry you anywhere, Mr. Kenny Kirtzanger. After all, the sunset stretches for miles and miles, but I would definitely say that gazebo where we had our Valentine's date last year. I love it, and I love you, my handsome Rusty Blade."

"I was hoping you would pick that because I love it too. It's such beautiful location and scenery. Do you know when I want to marry you?"

"Tell me, Kenny!"

"Valentine's Day."

"It's a perfect choice and only a week away. I am marrying you in a week, like really?"

"Yes, and that's why I wanted to file for our marriage license last week. That Valentine's date with you last year made me feel something for you. I knew I was starting to love you then, seeing you come down those stairs looking so lovely, so beautiful. That was the first real date that I had in a long time that I didn't want to end, and then when I opened that pen, just knowing that you went the length you did to find that for me really showed how much I mean to you. That pen is something I've wanted for so long and couldn't even find myself. I've never had anyone to go that far for me."

"I'll go to any length for you because I love you, and I'll do whatever it takes to make you happy. That's all I want is for you to be happy, and that makes me happy. Now I'm not perfect, and I don't try to be. I'm just me. What you see is what you get, but I will push hard for someone I love, and when it comes to you, I'll die trying."

"You make me happy, and as long as I have you and our son, I'll always be happy. I want that day to be our special day forever. I never thought I would ever get married. Just didn't think I would ever fall this deep in love. The thoughts literally terrified me at times. Especially when I did start having strong feelings for you. I remember a talk we had, and you told me that she might be right up under my nose."

"And the last person you ever expected, and here she is…me! Ha. I want to write my own vows to you, Kenny. My own words from my heart."

"Oh, I think that's a great idea."

"Let's do it!" she says, standing up quickly and running to the front door.

"Where are you going, Kiddo?"

"To work on my vows, silly. I only have a week, and they have to be just right," he says, winking her eye at him, giggling, and darting inside.

"Wait! I'm coming, then, ha."

22

Valentine's Day finally arrives, and tonight, Shannon Keeler will marry Kenny Kirtzanger privately under a sunset. Around four, Camilla and Paula take her out for pampering to get her hair, nails, and makeup done. She and Kenny have been apart since yesterday morning and won't see each other again until their meet at the gazebo this evening. She stayed at Carlos and Camilla's last night and will get ready at their house as well. Camilla asks her if she's nervous, and she says no—mostly excited and ready to become Kenny's wife. Meanwhile, Daniel and Carlos are hanging with Kenny at his house until it's time.

"Are you nervous, Kenny?" Carlos asks.

"Nope! Just ready to marry her."

"Never thought I would see this day, brother. It's wonderful, and I am so happy that you have finally found the right one to share your life with." Daniel says.

"Me either, and I only waited till fifty-eight years of age to do," he says with a giggle.

"Any time is a good time to give your heart to someone. Can't wait till the big wedding party, and I actually get to see you two get remarried," Carlos says.

"Yeah! Me too!" Daniel says.

Around six o'clock, Kenny, already showered earlier that day, heads to his room to get dressed; and even though Shannon told him he didn't have to dress fancy just to become her husband, he still wants to look handsome for her. While getting ready, he wonders what she'll be wearing and knows she will look beautiful regardless. As the time ticks by, he becomes more excited and anxious as he paces his living room floor. Daniel and Carlos say their goodbyes and wish them both a beautiful happy wedding before they leave first. With the sun expecting for sunset around 8:17 p.m., he heads out for the gazebo around 7:20 p.m., and she is supposed to arrive no later than 7:50 p.m.. He nor Shannon has seen it yet, since Camilla and Paula decorated it early this morning. He arrives twenty minutes later to find that the pastor and his photographer friend who will photograph the whole wedding are already there. He is stunned when he sees the gazebo and knows Shannon with just be in love with it. He waits up under the gazebo for her arrival anxious to see her. A part of him still can't believe he is getting married—that he found his complete soul mate. At exactly 7:50 p.m., Camilla pulls up, Paula gets out the passenger side, and opens Shannon's door; and she steps out completely focused on him and blocking out everything else. She sees the man of her dreams smiling back at her. The man she gave her complete heart and soul to. The man she'll take as her husband. She sees her Rusty Blade, and he's the most beautifully handsome man in the world. He's dressed in black slacks, black dress shoes, a white button-down dress shirt, and a long purple tie. He is completely taken aback at how beautiful she looks—wearing a floor-length white dress with layers that move in the breeze and a thin beaded belt that gently wraps around the top of her baby belly. Her hair is up in a soft bun with rings of curls all around and white pearls placed every few and a soft natural makeup. Not wanting to carry a flower bouquet, she opted for a white flower wrist corsage that she is wearing on her right wrist as well as her engagement ring that now sits on her right ring finger until her band is on. Camilla pulls away, and she begins her walk down the aisle of white rose petals to Kenny. The gazebo's posts are draped in white tulle, clear Christmas lights, white and red roses, and a huge crystal chandelier. White and red rose petals lie on the ground, and white rose petals lie on the floor of the gazebo. She finally makes her way up to him. Facing each other, they both hold each other's hands, and he lets a tear slip from his eye, which causes her to tear up, but they both hold them back.

"You look so beautiful, Kiddo."

"Thank you, and you look so handsome, and you wore purple, my favorite color. Is this really happening?"

"Just for you, and yes, this is happening."

As the pastor begins his introduction to the marriage, the sun starts to set around them, releasing colors into the sky for miles as far as the eye can see. It's time for them to exchange vows, and Kenny goes first.

"Kiddo, I spent two days trying to think of how I can express my feelings into words, my vows, and I found that it really isn't easy."

"No, it's not, ha."

"So I wrote you a letter instead that I would love to read as my vows, but I guess I can just try and recite it."

"No, you don't! You read that letter to me. I want you to. Those words are your vows to me, and I want to hear you read it to me."

"Okay, here it goes. Dear Shannon, my beautiful Kiddo, as you take this next step with me, here are some of the things you should know beforehand. I do cry sometimes when I am alone." She begins to tear up. "Whether it's during a movie, a stargazing night, or a sleepless night thinking about life. I cry even"—his voice breaks— "whoa, ha, when I speak of things that have hurt me, even if they no longer hurt anymore, and I now know that I can cry with you and that it's okay. I am at times afraid of being left, and I am afraid of not being good enough even for you. My career, fame, or popularity entitles me to always find true love. I feel that I no longer need to tell you in ways of how I myself or anyone else has let me down because I believe every single word you say when you disagree with each and every reason. You can tell me you love me countless times, and I don't have to be afraid of you leaving me. I fell in love with you. I love each imperfection of your skin and every sparkle of light in your eyes. I fell in love with the way you look while you're sleeping next to me and the way your mouth curves when you say my name. I fell in love with the way you smile at me across the room and how your face lights up just hearing my name. I will always raise my eyebrow each and every time I call you Kiddo. I will hug you every time you walk through our front door, and I will forever and always only be your Rusty Blade. I can be difficult to love, but for you, loving me will always be so easy. All I ask is that you continue to be patient with me and don't ever give up on me, and in return, I will never give up on you or our child. I promise to always love both you and our child with my entire heart. I promise to always protect you and keep you safe. I love you, Shannon."

"Sweetest most beautiful vows ever," she says as he wipes tears off her cheek. "Kenny, I never thought fourteen years ago, sitting in that movie theater watching you in that movie that here I would be marrying you. When you saved my life, I knew there was someone special I saw deep within your one beautiful brown eye that was visible behind that mask without even needing to see your face. You have given me inspiration, encouragement, happiness, my dreams back and after meeting you, you gave me a beautiful friendship. You picked me up during the darkest time in my life and gave me new life. I fell in love with you. I fell in love with the way you hug me. I fell in love with the way you smile at me. I fell in love with every laugh, every stare from you, your sweet gentle voice, and your soft caressing touch. I fell in love with how you always make me feel safe no matter where I am. I might not be able to give you the world, but I can share it with you for as long as we're both here. I promise to love you for the rest of my life even if I am the one here and you are the one gone. I promise to always be devoted, loyal, dedicated, and completely open and honest with you. As your wife, I promise to always make you proud, support you, take care of you, and be the best mother to our son. I will always work with you, make compromises, and only lift you up. I won't ever give up on you or turn away from you. My life with you has only begun, and I'll look forward to seeing what our future holds and where we go from here. I love you, Kenny."

Under the clear starry sky and a big full bright moon, the pastor hands them each their wedding band with Kenny going first, and they slip them into each other's left ring finger, sealing their vows and kissing as husband and wife. Kenny then moves her diamond from her right hand back to her left.

"You're my husband!" she says in excitement.

"Yes, I am, and you're my wife. Best feeling ever!"

After his friend takes a few more wedding photos, Kenny walks her to his car, and once inside, he surprises her with a trip to

Germany, a country he remembered from one of their very early conversations that she has always dreamed of visiting. They head back home for the night where they have their first dance in private to one of her most favorite childhood songs about finding love by looking through the eyes of love that he also fell in love with while out on the road with her. They fly out the next morning for their private two-week honeymoon.

It's the end March, and Shannon is halfway through her seventh month of pregnancy and due mid-May. With her body slowly breaking down from her autoimmune diseases due to being off her medication for so long to safely carry their son, Kenny made her come off the road to stay home and take it easy until after she deliverers and fully recovers. It's the day of their baby shower being held in their backyard, and she's superpumped, for this is a day she has always looked forward to. She's dressed in a baby-blue knee-length dress that sparkles with every movement. Different shades of blue and green balloons are tied off everywhere, blue and green tablecloths on all of the tables, and blue tulle tied to the back of each chair. Baby theme centerpieces and confetti decorates each table, and at each seat is a sealed card revealing their son's name to each individual person; it is to be opened at the same time with the rest. After waiting and hoping for this all their lives and not wanting to miss the day, all of Kenny's siblings fly in along with some of his nieces and nephews to meet Shannon in person and be a part of their baby shower. Carlos and Camilla also make the special day, and her mom and brother, Jeremy, also surprise her. It's a beautiful day filled with great food, joyful laughs, anticipating excitement of their baby's arrival, fun conversations, cute baby games, and opening gifts. Shannon takes Kenny's siblings and her mom in to see the nursery that's now complete with light-blue walls, a crib, rocking chair, dresser with changing station, baby swing, and other baby items. It's a long day for her as she fights through not feeling well. She feels joint pain, rash breakouts, and exhaustion; but she does her best not to let it show even though Kenny sees it. By late afternoon, he sends her in to lie down and asks everyone to let her rest. They all willingly pitch in to help clear up the tables and bring in the baby gifts. By this point, she is just ready to have their baby and get back to feeling better, which comes sooner than she expected.

One morning after reaching her eighth month, she passes out on Kenny after trying to get out of bed. He catches her just in time, and she is rushed to the hospital. She's four weeks from her due date, but her body just can't handle much more, for her immune system is attacking her and their baby. Her blood pressure is dropping, and both their heart rates are low. Even though she wants a natural birth, she understands that her body can't allow it, and she is prepped for a C-section. As she lies on the operating table nervous and excited to meet her baby boy, Kenny, now dressed in surgical scrubs, is sitting up close by her softly caressing her hair and speaking calmly to her. She can't see anything over the long wide blue paper tarp that's hung in front of her, but she can feel pressure through the numbness from her skin being pulled and tugged after being cut open. At four minutes after eleven that morning, their son, Bryson Rusty Kirtzanger, is welcomed into the world. Kenny steps around long enough to cut his cord. He weighs in at six pounds and nine ounces, and is twenty inches long. Looking up and watching Kenny's teary reaction to seeing his son through the nurses cleaning him is the most amazing feeling she has ever felt and what she has waited for, for the whole eight months. They are both overcome with uncontrollable tears as the nurse lays him next to her face. She kisses him on his tiny nose, and he's whisked away to be looked over by a pediatrician and to spend some time in the nursery while she is being closed up so she can recover as well. Kenny goes out into the waiting area to find Carlos, Camilla, Daniel, and Paula already at the window seeing his baby. They congratulate him and ask about Shannon. Daniel tears up seeing his nephew and causes Paula and Kenny to cry. Four days have passed, and it's their first night at home as a family. Shannon is already feeling better since being back on her medication. They are sitting on the couch, and Kenny is bottle-feeding Bryson.

"How does it feel to be a father, Kenny?"

"It feels incredible. A love like no other. Never thought I would ever have a child, but now that he's here, I'm never letting go."

"It does feel amazing to have this little life that we created. He's so beautiful like you. I've been thinking, do you know when I would love to have our big wedding party?"

"When's that, Kiddo?"

"August third! The day we met outside of that restaurant almost two years ago. Our first encounter with each other that started this journey that changed our lives. Just a fan who met her favorite actor."

"I think it's perfect, Kiddo."

"You never know when you meet someone just how much they can change your life. I was only hoping for communication and a possible friendship but never once thought I would end up being your wife and the mother of your child, but I wanted you, and I wasn't giving up."

"No, you didn't until it happened, and I'm glad you didn't give up on me. Thank you for choosing to be my fan and for trying so hard to have me know about you and never giving up on meeting me and having me in your life."

"You're welcome! I love you, Kenny!"

"I love you, too, Shannon."

Kenny goes and lays Bryson down in his crib and joins her back on the couch for a cuddle.

"Hey, Kenny?"

"Yeah!"

"Remember New Year's Eve a few years ago, out in Carlos's backyard, and I mentioned about writing a book but I wasn't ready to say what it was about yet?"

"Sure!"

"Well, I will have it finish soon, and I want to look into getting it published."

"Oh, that's fantastic, and you should."

"Want to know what it's about?"

"Of course!"

"It's about us, Kenny."

"Us?"

"Yes, but different names. I have journaled everything, Kenny, from our first time meeting to the birth of our son. As soon as I left after each visit, I wrote about what we did and talked about. I wrote about your sickness, my wreck, your conventions, and even my kidnapping. I have changed some of our talks and moments together just to keep some of it private, but for the most part, it's a book about a simple fan who meets her favorite actor and how this beautiful friendship blooms between them and they eventually find love in each other. It's to show that a fan can win even if she isn't perfect or in the business, ha. It's like looking through the eyes of love, Kenny, every time I look into your beautiful brown eyes. I don't see you as an actor or a famous person every time I look at you. I don't see your past or the pain that you have been through. When I look into your eyes, I just see you."

"No kidding! About us? I think that's pretty cool. I'm flattered! What an honor, and I'll look forward to reading it and seeing how you not only see me but also our relationship through your eyes."

"Be honest! Are you okay with it being out there for everyone including your fans to read?"

"Absolutely because I trust you, so go for it."

"Good because I wrote it for you. I'll go check on him," she says, hearing Bryson make a few sounds over the baby monitor.

"You sure?"

"Yeah."

"You really wrote me a book, Kiddo?"

Turning back from Bryson's doorway, she says, "Oh yes!"

"Well, I think that's so sweet. I'm touched!"

"It's just the love of a fan," she says, smiling at him smiling back in amazement.

"I feel lucky to have you."

"I'm the lucky one, Kenny, because I get to have you, my Rusty Blade," she says and walks in their son's room, and he hops up and heads in after her.

ABOUT THE AUTHOR

Shaina Keibler, born and raised in Loris, South Carolina has always dreamed of being a publishing Author. She was finally inspired to pursue her dream career after watching her favorite Actor Ken Kirzinger crossover from stunt work into main acting. He became the positive influence she needed to believe in herself and after years of battling depression, she finally had the courage and confidence to write Rusty Blade: The Love of a Fan. She loves creating writings from her dreams and imagination. She desired to create a masterpiece of love, tragedy, sacrifices, fantasy and adventure of being a fan. She hopes that the reader will not only enjoy her book but will also be inspired to follow his or her dreams.

CPSIA information can be obtained
at www.ICGtesting.com
Printed in the USA
LVHW020557010821
694125LV00003B/263